He Knew Her Name

A STORY OF LOVE, LOSS AND RESILIENCE

PENELOPE HILEMAN

iUniverse

HE KNEW HER NAME
A STORY OF LOVE, LOSS AND RESILIENCE

*This is a work of fiction. All of the characters, names, incidents,
organizations, and dialogue in this novel are either the products
of the author's imagination or are used fictitiously.*

iUniverse books may be ordered through booksellers or by contacting:

*iUniverse
1663 Liberty Drive
Bloomington, IN 47403
www.iuniverse.com
844-349-9409*

*ISBN: 978-1-6632-4157-3 (sc)
ISBN: 978-1-6632-4159-7 (hc)
ISBN: 978-1-6632-4158-0 (e)*

Library of Congress Control Number: 2022912673

Print information available on the last page.

iUniverse rev. date: 08/09/2022

This is dedicated to my mother Lorraine. Her strength is the inspiration behind this story. She continues to inspire everything I do. Thanks Mom.

Bea

Chapter 1

When Bea returned from the Oakwood home for troubled girls, no one expected her to have a baby girl with her. Her mother thought she had made it clear that the baby was to be place for adoption. It was bad enough that Bea had brought shame on the family by stealing money from the very bank that employed her, but after her father had sold the family farm to pay her debt, she would hide the fact that she was pregnant. Bea's mother was livid. Her father never really recovered from the shame and disappointment.

Bea was the first born of six children. To say that all their hopes and dreams were placed in her would be an understatement. Bea excelled at everything she attempted. Her good looks were only outdone by her drive to succeed.

Why do I feel like the weight of the world is on my shoulders? Bea's thoughts were always clouded with the feeling she must succeed, be the best. Being the oldest was not an easy position to be in. Times are tough and mom and dad put everything they have into my future, she thought. All in the hope that I will help financially with the rest of the kids. How is that fair? When is it my turn? She struggled to understand why.

Bea had gotten a job at the bank downtown after graduating. Her father was so proud of her. Unfortunately, she didn't like her job at all. She took the bus to work every day and although it was an annoyance waiting for it, she had to admit it was better than walking. When the bus finally came into sight Bea found herself wondering what her day would hold. Would Mr. Ellis let her work at the counter today as a teller as she had been trained to do or would he expect her to run his errands again? Married men, she thought as she shook her head.

As Bea took a step up onto the bus platform, she lost her footing falling forward right into the arms of Albert. Albert had been the bus driver on the Langley St. route for years, but today was the first time she really noticed him. He has incredible blue eyes and such a sweet smile she thought.

"Oh, my goodness, thank you."

"Are you alright?" He asked. She could feel the heat rising in her cheeks.

"Um, yes. Just embarrassed."

She couldn't stop looking at his eyes, they were captivating. After regaining her composure, she straightened her skirt and made her way to the middle of the bus and promptly sat down. When she felt it was safe to look up, she instantly looked into the bus's huge rear-view mirror, only to see Albert looking back at her. She quickly looked away when their eyes met. What on earth was she doing he was a bus driver? She looked out the window trying not to think about his eyes.

"Happy Birthday!" Agnes yelled across the bank as Bea walked in.

"Agnes, I can't believe you remembered."

"Of course, I did Bea, you're my best friend. And lunch is on me today."

Agnes loved to go to the Woolworth lunch counter, partly because the food was always so yummy, but mostly because she was sweet on Malcolm, and he would surely be there. All the boys from the law office down the street came in for lunch. Mainly to be seen.

"All part of the law business," he would say.

After an uneventful morning, thank goodness, the two girls hurried out the door giggling while running the block and a half to Woolworths'. Timing was everything, two minutes late and your whole lunch was taken up waiting for a seat. Agnes was not going to let her friend down today. She took Bea's hand in hers and practically dragged her the whole way. Once situated at their favorite spot Bea was bombarded with well wishes. Was she really that popular? She thought. Lunch ended way to soon and the girls found themselves running back to the bank to avoid being late. The afternoon seemed endless. Finally, the clocks hands reached four o'clock and the doors were locked.

With feet hurting, Bea headed for the bus stop. Is it always going to be this way? It's 1934, I'm seventeen years old. I finished school top of my class, I have lots of friends and yet I still feel so alone. Mom will be waiting for me to get home so I can help with dinner, get the kids bathed and into bed. Her thoughts quickly turned to getting out of this town. Oh, how she wanted to move to Toronto. That's where she belonged, not here. Sure, she was grateful for everything her parents had sacrificed, but she didn't ask them to. When would it be her turn? When the bus pulled to a stop Bea had to admit she was happy to see Albert again. This time he had a big smile on his face.

"Watch your step Miss." His eyes were laughing, and it was so unnerving.

"Thank you, I will." Bea wasn't used to feeling like this. She was always in control, but this was different. She kind of liked it.

Two weeks passed and Bea and Albert were inseparable. Well as much as they could be. Between work and Bea's responsibilities at home, time was limited, but that didn't stop them. Bea hurried to the park to meet Al for lunch. Agnes was disappointed that Bea had abandoned her, but she was a good friend, so Bea knew she would understand. She had asked to meet Al, but Bea explained that he was shy, and since their time together was so limited, he just wanted Bea all to himself.

Bea waited patiently but, on this day, Al was nowhere to be seen. It was so unlike Albert; he was always here before she was. How did I get so lucky? She thought. He is so kind and caring. Their relationship was moving so quickly and although she had always seen herself as a professional woman, she couldn't help feeling that he was "the" one. She waited as long as she could, but she had to return to work.

Bea's thoughts were a jumbled mess all afternoon. She tried to stop worrying about Al but couldn't. What could have happened? That's when Bea realized she didn't know any of Al's friends or exactly where he lived. They had become so close, but he was private. She didn't want to appear needy, so she didn't ask to many questions. But where was he? Was he okay?

Bea hurried to the bus stop hoping to get answers. Was she making too much of this? She was getting nervous. What if he had just forgotten, what would she say? Or worse, had he intentionally stood her up? And now she would have to face him. As the bus pulled to the curb Bea found herself wanting to turn and run. Why wasn't she angry? She thought. After all he was the one that missed their lunch date. The door swung open and there sitting in Al's seat was a man Bea had never seen. Before she knew it Bea asked where Al was.

"Al?" He asked.

"Yes, um Al, the driver that has this route."

"Oh, sorry, I don't know the guy's name. They just asked me to take this route today because his kid had an accident at school. He and his wife had to go to the hospital." Bea's face must have shown the shock because he immediately told her the little girl was fine, just a broken wrist.

Bea didn't remember finding a seat. She felt as though someone had just punched her in the stomach. Maybe this guy was mistaken. People make mistakes all the time. Al couldn't be married, and a child. No, this had to be a mistake.

Bea spent a long night tossing and turning. Sleep wouldn't come, but tears did. And so did anger. Then more tears.

"Bea, are you alright dear?" Mrs. Ledoux had a look of concern on her face.

"Yes mother, maybe I'm catching something."

"Oh no Bea, I need you to watch your brothers and sisters tonight after work."

"Mother I have plans. Besides are they old enough to care for themselves?" Bea knew she was being selfish, but she just didn't want to care for anyone tonight.

"Not tonight you don't." Her mother said as she turned and left the kitchen.

Three days had passed. Three long frustrating days. The tears had stopped, and the anger had subsided. Now all that was left were questions.

Agnes was busy at lunch now with Malcolm, after all Bea had abandoned her for Al. Bea walked to the park bench where she and Al were supposed to have met for lunch and there he was.

"Bea, Bea I'm so sorry. My mother was ill and there was no one to care for her but me."

"Lies." She said calmly.

"What?" His face looked stricken.

"Why are you lying to me?" Her question was so direct he looked off balance.

"I, um, I" Words were failing him just when he needed them the most.

"I know Al. I know. A wife, a child? How could you? I fell in love with you, and you lied." Bea was close to tears.

"Oh Bea, oh God, I'm so sorry." He truly seemed contrite. Bea was sobbing all over again. He took her in his arms. She tried to resist but quickly melted into him.

"I wanted to tell you; I just didn't know how. Before I knew it, I had feelings for you, feelings I had never had for Roberta. But the children."

"Children? I thought you only had a daughter." She couldn't hide her anguish.

"I have two. Two girls."

Bea felt as though her world was crumbling around her and she need to be saved. But who could save her? She was stuck and she knew it. Al told her how his wife Roberta only cared about what other people thought. They both knew they were in a loveless marriage, but saving face was much more important to her.

Bea was in no shape to go back to work, but she had no choice.

"Please Bea, meet me after work. I'll explain everything. I promise. Please." His blue eyes were pleading with her, and it broke her heart. Should she hear him out? She wondered. What could he say to fix this?

"Please Bea, I love you."

At the end of her workday Bea made the decision to end this misguided romance. She would somehow forget this man.

The next few days were a blur. Bea simply went through the motions of her mundane life. Before she knew it a week had passed then two and the thought of him came with less sting. Albert had transferred to another route almost immediately which explained everything. How could she have been so gullible?

Chapter 2

Months had passed, and Bea found her way back to normalcy. No more tears. Sometimes whole days would pass without a memory creeping in of the hours at the park or the long walks by the river. The scent of his aftershave against her cheek. Bea was moving on.

It was a cold blustery Monday morning; the snow had drifted overnight so the sidewalks that had been cleared were covered again. Bea was having a terrible time navigating her way to the bus stop. She wrapped her coat around her slender body as tightly as she could. Her galoshes were filling in with snow and now she would have to deal with cold wet feet at work.

The bus of course was late because of the snow which was adding to her already bad mood. Is this it Lord? Is this how my life is destined to be? Her frustration welled up in her until she swore she could taste it. Finally, the bus pulled to the curb, splashing slush as it came to a stop. Bea could hardly feel her toes and as she tried to get over the curb and onto the first step of the bus, down she went. Bea thought for a second, she was in control of her fall but before she knew it, she was lying flat on her back with her legs under the bus. There was an awful ringing in her ears and a burning pain in the back of her head.

"Don't move her! Careful, Bea! Bea are you alright?" What's going on she thought. What happened? She must be dreaming, because the voice in the background sounded like Al's. People were now helping her up.

"Are you sure you're, okay?" She wasn't dreaming. It was Al's voice. "What happened?" she asked

"You fell, lost your footing in the snow. Really Bea, are you alright? You went down hard." Al's face was filled with concern.

"What are you doing here?" She was shaking as she asked.

"Robert got a better job and moved on. They said I had to take this route back. I'm sorry Bea."

"Hey let's go!" Yelled a man who hadn't moved from his seat to help. "I've got a job to get to!"

Al helped Bea onto the bus, and into a seat. As she sat down the ache, she had felt in the back of her head began to subside. However, she was soaked through. Al took his seat but kept one eye on her as if she would disappear if he looked away. He looked at her as if she was the most beautiful woman he had ever seen. She returned his gaze, and she knew she wanted to spend the rest of her life with him. She only hoped he felt the same way.

There was no one left on the bus but Bea. She hadn't uttered a word since he sat her on the bus and her stop was next. Most businesses were closed because of the weather. When the bus stopped in front of the bank, they both realized it was closed as well. She thought about getting off but to go where? She returned to her seat not knowing what to do she tried to focus on the passing scenery. Anything so she wouldn't have to look at those eyes. Unfortunately, Albert had other plans. Bea didn't even notice that Al had driven past her stop. And now the bus was listing as it bounced over a curb on its way to an empty parking lot. The storm was getting worse, and the streets were abandoned.

"Albert why are we stopping?" She was truly nervous.

"Because if I don't talk to you now, we may never get another chance and I have to explain." Bea didn't want to understand, she wanted to hate him. But when he spoke with such pain about the situation, he found himself in she wanted to forgive him. He assured her he didn't love his wife and that if it wasn't for the children, he would have left her years ago. He told her how he loved her, and he couldn't stop thinking about her. How his days were nothing but hours that passed in a fog of regret. How he wished there was some way they could be together. Before she knew it, she was crying again, and he was sitting next to her.

"Please Bea, forgive me." She was shaking with the cold and overwhelmed with emotion. He took her hand in his and she felt the warmth of him. She could smell that familiar scent of his aftershave. It was in that moment that she knew she was lost to him forever.

Months had passed since the day on the bus. Albert and Bea had become adept at hiding their relationship. Meeting at out of the way places. Steeling away any time they could together. Then one night with a look of anguish on his face, Albert explained that his wife Roberta had begun to question their finances.

"She wants to know where the money is going." He said. "I'm running out of excuses Bea. I don't know how I can continue to pay for our time together without her finding out." Bea couldn't imagine her life without Albert. The time they spent together was all consuming to her. If she couldn't at least have this time with him, she would just die. Albert took her from a girl to a woman. They were careful of course, but he was like a drug to her. When he made love to her, she knew there was nothing she wouldn't do for him. Bea was not needy in the sense that she would beg or plead with him to leave Roberts, but it was very clear to her that she did indeed need him.

Chapter 3

Mr. Ellis, the bank manager, didn't see it coming, not really. Bea had decided she would do whatever it took to continue seeing Albert Even if that meant she had to flirt with a man she could barely stomach.

"Oh, Mr. Ellis, that tie looks wonderful on you, it really compliments your eyes. Can I get you a coffee? Do you need anything today Mr. Ellis? Your wife is a very lucky woman, Mr. Ellis." Was she really saying these things? Bea understood the only way she was going to be able to work as a teller was to flatter this smarmy old man. And it worked. Bea managed to gain his trust without even trying that hard.

It wasn't long before Bea managed to swap forged checks for cash without anyone noticing. It was like taking candy from a baby, she thought. Just a few smiles in the right direction or a little bite of the lower lip and Mr. Ellis didn't know if he was coming or going.

Bea had managed to steal enough money that she and Albert were able to run off for a weekend in Niagara Falls. Bea's mother was easy to fool. A story of how the bank was sending her off for training was believable enough. She was becoming quite good at lying. Roberta was a little harder to convince. Once Albert assured her that with extra training, he was assured a promotion, she was putty in his hands. She practically pushed him out the door.

Albert pulled up to the corner one block away from Bea's house. They had agreed to meet there so her parents wouldn't see him. When she walked out the front door her heart was pounding with excitement. Bea's mother was yelling instructions as the door slammed shut behind her. Bea didn't want to run to him, but she couldn't help herself. There he was, right on time. As she got closer, he leaned over and pushed the passenger door open. She jumped in and they were on their way.

"You look beautiful Bea." He smiled at her.

"Do you really think so?" She was glad her found her attractive.

"More beautiful than I've ever seen you look." She snuggled as close as she could and settled in for their journey. When they pulled up to the hotel Albert gently shook her awake.

"Where are we?" She asked with a sleepy voice.

"We're here my love." Bea looked around, happy with what she saw, she retrieved a stack of bills from her handbag.

"Al, here's the money. You handle it for us, okay?" Al looked embarrassed but took the money anyway.

"I love you." He said and let his gaze wash over her.

"Oh, my darling, I love you too. Wait, I almost forgot to put my ring on." She dug into her handbag and slid the diamond ring her grandmother had given her for her sixteenth birthday on her ring finger. "There now we're ready." Albert walked to the front desk like a man on a mission.

"Reservation for Mr. and Mrs. Sander please."

"Yes sir Mr. Sander. We've been expecting you." The desk clerk gave Bea a welcoming smile and handed Albert the key. "If there's anything you need, please don't hesitate to let us know. Can we get your bags?"

"Oh no. I have them, thank you." When the key turned the lock and the door swung open Bea realized they had pulled this off.

She would sleep in his arms tonight. She would wake next to him in the morning.

"Are you alright Bea? Can I get you a drink?"

"I'll have what you're having." Bea had never had alcohol before, but she was ready to relax and enjoy herself. Albert handed her a glass half filled with whiskey and ice.

"Sip it Bea, it can sneak up on you."

"Mm, a girl could get used to this." It warmed her throat and then all the way to her toes. "I wish it could always be like this." She whispered.

"So do I, my darling. Let's just enjoy each other and not think about anything else." He took her by the small of her back and pulled her close. Their breath was warm with the scent of whiskey and heat was rising between them. They melted into each other, lost in their love making the world disappeared.

Saturday morning came too soon. Bea felt a little foggy and there was a dull ache in her temples.

"Good morning sweetheart." Albert was caressing her cheek. "Did you sleep alright?"

"Oh, yes darling." Suddenly self-conscience Bea touched her hair. "I must look a fright."

"You couldn't if you tried." His smile turned to a grin and before she knew it Albert was touching her just the way she liked.

Albert had fallen back to sleep and Bea took this time as an opportunity to hurry into the bathroom to shower. She quickly removed the shower cap that the hotel had supplied and began to fix her hair. A little makeup and she was ready for whatever the day held. When she opened the bathroom door, Albert was sitting on the bed dressed.

"Hi beautiful. Are you hungry?" He asked as he ran a comb through his hair.

"Starving."

"There's a diner on the corner, we can walk." He was standing putting the comb back in his pocket. He reached out to her, and she took his hand. They strolled to the diner still hand in hand. She could get used to this she thought. They couldn't be seen touching at home, but here they were just another married couple. Sitting across from each other in the tiny booth, they laughed and talked about a future neither of them ever believed would come true. But wanting to keep the fantasy alive the knew not to talk about it.

"Let's go see the Falls." He suggested.

Oh, I'd love to." She had only seen them in pictures.

The day couldn't be better, Bea thought. The mist coming off the Falls was exhilarating. Bea felt like she was living a dream. One she never wanted to wake from.

"Excuse me Miss. How would you like to enter Miss Niagara Falls?"

"Are you talking to me?" Bea looked around to see if there had been a mistake. In that moment Bea realized she had forgotten to put her ring back on after her shower.

"Let me introduce myself. My name is Mr. Neil Blackwood. I'm with the Niagara Pageant Committee and we have a last-minute opening. I was wondering if you would be interested in taking that spot?"

"I'm from out of town and only here until tomorrow. I couldn't possibly." Although flattered, Bea didn't know if it was a good idea. "Albert, what do you think? Should I do it?"

It was obvious that Albert didn't really want to share her, their time was so limited, but he could see the excitement in her eyes. "Well, I think it might be fun."

"We have everything you need. Please, if you'll both come with me, I'll get you registered." The next few hours were a complete blur. Bea was on the stage and her name was being called. "And the winner of our 1935 Miss Niagara Falls Beauty Pageant is Bea Ledoux." There was a loud cheer, and a banner was being draped across her trembling chest. Flowers placed in her hands and a trophy shoved in her arms. What! Oh no, there must be a mistake, were the only thoughts coming to her. Then laughter, a lot of laughter.

She spotted Albert from the corner of the stage, and he was smiling from ear to ear. Her heart was soaring.

When they arrived back in their room, it was after midnight. They were giddy and exhausted at the same time. The prize was a check for seventy-five dollars. And an eight by ten photograph of her with her trophy. What started as the perfect day was about to get better. They fell into each other's arms and again the world fell away. Sleep didn't come easy. Bea felt as though her life was perfect. She also felt more beautiful than she ever had. Not because of the pageant, but because of the way Albert looked at her. How was she ever going to go back to her mundane life? How was she going to be able to stand the thought of Albert warming the bed of another woman? Even if that woman was his wife. Why didn't she feel guilty? She didn't. Bea felt like she deserved to be Albert's. It wasn't fair she thought. He loved her. She was a good girl. Well aside from stealing and being the other woman. Anyone in her position would do the same thing right?

The drive home was uneventful. They didn't really speak and the quiet was deafening. Finally, the tears began to stream down Bea's cheeks.

"Please don't cry Bea. Everything will be alright. I'll find a way to make it work." He looked like he had the weight of the world on his shoulders.

"There is no way. Don't you see, I'm the other woman." She was sobbing now. "I can't believe this. I love you and I'm the other woman."

Albert slowed the car down and pulled off the highway. He took her in his arms and let her sobs wash over him. How did this happen? How did they make such a mess of things? "You're the only woman I love Bea, more than you'll ever know. But when we get home, we need to forget each other. I've done nothing but drag you into an impossible situation. It's time for me to take responsibility and let you go."

"What! No! You can't mean that Al! We love each other. I'll wait, I'm sorry I don't know why I'm crying. Look, see I can stop." This couldn't be happening. How could she have been so stupid, letting her emotions get the best of her?

Bea, we need to do this. It will be years before the children will be grown. I cannot and will not let you through away your life waiting for me. You have a beautiful, wonderful life ahead of you. I want you to live it, Bea. That's the best way for me to show you how much I love you." He looked like he had just lost his best friend.

"So, I have no say in this? You decide what's best for me?" Her anger was blinding. Her head was pounding, and she was shaking. "But I love you, Albert." Her words fell flat. Even as she said them, she knew he was right. How could they continue?

The rest of the trip home was miserable, partly because it was going to come to an end and partly because she wished it was over. Albert pulled up to the corner where just two days ago he picked her up. Now there was nothing left to say. His hands were on the steering wheel and his knuckles were turning white. "I'm so sorry Bea." These were the final words he spoke to her. She looked into those blue eyes one more time and her heart not only broke it hardened in ways she could not imagine.

Chapter 4

Monday morning all Bea could think of was how she would have the strength to face Albert on the bus. With her purse in hand and a light sweater over her shoulders, Bea opened the door to a beautiful June morning. The sky was blue, and the birds were singing songs of love. Love, ha. There is no such thing as love. She pulled the door behind her and when she turned, she was met by two men wearing dark suits.

"Are you Beatrice Ledoux?"

"Yes, who's asking?" What happened next was a bit jumbled in Bea's mind. She found it hard to breathe and there was a piercing ringing in her ears. The detective allowed Bea to re-enter the house where her mother was busy getting the children ready for breakfast. Without turning around Bea's mother asked if she had forgotten something.

"Mother I'm in trouble."

The detectives explained to Bea's parents what Bea had done at the bank. She had managed to steel fifteen hundred dollars and that was punishable by up to ten years in prison. They had to take Bea with them. She would be in front of the Judge Irving first thing

Wednesday. She would be held at the county jail unless they could make bail. Bea stayed locked up for the next two days. Wednesday was another beautiful June day, but this time Bea was seeing it through the courthouse windows. How did she let this happen? What had she been thinking? Well obviously, she thought, she hadn't been thinking at all. She really thought she had gotten away with it. The bank manager had suspected Bea, but it was over the weekend as they poured over Bea's transactions that they found the discrepancies. Mr. Ellis wanted to believe that a beautiful young woman could find him attractive, and he also wanted to believe he was that attractive. He knew neither to be true. He played along because it was flattering, but Bea was a little too good. Even Mr. Ellis had to question her motives. When he saw the discrepancies, he didn't want to believe that she was capable of such deceit. He let it go on for a s long as he could. But when the loss became obvious, he had to bring the police in.

Judge Irving knew Bea's father. They had grown up together. Although their lives had taken different paths, they still had a mutual respect. Bea's father had taken over the family farm, while Judge Irving went on to law school. Now they were face to face after all these years.

"This is a hearing for Beatrice Ledoux, Beatrice do you understand why you're here? The Judge asked as gently as he could without showing favor.

"Yes sir, I do." She answered.

"I would like to speak to your father about this matter. Do you have any objections to this?"

"No sir."

"Mr. Ledoux are you aware of what your daughter is being charged with?"

"Yes I am." His face filled with shame.

"I would like to work something out with you if I could. Mr. Ellis and I have spoken, and he is willing to let Beatrice go if you are willing to pay the bank back all the money with interest. I however feel that Beatrice will not learn anything if there are no consequences. Beatrice you will have to go to Kitchener's reformatory for girls for one year. Then your record will be expunged. Do you agree with these terms?" He asked.

Mr. Ledoux stood still for a very long moment. Bea wasn't sure what his response was going to be. Then the silence was broken.

"Your honor I don't have that kind of money, but if you can give me a few days I have someone who has wanted to buy my land for some time now. I'll reach out to him, and I will get the money." Mr. Ledoux lowered his head in total defeat.

Bea's heart sank. He was going to give up the family land. For her? Oh, what had she done?

Judge Irving looked at her father with compassion, then her, and simply said "Miss Ledoux you are to be taken to the Oakwood Reformatory in Kitchener where you will be held for one year." He slammed his gavel down and said, "this hearing is adjourned."

Bea looked at her father with tears streaming down her face. But the look she got in return was devastating. All the hopes and dreams he had for his oldest child, all the hard work, long hours working in the fields so he could afford to send her to the best school. All the while the rest of the family went without. All that and so much more came through one disappointing, piercing look.

"Bea" he said

"Yes Father"

"I don't ever want to see you again." He turned and left the room.

The guard the had been holding Bea's arm was now holding the whole weight of her.

Chapter 5

The bus ride to Kitchener was hot and bumpy. There was no comfort afforded here. How she longed for Albert. She wondered if he had any idea. Surely, he would have thought something was wrong when she didn't get on the bus that awful Monday morning. She wondered how Agnes had taken the betrayal. Would she ever see her again? As she pondered her fate, she had to think how ironic it was that she had so desperately wanted to get out of town and look at her now.

The bus pulled up to a large gate surrounded by a fence topped with barbed wire. This is not at all what she thought the next year of her life would look like. A large woman with the hands of a man greeted Bea. "Follow me" was all she said. Bea did as she was told. And she continued to do as she was told because she was scared to death. This was only the second time she had been away from home. She was desperately trying not to think of the first time.

Days passed then weeks. Bea kept her head down for the most part. She had to work in the kitchen along with one other girl. They were paired off, so they had to be responsible for one another, You broke the rules, and your partner received the same punishment as you. Bea's partner was a real law breaker named Sheila. She had been caught stealing four times. The last time she got caught she had pulled a knife on the man she was robbing. Her parents were big shots in her hometown, so the judge to keep things quiet.

Sheila and Bea had become fast friends mainly because Bea had done most of Sheila's work. Bea didn't really mind though since it kept her busy. Less time to think. Bea had been so busy however that when Sheila asked if she had an extra rag Bea realized she hadn't had her period. Fear washed over her, and suddenly she felt faint.

"Hey are you alright?" Sheila could see something was upsetting Bea.

"Um, I don't know." Bea was close to tears now. Could she really be pregnant? Albert would surely marry her. Oh, the thoughts were coming so fast she could barely contain herself.

"Bea, snap out of it. What's going on?"

"I haven't had my period." Saying it out loud seemed to make it real.

"What? Holy shit! If your pregnant, you'll get out of here!" Sheila was jumping up and down. Could she be right? Bea thought.

When the doctor entered the room, his face gave nothing away. Hardened from all he had seen in here; he was in no mood to sugar coat this. "Miss. Ledoux you're pregnant." Bea didn't know what to say or to feel so she just sat still.

"I will be in touch with your parents, and we will then discuss our next steps."

"Next steps? What are you talking about? This is my baby!" Bea didn't understand.

"Well as long as you're here the decision is not yours. Now if you have any other questions?"

"I don't understand!" But with that Dr. Patterson turned and left the room. The nurse entered the room along with a guard and told Bea to get dressed.

"What's going to happen to my baby?" Bea's questions were left unanswered.

"They won't tell me anything." Bea said to an anxious Sheila.

"Don't worry Bea, those bastards can't do anything to your baby. They'll tell your parents what's going on but ultimately the decision will be yours." Sheila tried to reassure Bea.

What decision she thought. This baby is mine.

Two weeks passed without a word. Bea was scrubbing the last pot when a guard called her name. Startled, Bea turned to see the guard waving her hand from across the large kitchen. Bea quickly wiped the dirty dishwater from her arms and slung the towel over her shoulder as she made her way a to the guard.

"Yes?" she asked.

"Follow me." As usual, no explanation. Bea stole a quick glance at Sheila as she let the kitchen. She was led down a long corridor and then up two flights of stairs.

"Wait here." Bea stood still as she waited to be told what to do next. A large door swung opened and behind it was a small office with a kind looking woman sitting behind a desk.

"Come in please Bea. The warden will be right with you." Warden? Why Bea thought. She hadn't done anything wrong. A busser sounded and Bea was led into the Warden's office.

"This is Miss. Ledoux, Warden Jeffrey." The kind lady then left the office closing the door behind her.

"Have a seat Miss. Ledoux. Do you know why you're here?"

"No sir."

"I've been in contact with your parents, and they are now aware of your situation." It was obvious he was uncomfortable having to have this conversation.

"You told them?" She managed to whisper.

"Well of course. They have instructed me to inform you that you are to relinquish all parental rights upon the birth of the child. We will, of course, handle everything from here on. We have a relationship with a suitable agency. The child will become a ward of the province. You won't have to worry about a thing." Bea's head began to spin. What was he saying? They couldn't do this. They couldn't take her baby and give it to strangers. She could taste the bile welling up inside her. She couldn't focus on the words that floating around the room. I don't feel well was the last thing she remembered saying.

"Miss Ledoux. Are you alright? Miriam, get in here. Get her a glass of water." She was laying on the floor and the Warden was holding her head in his hands. A guard was shaking her shoulders.

"What happened? She asked

"You fainted." Miriam answered as she handed her a glass of water. "Drink this."

"You can't have my baby. I won't let you take my baby!" Bea was suddenly very angry.

"Miss Ledoux, you just turned eighteen and although this is 1935, there is no place for a fatherless child in society."

"What makes you think my child is fatherless? When I tell him he'll be very happy." She almost believed what she was saying.

"It's our understanding that he is a married man."

"But when he finds out about our baby everything will change." Bea was seated now and very defiant.

"He knows. Your parents informed him. He wants nothing to do with you or the baby."

The words hit Bea with such force that she thought she might scream. But she didn't. Instead, she became very quiet.

"Do you have any further questions?"

Bea thought for a long moment. Then with newfound strength she said, I'm eighteen years old and this baby is mine. I will decide what I want to do with it. "Can I leave now?"

Chapter 6

The months were flying by. Bea's feet were swollen but as the saying goes, there's no rest for the wicked. After her meeting with the Warden, Bea began to write letters. One a day for the next two weeks. She pleaded with her mother to let her keep this baby. She also wrote to Albert. Bea's mother was adamant about her decision for adoption. If Bea would agree, she could come home. But she had caused their family enough shame, so she was absolutely forbidden to keep that baby. The letters she had written to Albert all came back unopened, marked return to sender. All but one. The first one. The response wasn't from Albert, it was from Roberta. Her answer was clear. Bea was to stay away from her husband and her family. If indeed the child is Albert's, he doesn't want it. There is to be no further communication.

Bea was alone. Completely and totally alone. The baby growing in her belly was nothing more than a reminder of everything she had lost. How could she ever love it? Why should she keep it? Her love for Albert had turned to disgust. He was a coward. Plain and simple, He lied to Bea, and she had been gullible enough to believe him. Everything she was, was a lie. Her own mother only wanted her to care for her brothers and sisters. She went to work every day and handed her paycheck over to her father. Had she not paid them back? If they thought, she was going to return to that life they had another thing coming.

Sheila turned out to be a better friend than Bea could have dreamed. She worked twice as hard so Bea could back off a little. On days that Bea couldn't get out of bed, Sheila would rub her back. When Bea couldn't get her feet into her shoes it was Sheila who demanded larger shoes for Bea. And when Bea didn't think she could find the strength to follow through with her plan, it was Sheila who convinced her she was doing the right thing. Bea was extremely tired. It took all her strength to make her own bed. As she reached over to tuck the blanket under the thin mattress, a stabbing pain almost took her to her knees. She was careful not to bond with the baby growing in her swollen belly but in this moment, she couldn't help thinking this was payback. Before she could catch her breath, she felt a rush of hot liquid run down her legs.

"Sheila! Sheila, I need you!" Bea was sure this was it.

Sheila was by her side in no time. "I'm here Bea, I'm here."

When Bea awoke there was a nurse checking her blood pressure and another was fidgeting with papers.

"Miss. Ledoux, you've had a baby. Everything is fine. We need you to sit up." Sit up she thought, I can barely feel my legs.

"Come on now, you need to sign these papers." The nurse sounded annoyed.

"What is it?" She was trying to find her voice, but she wasn't sure if they heard her. "What is it?" This time she was loud and clear.

"Are you sure you want to know? After all, when you sign the papers, you'll never have to know." The nurse was pushing the papers toward Bea.

"I'm not signing any papers. I want my baby!"

"This is very unexpected Miss. Ledoux, we thought..."

"Well, you thought wrong. Now what is it?"

"You've given birth to a healthy baby girl." The nurse was now reaching back for the papers.

"Mary Ellen, her name is Mary Ellen." Then Bea fell fast asleep.

Miss. Ledoux wake up; Warden Jeffrey is here to see you." Bea sat up and tried to shake off the sleep.

"Warden Jeffrey, is everything okay?" Can I see Mary Ellen?"

"Your baby is fine. I'm here to make sure know what you're doing." He sounded genuinely concerned.

"Yes, thank you. I know exactly what I'm doing." But she wasn't sure she did. "I want my baby." Bea did appreciate his concern, but she had to do this.

"Well, I had to be sure. As soon as you can travel, I'll sign your release papers. We aren't in the business of caring for babies, you have been here for eight of your twelve-month sentence. We believe it is in everyone's best interest to release you."

"Thank you, Warden Jeffrey."

"Don't thank me young lady, I don't think you know what you're getting yourself into."

Oh, how she knew he was right. Two weeks had gone by, and her release papers had been signed. Bea asked the Warden to let her tell her family that she was being released early and thankfully he had agreed. Her letter to her mother was short and to the point.

Mother, they have released me early and I will arrive by train on 19th of February at 4pm. Please meet me. Bea.

Bea was sorry to leave Sheila; besides Agnes, she was the only friend Bea had every really had. The memory of Agnes only caused Bea pain. What must Agnes think of her? She shook off the feeling. She was going to need all her strength to pull of the next part of her plan. She pulled her collar high against her cheeks to fight against the cold wind that stung her face. She also held tight against her chest the warm little bundle that she was desperately trying not to bond with. The first time she laid eyes on Mary Ellen her heart soared. Mary Ellen was a good baby. She didn't cry once on the long train ride home. Bea was careful not to look at her too much, but she was so drawn to her. This was for the best; Bea was sure of it

Chapter 7

The train arrived at precisely 4pm. Bea could see her mother and two sisters waiting on the platform. Her father was still not ready to face her. Would he ever? She couldn't worry about that now. The train came to a stop with a bit of a jolt. Mary Ellen fidgeted in Bea's arms.

"This is it, Mary Ellen. I do love you." Bea held her close for a brief moment, and then with all her resolve stepped off the train. The look of shock on her mother's face was a little unsettling to Bea, but after all what did she expect.

"Beatrice what is going on here?" Her mother voice was full of pain. "Why? What are you doing?"

"Mother this is Mary Ellen. Your granddaughter. I will not be coming home with you, but Mary Ellen will." She handed Mary Ellen to her mother and walked away.

"Bea! Bea! Come back here. Where are you going?" She could hear her sisters' questions but would not look back. Bea knew Mary Ellen would be cared for she would be surrounded by family. If her mother wanted Bea to give her baby away, she would, to her.

Sheila had given Bea the name of one of her father's friends who owned a chain of hair salons. Bea had a job waiting and one of

Sheila's friends was willing to share her apartment with her. Sheila had thought of everything. Bea jumped into one of the many taxies waiting and handed the driver the address to her new home.

When Bea arrived at the apartment building, she was full of emotion. Fighting back the tears that were welling up in her eyes she pressed the buzzer alerting her new roommate of her arrival.

"Hello." The voice coming out of the box sounded friendly.

"Hi Mary? This is Bea." The door clicked and Bea entered her new life.

Chapter 8

"Bea. Come in." Mary was a pretty girl. Not as pretty as Bea, but she had a confidence that Bea was immediately drawn to. "Sheila has told me so much about you I feel like we already know each other. If you're a friend of Sheila's you're a friend of mine." Mary said. "Is that all you have?" Pointing to a little bag that Bea had forgotten she was carrying.

"Um, yes. I'll get the rest of my things from my parents as soon as things settle down." "Oh ya, Sheila told me all about your little situation."

"She did?" Bea was a little surprised but still thankful.

"Don't get your panties in a bunch honey, you're not the first girl to give up a kid." What did she mean, Bea hadn't given up a kid, she simply gave Mary Ellen to her mother? That was different. She wasn't like those women. Bea would get on her feet and then take Mary Ellen back. Then her mother would feel how crazy it was that she had told Bea she had to give her up. After a restless night Bea was ready to get started on her new life. "Coffee?" Mary asked.

"I've never tried coffee."

"Well today is the day you will." Replied Mary. It was a little bitter to Bea, but she liked the way it made her feel. Like she had more energy or something. This day was starting out perfectly. They grabbed their purses and headed out the door for the five blocks walk to work. Living downtown was going to be exciting. There was so much going on. People coming and going. Everyone in a hurry and moving with a purpose. Bea was careful to avoid walking past the bank that she had worked at hoping she wouldn't be spotted. Mary didn't mind going a block out of their way if it meant helping her new friend. Bea's first day at the salon was exhausting. She had forgotten what it was like to be on her feet all day. Bea was responsible for washing the patron's hair. After Lidia, the manager of the salon, showed her around she was left on her own. In between shampoos she had to sweep up the hair. Washed towels and answer the phone.

It was seven pm when the last customer left. Bea was dead on her feet; Mary had left hours ago after her last client. Bea had to walk back to the apartment alone. She didn't have to worry about the bank though since it had closed hours earlier. Bea stopped at a little fish and chip joint and grabbed dinner to go. It would be cold by the time she got home so she nibbled on it as she walked. When she put the key in the door, she could hear laughter coming from inside. Oh no she thought, company.

"Hey Bea, come on in I want you to meet some friends. This is Sue and Jack and Ronny and Phil."

"Ah, hi everyone. I'm sorry but if you'll excuse me, I'm a little tired. So, I'll get out of your way."

"Oh no you don't Bea. We're celebrating." Mary announced.

"Celebrating what?" Bea questioned

"Your new job, of course silly. Now sit down here next to Ronny and have a drink with us." Bea had only drunk once in her life and that was a memory she did not want to recall. "What's your poison?" Mary inquired

"Um, Whiskey?"

"Oh, hey boys, we've got a live one. Sure honey, how do you want it?"

"Ah, over ice?" Ronny smiled at Bea in a way that made her a little uncomfortable, but she didn't want to upset the party, so she just pushed that feeling aside. Music was playing on the radio, Fred Astaire, followed by Benny Goodman. One after another. Her glass didn't have a chance to empty before Ronny was filling it for her. She was warm and relaxed. Ronny was sitting very close, but she really didn't mind. His eyes were dark, and his teeth were crooked. His dark hair fell in waves over his forehead, and she thought he was kind of cute. When Bea looked around, she realized Mary and Phil were gone and Sue and Jack were smashed together so close no air could pass between them.

"Ah, I think I should go to bed." She said. Although the words came out a little different than she heard in her head. What was going on.

"Perfect" Ronny said, "I thought you'd never ask"

"What?" Fear gripped her throat. Before she could say anything else, she stumbled.

"Here let me help you." Ronny said. He had his hands around her waist and was leading her to the bedroom. Once inside he closed the door behind her. It all happened so fast Bea was in shock.

"You're so beautiful" he said. His hands expertly hovered over her blouse until they found the buttons. One quick tug and her breasts were exposed.

"Wait, wait." Her words fell on deaf ears. He moved to the button on her skirt and then to the zipper. Down it fell.

"Please" she whispered.

"Shhh, you'll love it." He was hot and hairy, and she couldn't focus. When he entered her, she began to pray, pray that this would be over soon. She prayed that he wouldn't hurt her. She prayed she would find the strength not to cry. The curtains moved slowly as the warm night air filled the room. Bea focused on the rhythm of their movement. It was over. It was nothing like when she and Albert made love. This was animalistic. Pure and simple. He rolled over and said.

"Baby that was great. Thanks, but I gotta go. Got to work in the morning."

What was he saying? Did he really think she wanted him to stay? Oh, she didn't feel very good.

"Bye baby. See ya round." The door closed behind him, and Bea grabbed her garbage can and threw up. When the alarm rang the next morning, it almost shook of the nightstand. It also shook Bea to the core. Ahh, she said as she grabbed her head with one hand and searched for the alarm with the other. It felt like she had just closed her eyes. Her teeth hurt, how could her teeth hurt. Whiskey she thought. So, this is a hangover. Bea eased herself out of the bed and a wave of nausea washed over her. Thankfully it passed. There was a light tap on her door. Mary peaked in

"Morning, how ya doin?"

"Not so good I'm afraid."

"Ya, you were putting them away pretty good last night. Not that I want you to kiss and tell but what did you think? Isn't Ronny dreamy? I knew you'd just love him."

"Ya, ya, he's great."

"Okay girly let's get going, the rent doesn't pay itself."

Wow she had to work. What was she thinking? Tuesday was harder than Monday. And Wednesday was harder still. Bea learned that the salon got busier as the week progressed. Friday was the worst. The salon opened at 8 am and closed at 9pm. Woman needed to look good for the weekend.

One month had gone by when Lydia approached Bea and said, "I'll need you to stay late tomorrow night Bea so I can start training you to be a beautician."

"Sure" Bea replied. This is what she had been waiting for. She knew not to overstep though; this was a means to an end. An end that would get Mary Ellen back. Summer turned to fall, and Bea was nearing the completion of her training. All that was left was the test that she was sure she would pass. When she had her own chair, she would start making some serious money. And money meant Mary Ellen.

Parties were becoming a way of life. Bea had put her foot down about drinking through the week, but the weekends were a different story. Bea had no idea life could be so much fun. Mary had introduced her to a whole new way of life. Work hard, play hard. Ronny was still hanging around and she had entertained him a few times since that first night but now it was on her terms. She was becoming a party girl. Unfortunately, she didn't understand all that came along with that. Bea was building up a sizable clientele. She was in high demand and was able to charge a fair amount for her services. It was taking her longer than she thought though to save money to start a life with Mary Ellen though. Between rent, groceries, the cost of renting a chair at this salon. All the weekend jaunts, money was tight. Bea was hard at work on blustery night in late November when the door swung open letting a cold blast of wind come rushing in. She turned quickly and was shocked to see her brother standing there.

"Ernie! What are you doing here? Is Mary Ellen alright?"

"It's not Mary Ellen Bea, its dad." Tears were welling up in her brothers' eyes. Ernie was 3 years younger than her, and she had been very close to him.

"Dad? What are you saying Ernie?"

"Oh Bea, dad is gone. He had a massive heart attack. He's gone." Bea stopped breathing. No this can't be happening. She had so much to say to him. She couldn't bear the thought of the last words he spoke to her.

"How's mom?" She asked.

"Not good, Bea. Can you come home?"

"Does she want me home?" She asked

"She doesn't know I'm here. Please Bea." Bea didn't know how she would face her mother. This isn't how she planned to see Mary Ellen either, after all this time. One foot in front of the other. Those were the words her father used to say to her when she was a little girl. If things were hard and she questioned what she could do, he would always tell her to put one foot in front of the other. Here she was and she wasn't sure she could do it.

Ernie opened the front door and went in first. There sitting in the living room was her mother. She looked older, a lot older. Her mother's sister was sitting next to her. Bea was shaking.

"Mother" was all she could say. Mrs. Ledoux couldn't believe the nerve of her oldest child. Hadn't she done enough.

"What are you doing here?" Her words were cutting and filled with pain.

"Mother, I'm here for you."

"Then you should leave, because I don't need you here or want you here."

Tears began to stream down Bea's cheeks.

"Don't you dare cry. Your father died of a broken heart. He loved you and you broke his heart."

"Mother, please." Bea whimpered.

"I'll let you come to the funeral but that's it. Do you hear me?"

"Can I see Mary Ellen?"

"No." Was all her mother said as she turned and left the room. Bea's aunt Mirna came to her, took her hand.

"Bea your mother is in a lot of pain. Please don't make this any worse than it already is. Mary Ellen is fine. Your brother will let you know when the arrangements are made. Now please leave." Bea walked out the front door. She now had a better understanding of the pain she had caused. What must her father have gone through? She had been so selfish and naïve. What was to become of her family. Her mother? Bea walked a long way until she finally saw a taxi stand. She got in and began to weep. The funeral was held in the large Catholic Church that her father had given so much to. He gave his time and his money. Bea hadn't been here in almost two years. She was overwhelmed with all the people who had come to say their final goodbyes to this good man. Her mother sat erect in the first pew with all her children next to her in a row. Bea was led by the arm to the opposite end of that same pew. They were like book ends. Holding up a bunch of broken, tattered books. Her youngest sister Louise leaned forward when Bea sat down and smiled at her through tear-streaked eyes. Bea missed her so much. She hadn't realized how much until this very moment. She spotted Mary Ellen in the arms of her aunt. It would be impossible for Bea to go to her now the funeral procession was coming up the center aisle. Her father, the man who had given so much, all so she could have everything, was lying in that box. He is lying there because of me she thought. Mother is right I did this, I killed him. When the funeral mass was complete the family marched out of the church behind the casket. Bea was the last one so as she stepped into the isle her aunt stepped out right behind her. Bea looked at her beautiful daughter for the first time in months. She had his eyes. She was beautiful. Full round face and blonde curls in a crazy mess atop her head. Bea stopped to touch her, but her aunt shot her a look much like her mother could. Bea knew better. Once out of the church Aunt Mirna and Mary Ellen disappeared in the crowd. Bea was mobbed by people wanting to give they're sympathy

Chapter 9

When Bea got back to her apartment, she was alone. She walked directly over to the little liquor cabinet and pulled out a bottle of whiskey. Without a thought she took a long swig. It burned all the way down. It felt good. Really good. She took another on the way into the kitchen to get a glass. She poured until it reached the top. And slowly moved to her room. Bea didn't hear Mary come home that night. Or leave for work the next morning. When she did open her eyes, the sun was high in the sky. And she wasn't interested in seeing it. There was a little left in the bottle that kept her company last night, so she finished it off. When Mary came home that night, she knocked on Bea's door.

"Bea are you alright? Do you want to talk about it?" Bea swallowed hard fighting back the tears. Mary peaked her head in the door.

"Bea darling please talk to me."

"I killed him." She managed to whisper.

"Killed who?" She asked shocked

"My father" Bea whimpered.

"Bea don't be ridiculous. You didn't kill your father."

"I did. His heart was broken by what I did and now they won't let me see Mary Ellen. I've made such a mess of things." Mary moved to the bed where Bea had taken refuge.

"Look Bea, things seem like a mess right now but give them time. Your mom is grieving, and you've lost your way, but you'll find it. Now come on get up and wash your face we need to go out. My treat." Bea was so grateful she had a friend like Mary. A drink and a few laughs were just what she needed.

The juke box was blasting out the latest greatest hits of 1937. People were talking about some guy named Hitler and what would happen if he was able to win his party in Germany. Why did they care she thought? Let's dance and have another drink. There was a tall handsome looking fellow who hadn't taken his eyes off her since she walked in and now, he was coming her way.

"Wanna dance?" His hand was outstretched, and she willingly took it. The dance was the beginning, the drinking continued and once the whiskey took full affect, she was like putty in his hands.

"Wanna get out of here?"

"Sure." She slurred. They were driving down a road that Bea didn't recognize but she really didn't care. The car pulled to a stop, and he slowly looked at her.

"This is as good a place as any, right?" She knew what he wanted, and Bea was more than willing to give it. She slid her panties off and lifted her skirt. She expertly climbed over the gear shift and onto his lap. He was trying to undo his belt when Bea pushed his hand away. With one hand she expertly undid his belt all the while she was rubbing his growing hardness. Bea reached it to his pants and released his yearning. She knew what a man wanted. What he needed and she needed it to. She mounted him and the rhythm began. The windows were steaming up and the drops of sweat were sliding between her firm breasts. He took her nipple into his mouth and began to suck. One hand on her breast and one on her ass. He was pulling and pushing right along with her. Then it was brought to the climax they both needed. An amazing release. She felt empowered, like a new woman. In that moment Bea decided no one would hurt her again, ever.

She climbed back over the gear shift and retrieved her panties, slid them on and then without looking at this man she barely knew told him she was ready to go home.

Chapter 10

Work was going along fine but no matter how hard she worked she couldn't seem to get ahead. Six months had passed since her father's funeral. She knew it was well passed time to take charge of her daughter but how could she if she had nothing to offer her. She wrote her mother asking to see her, but she got no response. She wasn't going to be ignored. She would go to her mother's house on Sunday and insist. Sunday morning found Bea with a bit of a hangover. Saturday night started in the usual way. After work she'd stop at the liquor store get two bottles of crown royal and a pack of smokes. Next, she'd stop and grab some fish for herself and Mary. Once they had finished sharing the piece of battered cod. They would pour themselves a drink. One for the road they'd say. By eight thirty they were headed down the road to their first bar. A little hole in the wall that was frequented by the local dock workers. They had all gotten their pay so the drinks would be flowing. After a bit of flirting the men were lining up to by the girls a drink. Men were so stupid. When Mary and Bea knew they had gotten out of them all they could without having to give back anything the headed out to where the real party was starting. By ten o'clock they stepped into a real hot spot in the heart of the city. It was filled with sailors looking for a good time and these were the girls who knew how to give it.

Now, Bea knew the perfect way to stop the dull ache that nagged her. Besides a little hair of the dog, there was nothing wrong with a little liquid courage. Two birds one drink, or maybe two.

When Bea arrived at her mother's house she couldn't help feeling like a scared child. She was a grown woman, and she would put her foot down. Louise was outside with Mary Ellen playing. Bea stopped dead in her tracks. She had grown so much. Had it really been over a year? Fifteen months, to be exact. It was May 1937. Bea had been so caught up in her own life that she didn't realize her daughter wasn't going to stay a baby forever.

"Louise!" Louise looked up and then ran to Bea. She was almost twelve years old now. The youngest of all her siblings. She missed her so much. Louise hugged Bea and began to cry.

"Shhh. Darling its ok I'm here."

"Are you staying Bea? I miss you, please stay." She pleaded. Bea couldn't answer her. All her attention now focused on the blue-eyed beauty staring at her.

"Hey, is this my Mary Ellen?" Hi Mary Ellen, I'm your mommy."

Just then her mother yelled out the window for them to come in to eat Sunday dinner. Bea stood up and then reached down and picked up her daughter. She turned and walked into her mother's house.

"Louise, go wash your hands and bring Mary Ellen to me." Her mother said as she mashed the potatoes with the same potato masher her mother had used and her mother before her.

"Hello mother." Bea said. Mrs. Ledoux turned around and shook her head.

"What do you want Bea?"

"I just want to see my daughter. I don't want any trouble mother."

"Trouble follows you, Beatrice. You have your daughter in your arms, now what do you plan on doing with her?" Had she really called her bluff? Shit, shit. Think.

"I thought I could take her home with me for the afternoon." She hadn't planned that, but she wouldn't let her mother know.

"Fine." Her mother said. "Take her"

"Um, now?" Bea's mother didn't respond. Bea turned and walked out the door. Mary Ellen began to cry, her outstretched arms reaching for her meme.

"It's ok Mary Ellen, I'm your mommy. It will be fun. Please stop crying."

When Bea got back to the apartment Mary, Phil and Ronny were sitting at the kitchen table helping themselves to her whiskey.

"What have we got here?" Ronny slurred

"This is my daughter. Now pour me a drink?" Mary Ellen fell fast asleep on a makeshift bed Bea made on the floor of her bedroom.

"Aren't you afraid she might wake up?" Ronny asked

"She's just a baby, she won't remember anything if she does. Now shut up and get on with it."

Even Ronny didn't feel right about this, but he knew he wanted her and after a night of drinking he really didn't care who watched. It was after midnight when Mary Ellen began to cry.

"What the hell?" Ronny was not happy. "Make her stop." He barked Bea rolled over and grabbed her robe.

"Mary Ellen shhh. It's okay I'm here." Her eyes were swollen, and her cheeks were red.

"Meme." Oh, my she smelled like something the cat dragged in. Bea hadn't thought about grabbing diapers or her bottle or anything. She simply walked out of her mother's house because she had a point to prove. Bea cleared the table and grabbed a couple dish rags. She had changed enough diapers in her day to know what had to be done. "Shhh Mary Ellen."

Mary came stumbling out of her room.

"What the hell is going on?"

"Sorry Mary. I'm trying to settle her down." Bea said. "She's just scared."

"We have to work in the morning Bea. Please make her stop." Just then the buzzer to the apartment sounded. What on earth she thought. It's after midnight. She gathered Mary Ellen in her arms and went to see who in their right mind would be out this late.

"Yes? Can I help you?" "Miss Ledoux, this is Officer Pickford. I'm here with your mother. Please open the door." What! Oh no! Bea pushed the button to release the lock and began to pick up the empty bottles and glasses.

"What the hell is going on?" Mary and Ronny were now both out of bed looking very irritated. Then there was a knock on the door. Mary Ellen began to cry again. Mary demanded an answer.

"Bea, who's that?"

"Please go back to bed, both of you. It's my mother." Then the knocking got louder. Bea shot a pleading look at Mary who in turn grabbed Ronny and headed back down the hall. Bea took a big breath and opened the door.

"Mother, ah what are you doing here?"

"Give me Mary Ellen now." She barked

"What? Why?" Bea couldn't believe the audacity of her mother. Office Pickford stepped in and reached for Mary Ellen.

"What do you think you're doing?" She demanded.

"Miss Ledoux, you told your mother you were going to take Mary Ellen for the afternoon. We had some trouble finding you since you left no address." He took Mary Ellen from Bea's arms and handed her to her grandmother.

"Mother, I ah." Words weren't coming to Bea. She was still a little drunk. Bea's mother looked at Bea for a long moment and then turned and walked out the door. Officer Pickford tipped his hat and followed. Bea was left standing in her apartment alone with the smell of Mary Ellen still clinging to her. Bea slowly walked to the kitchen and poured herself a stiff drink.

Chapter 11

Time is a funny thing; it seems like it's dragging on but when you look back you can't believe how quickly it goes bye. Mary Ellen's third birthday was just days away. Has it really been three years Bea thought? She hadn't seen or heard from Albert since that day in the car. She could still hear his final words to her. "I'm sorry." She bet he was. She wondered if he ever thought of them. Bea still had a hard time believing he could just walk away from his own daughter. Why was she doing this to herself? She had the day off and she was going to go shopping for the perfect gift for Mary Ellen. It had to be better than anything her mother would give her. Bea would show her up and Mary Ellen would love it. Bea had only seen Mary Ellen a few times since the night her mother came to get her. Things between Bea and her mother were cold to say the least, but she never stopped her from seeing Mary Ellen. Bea tried but there just always seemed to be something that got in the way. If it wasn't work, it was a party here, or a few days away there. Time is a funny thing. When Bea arrived at Woolworth's she didn't realize it was close to lunch time. She hurried passed the lunch counter trying not to look in the direction of the people trying to get a seat.

"Bea! Bea!" There was a woman waving to her.

"Bea, oh my God is that you?" It was Agnes and she looked fantastic. Why hadn't she paid more attention to the time? Now she had no way out.

"Agnes?" Bea tried to look happy, but she really wasn't ready to face her old friend. Agnes was wrapping her arms around Bea, and she smelled wonderful.

"Oh, Bea it's so good to see you. How are you? Where are you living? What are you doing these days?" Agnes had so many questions. Bea was overwhelmed with emotion.

"Oh, Agnes I'm so sorry." Tears were welling up in her eyes. Agnes took Bea by the arm and led her outside. They walked arm and arm to the park where they found the same bench she used to share with Albert.

"Where do I begin" Bea questioned? Agnes took a hanky out of her handbag and patted her cheeks. She was already late getting back to work, but she couldn't leave Bea. Bea began the whole sorted saga.

"I had no idea, Bea. Albert came into the bank looking for you and when I told him what happened he turned white. He really had no idea. He had been worried sick. We went for lunch, and he told me he broke up with you but that he couldn't get over you. He went to the park everyday hoping you would show up. When you didn't, he thought he would come by the bank. None of us knew what happened to you. We were told you quit and moved. When I went to see your mother. She said you had an aunt that lived out of town who had become ill and needed you to care for her children."

Bea was shocked. She thought everyone must know. She had been so ashamed. Her mother had never said a word.

"Agnes, don't you hate me?" Bea's question was sincere.

"Bea, I don't like what you did. But I think you've paid for your mistake. And my God you have a daughter. I can't wait to meet her." Bea knew Agnes must be late getting back to work; besides she could barely feel her fingers and toes. It was a beautiful sunny day, but it was February after all. They agreed to meet for lunch at a little diner so Agnes could meet Mary Ellen later that month and she was off. Bea realized she hadn't asked Agnes one question about herself. Had Albert really missed her? Why was he so adamant about not wanting Mary Ellen? Well, it really didn't change anything did it? He made himself perfectly clear not once but twice. Bea found a little baby doll that she just knew Mary Ellen would love. It wasn't exactly the fantastic gift she had hoped for, but as usual time had gotten away from her. She was too exhausted to go back to the department store after meeting Agnes. Then she got busy with work and stuff. Well, that's alright the thought. She's only three she probably won't even remember.

It was Saturday night and the fun had begun. Mary was well on her way when Bea got home from work.

"You started without me?" Bea stated.

"Well maybe a bit, I wasn't sure if you were going to make it tonight with the kids' birthday tomorrow and everything." She answered.

"When have you ever known me to miss a good time?" She said with a wry smile on her face. "Just give me a minute to freshen up and I'll be ready." They were out the door in no time.

There was a dance going on in the French Club right down the road and these girls loved to dance. The boys were all coming in in their uniforms. There was a lot of talk of Canada entering the war and young men were lining up at recruitment centers across the country. Even Bea's three brothers had signed up. Much to the disappointment to her mother. The drinks were flowing, and the music was melodic. Bea was dancing with a handsome young man who'd recently received his Canadian citizenship. He had a fabulous Italian accent. He had dark eyes and dark curly hair. The sides were slicked back with pomade, and he smelled like a dream.

"Is there somewhere we can go?" He asked

"Sure, I live right down the road" she said with a sexy little grin. With a wave to Mary, they were off. Bea put the key in the door and Mario held it for her. He was a real gentleman. Once inside Bea offered him a drink.

"Yes please". Please? She thought. He has manners. Even mother would like this one. She assumed he was catholic which was an absolute must for her church going mother. How funny she thought. She handed Mario his drink and he threw it back, then handed her the glass and said another please. Bea hadn't even had a sip of her drink yet.

"Sure" she said. This time he drank it a little more slowly, but he still finished it before she was able to sit down. As she moved toward the couch he stood. Bea didn't know what was going on with this guy, but she needed to sit down. "Hey why don't you relax.? She said. He shot her a look that made her blood chill. His once dreamy brown eyes seemed to have turned black.

"Don't tell me what to do." The words were cold and deliberate. Before Bea knew what was happening, he slapped her right across the face. The pain shot up her jaw and into her eye. Followed immediately by another blow. This time it was a full fist. Now she was on the floor. Bea scrambled as fast as she could, but he was faster. He grabbed her by the back of her head taking a full fist of her hair in his grasp.

"Don't fight me." He barked. Bea went limp. When she did, he kicked her in the side. "Roll over bitch." Bea wasn't sure what was happening, but she did as she was told. When she did, he reached down like a mad man and pulled her skirt up.

"Why? What?"

"Shut up" he said almost calmly. Then he hit her again. This time there was darkness.

Chapter 12

When Bea came to, she was alone there was pain shooting though her whole body. Her mouth was bleeding and the pain coming from between her legs was excruciating. Tears were welling up and then the sobs began. Just then the door opened, and Bea screamed. She tried to move but was unable to lift herself.

"Bea! Oh my God Bea!" Mary couldn't believe what she was seeing. Mary came home with a sailor she met at the club and now they were both at Bea's side.

"Don't move her" he said. "I'm a medic. Get some ice quick". Mary did as she was told. "Bea, can you move" he asked.

"It's ok Bea, I'm here. Mary took her hand. They managed to get her onto the couch.

"Bea what happened? Mary asked. All the while Mary's new friend was examining her.

"Bea does this hurt?" He asked.

"Please leave". Was all she could say. He shot Mary a look.

"I think she should go to the hospital Mary"

"No, No. I can't. Please Mary." Bea was crying now.

"Okay Bea". Mary led him to the door.

"She could have internal bleeding." he whispered, "And if she was raped, which I'm sure she was, you need to get the police." He turned and walked out the door.

"Wait!" she said, "Can you drive us?" Bea wasn't happy about going, but Mary insisted.

The doctor came out of the exam room and found Mary sitting alone in the waiting room.

"Can I see her?" Mary was frantic.

"Miss William, your friend has had a rough time. She has two broken ribs and a lot of bruising. She was raped and I've contacted the local police. They will be here tomorrow. Is there someone else, a family member maybe her mother or father we should call?" He asked.

"No, please, Bea is an adult. There's no one. Now can I see my friend"

"She's resting. We've given her something to help her sleep. But you can go sit with her."

Bea looked worse. The swelling had shut her eye and her lip was split open they had her torso bound with bandages. Thankfully she was sleeping. Mary pulled up a chair and laid her head on the bed next to Bea. The next morning the police arrived to interview Bea. It only took a couple of questions before it was apparent, they were blaming Bea.

"So, let me get this straight you invited him into your apartment?" His accusatory tone spoke volumes.

"I don't want to press charges. I don't want to do anything. This was all my fault." Bea was taking charge. She was nobody's victim. "I would appreciate it if you would leave."

"Well, if you're sure miss." He was already closing his note pad and turning to leave. "I think you've made the right decision Miss Ledoux. Be a little more careful who you associate with."

Bea looked at Mary who was standing in the corner of the room. "Thank you, Mary."

"For what?" She asked. "You would have done it for me. I'm so sorry Bea." There was a little catch in her voice. Bea waved her over and took her hand.

The Doctor softly knocked on the door.

"Come in" Bea said.

"Miss Ledoux, can we talk privately?" He asked,

"Whatever you have to say you can say it in front of my friend." She was still holding Mary's hand when the doctor closed the door.

"After I examined you yesterday, I ran a couple tests and I'm sorry to say you will not be able to have children." Bea sat still for a long time. "Do you have any questions?" He asked. Then the doctor left the room. Mary continued to hold Bea's hand.

"I think I would like to be alone Mary."

"Of course, Bea, I'll be right outside."

"Go home Mary, get some rest. I'll be okay." Mary left, not because she wanted to but because Bea needed to be alone. Bea laid in the bed replaying the events that led up to last night. Did she deserve this? She had given away her precious baby girl and now she was told she'd never have another. Oh my God Mary Ellen. Her birthday. Bea began to cry. The release papers were signed, and the nurse was wheeling her down the corridor. There was a waiting taxi on the other side of the glass doors.

"Now go slowly Miss Ledoux". The nurse bent down to release the footrests and Bea couldn't help but notice the perfectly white starched uniform, the white stockings, perfectly polished white shoes all topped off with a white cap pinned atop her head. It was a strong contrast to how dirty Bea felt. Would she ever feel clean again?

"Thank you." She said as she lifted herself out of the chair and into the backseat of the cab. Nothing was ever going to be the same.

Chapter 13

Months passed and although the visible scars were gone Bea would never be the same. She was drinking more than she ever had. But now there were no parties. No men. Mary and Bea were finding it hard to live under the same roof. The unspoken words were dripping off the walls like wet paint. Neither spoke about that night but the strain was apparent to each of them. Bea stayed home while Mary found new friends to go out with. The distance growing between them was great.

War was imminent. Canada entered the fight in September 1939. All three of Bea's brothers had signed up and were now somewhere in Europe. Christmas came and went, then spring and summer. Bea had gotten her own little apartment over a grocery store. It was one room with a very small bathroom. It was enough for her. Bea's focus was gone and so were about half her clients. To make matters worse her mother had decided to make extra money running a bootleg. How dare she? Miss holier than thou! They were in the heart of the Great Depression now. With all the boys gone to war and money scarce Bea had to find something else to do to earn money.

It was a long winter. Bea saw Mary Ellen as much as she could. Her mother was a little more accepting of the relationship she had with Mary Ellen. Mainly because she didn't really want Mary Ellen around all the men coming and going for a drink. Bea understood that her mother was just trying to make a few extra dollars, but she wouldn't let her know that. It was a little easier with Mary Ellen now that she was almost four. It was obvious to Bea. that she didn't want to be with her but that was irrelevant. So long as Bea could take her from her mother, she had the power. And she would never give up her power not anyone not even to her own mother.

Bea realized that she in fact didn't want to be a mother. She didn't like being restricted by the responsibility of a child. She loved working and drinking and neither of those things included a child. This was a hard thing for Bea to accept at first because in her heart Mary Ellen was a part of Albert. And to admit that she didn't want Alberts child was like admitting she didn't want Albert.

Christmas was the first she spent with her family in years. Her little sister Louise insisted they come together as a family. Since the boys were fighting with the allies the girls needed to stick together. Bea was a little overwhelmed when she saw her whole family come together around the table without all the men. Her mother had made a wonderful dinner. She must have sold a lot of booze she thought.

"Sit next to me Bea." Louise was a young lady now and was like a little mother to Mary Ellen. Roselyn was beautiful and she knew it. She always thought she was better than everyone else. She had a steady boyfriend and he had asked mother for her hand in marriage. Mrs. Ledoux said yes of course because he was a good catholic boy who came from a very good family. His only shortcoming was that he was flat footed and was not accepted into the army. He would join them after dinner. It bothered Bea that he came in and acted like the man of the house and worse, her mother allowed it.

"Mary Ellen, you have to go with your mother. Now get your bag and don't argue with me." Mrs. Ledoux didn't want to let Mary Ellen go with Bea, but she really didn't have a choice. Her one regret was that she didn't insist on adopting Mary Ellen when her husband was alive. She hated that Bea could use Mary Ellen like a pawn. She knew however if she fought Bea on this, she might take Mary Ellen for good. Mary Ellen was being difficult because she didn't want to be with her mother. She wanted to sleep in her own bed and play with new dolly.

"Mary Ellen, I have to go out for a bit, now get into bed and I'll be right back." Bea knew that if she didn't get out and have a drink, she would go crazy. Mary had moved and was having a few friends over to celebrate Christmas and she wasn't going to miss it. Mary Ellen began to cry, and Bea couldn't take it.

"Ok I'll stay but you have to go to sleep now." Mary Ellen crawled into Bea's bed and in no time fell fast asleep. Within minutes Bea was quietly slipping out the door locking it behind her. The party was well on its way when Bea arrived.

"Bea, you made it." Mary was genuinely happy to see her old friend. Ronny was leaning against the fridge when he saw her.

"Hey beautiful. Long time no see."

"Hi Ronny, it's been a while hasn't it."

"Boy you're a sight for sore eyes." He was smiling at her the way she remembered.

"I thought you enlisted?" Bea questioned

"Yea I did, I leave in two weeks. Guess they thought they'd give me one more Christmas as a civilian."

He seemed like a different person. Grown up she guessed. They stood in the kitchen and talked and drank and laughed and drank and kissed and drank. This was the first time she felt this way since that horrible night eight months ago. Could she go through with it she wondered. Ronny took her hand.

"Can we go to your place?" He asked.

"My kid is there." She answered.

"That never stopped us before," he said with a dirty laugh. They said their goodbyes and left.

There were no buses, so they had to walk. It was a little refreshing after being in the smoke-filled apartment.

"It's really nice to see you again Bea. I've really missed you." She could tell even though they had consumed a lot of alcohol he was sincere.

"I've missed you too Ronny. Things are so different now." He put his arm over her shoulder and pulled her close as they walked. When they arrived at her apartment she turned to him,

"Now you'll have to be quiet, okay?" She whispered. He smiled in response. Bea made a bed in the bathtub for Mary Ellen and gently placed her little body into it. She then covered her with a bath towel. When she returned to the living area Ronny was pouring her a drink.

"Thanks" she said. Ronny made love to her that night. It was the first time since Albert she felt cared for. They laid in each other's arms for a long time after in total silence.

"Bea are you awake?" He asked

"Yes".

"Will you wait for me?"

"What?" Did she hear him right? Was he serious?

"Look I know you could have anyone you want but I'm in love with you. I don't want to leave if I don't have you to come home to." He was showing her his heart. She laid the for a long time and he started to fidget

"Bea?"

"Yes darling, I'll wait." They made love again and then exhausted they slept.

Chapter 14

The war was well underway, but the Americans still hadn't entered. Things were so uncertain. Bea's mother would sit with the newspaper and her world map trying to figure out where her sons were. Ronny would send Bea letters when he could but there was no talk of what he was really going through. The letters were light and filled with his hopes and dreams for their future. Bea would respond accordingly. She didn't tell him how lonely she was or how difficult things were here at home. Everything was being rationed and the government had enacted conscription. So, boys that hadn't signed up were now being forced to go.

December 7th, 1941. The day the world changed. It was all over the news, Pearl Harbor in Hawaii had been bombed. There was death and destruction everywhere. Oh my God, were they safe? What if it happens here? People were in shock. The radio crackled with the reports coming from the States. Then it happened, America was joining the allies in Europe.

"Have you heard from any of the boys?" Bea asked her mother.

"Not in a few weeks." Her mother looked very tired. Mary Ellen was almost six now and had grown up very quickly. Bea took her when she could, but it was still obvious Mary Ellen really didn't want to go with her. Bea left and walked to the bus stop. She started taking the bus again when the war started. No one could really afford a taxi anymore and she had heard that Albert was now an electrician so there was no chance of running into him.

Her thoughts were on Ronny now. When he came home, they would start a life together and she would tell her mother Mary Ellen would be living with them. Maybe they would get a nice little house in Tecumseh near her mother so Mary Ellen could still visit her whenever she wanted. Things were looking up. The war would surely be over soon now that America was in it.

May of 1942 started off like any other spring day. The allied forces were on the march, but things weren't going as smoothly as they thought. Boys were coming home in caskets or not at all. Mrs. Ledoux had lost a lot of weight, everyone had really. She was filled with worry. Mary Ellen was a mere after thought. Instead of losing weight though Mary Ellen was gaining. She had turned into a little butter ball. She was so beautiful that wherever Bea took her people gave her candy. When Bea took her to the hotel in the afternoons she sat like a little angel. Men would order her milkshakes or soda's. It had taken its toll. When Bea dropped her off late one Sunday, she found her mother crying in the kitchen.

"Mother what is it?" Fear gripped Bea. There was a letter laying on the table. Bea picked it up. It was from her brother Peter; he had been shot but was on the mend. He was coming home. Bea dropped the letter and embraced her mother. The two women hadn't touched in years and for a brief moment all the hurt slipped away. But the moment quickly ended when her mother pulled away.

"Well, the important thing was that he was alright, and he is coming home mother." Bea was trying to gain composure.

"Yes, yes of course your right. I will go to the church in the morning and light a candle for him and your other brothers." Ernie was the third child after Roselyn then Peter then Lewis and finally her baby sister Louise. Roselyn had gotten married in a civil ceremony the fall before. Money was tight so Bea gave Her sister enough to pay for a small reception. Nothing was said. They didn't feel it was right to make a big fuss not with the war and everything. That only left Louise and Mary Ellen at home. Louise was sixteen almost seventeen now and about ready to graduate. Her mother insisted she stay in school. But she did have a job cleaning after school for one of the wealthy families in the city. Every bit helped in these difficult times.

When Bea arrived home, there was a tall older man waiting outside the grocery store. She slowly walked to the door which opened to a staircase that led to her apartment.

"Miss. Ledoux?" He called to her.

"Yes, can I help you?" She said guarded.

"I'm Mr. Walter." He said. Walter, was this Ronny's father? Bea began to shake.

"Ronny?" She whispered,

"Can we go somewhere to talk?" She led him into her apartment. The resemblance was startling. His hair was going grey, but it was wavy just like Ronny's. And he was tall, and his nose was the same. Is this what Ronny will look like she thought. Then reality slapped her. Once inside her apartment she offered him a drink.

"No thank you" he said, "Ronny has written us about you Bea, can I call you Bea?" She shook her head yes. "He said if anything ever happened, we were to find you and let you know." He was fidgeting with the brim of the hat he had taken off upon entering her living room. He then pulled out a letter from his pocket and handed it to her. "We got a telegram two days ago. This was the first chance I've had to come to you. I'm really sorry dear."

What was he saying? Bea took the letter into her trembling hand. She tried to read it, but her eyes wouldn't focus.

"What are you saying?" She demanded

"Ronny is gone Bea; he wrote you this letter and told us to make sure you got if he didn't make it home." Tears were streaming down his cheeks as he crushed the hat in his hands. Bea became very stoic.

"Thank you, Mr. Walter. I'm very sorry for your loss." Bea led him to the door.

"Are you sure you're alright Bea?" He asked. But Bea couldn't answer. She quietly closed the door behind him and then poured herself a drink. Bea sat at the table and opened the letter again.

My beautiful Bea, if you're reading this, well I guess you know I'm not coming home. I want you to know that I really love you Bea and you are everything I could ever have hoped for. I will never forget the times we've shared, and I will never forget you. All my love, Ronny.

Bea sat shocked for a long time. Even the drinks weren't helping. Then the sobs came. Like waves crashing into her heart. She let them wash over her. She wanted to drown. Instead, she drank. Bea woke up with her head in her hands resting on the table. The letter staring up at her. For a brief second, she thought it had been a dream, but she was looking at the proof of her new reality. Alone, totally and forever alone.

Days had gone by before Bea made it into work. Lydia shot her a look. Then softened when she saw the state Bea was in.

"Hey are you alright?" She inquired.

"No not really but I will be." She said with more determination than she had.

"Do you want to talk about it.?" People knew it was war time and anything could happen.

"Ronny" was all Bea could manage to say. Lydia took her in the back room and sat her down.

"Oh Bea, why didn't you let me know. I would have come to you." Bea had really never thought of Lydia as a friend, so it never occurred to her. Mary had moved and left no forwarding address so there was no one. "Are you sure you want to be here?" I have nowhere else I can go Bea thought. So, she simply said "yes."

Chapter 15

Bea picked Mary Ellen up in a car she had borrowed from Lydia the week before Christmas and with nowhere to go she stopped at her favorite bar. It was December 1944. Was the war ever going to end? she thought. So many lives had been lost. Thankfully her brothers were okay. Peter was home but he wasn't the same. The war had taken its toll. He drank too much and slept too little. He had a terrible limp from where he had been shot.

"It could have been a lot worse" was all he would say. When Bea tried to talk to him about it, Peter would get a blank look on his face. It was like he was reliving the horrors he had seen all over again. Bea stopped asking. Then they stopped talking. They just drank.

Mary Ellen sat quietly across the booth from her mother. She was getting so big she was nine years old now and very pretty. All the baby fat was gone, and she could have been in movies, like that Shirley Temple Bea thought. Someone put a nickel in the juke box and the sound of Bing Crosby's crooning voice filled the dark room. *"I'll be home for Christmas, you can plan on me"* was playing loud and clear. Bea was now singing and crying as she let the lyrics seduce her. Mary Ellen was visibly uncomfortable but who cared? Bea needed to feel something, anything. Her father was gone, Albert had abandoned her, Ronny was dead and her brothers, oh her little brothers. She couldn't bear the thought that something might happen to them. The booze was doing its job. The bar tender brought Mary Ellen a sandwich and a soda. She was fine Bea thought, spoiled even.

Just then the door swung open with a cold rush of air to follow. It was hard to see when the light shone in since Bea's eyes had adjusted to the dark, but she had a funny feeling in the pit of her stomach. There was a group of men coming in from work and one of them was staring directly at her.

"Bea? Is that you?" Bea looked up and swallowed hard. It was Albert. Standing right in front of her. After all these years he was still as handsome as ever.

"Albert" she said trying not to slur.

"Oh my God Bea where have you been?"

"Oh around" she answered. "I'd like you to meet your daughter" she blurted. Mary Ellen was frozen. The look of shock on her face was only matched by his.

"What? What are you talking about?"

"Well just like I figured, you're going to pretend you didn't know." She spat the words at him.

"Bea, I didn't!" He insisted. But when he looked at Mary Ellen, he knew she was his. She looked just like her two sisters.

"Oh my God" he said, "Can I sit down?" He didn't wait for an answer he slid into the booth next to Mary Ellen.

"How? When?" Bea's head was spinning. Is it possible he didn't know? But her parents told her they spoke with him and what about the letters she had written? Could Roberta really have been that cruel? Bea didn't want to say anymore in front of Mary Ellen.

"Can we meet for a drink tomorrow? I will explain everything then."

"Yes, of course. I understand. Here? Same time?" He took Mary Ellen's hand and looked deep into her beautiful blue eyes and said, "You have my mother's eyes" and then left.

Bea ordered one more drink to shake off the nerves. When Mary Ellen tried to ask questions, she told her to mind her peas and cues. The next day Bea took a little more time getting ready. Her hair was perfect, and her lipstick was applied expertly. She arrived at the bar and Albert was already there waiting. Sitting in the same booth. He stood when she came in.

"Bea please have a seat. Can I get you a drink?"

"Whiskey" she said with a wry smile. Albert caught on right away, he was taken back to that night in Niagara Falls when he poured her first glass.

"On the rocks?" He smiled

"Look she said I don't know what kind of game you think you're playing here but I'm not stupid. You had your kids, and you didn't want any more. Just please don't lie to me. I know you told my parents you wanted nothing to do with me or Mary Ellen. Then you had your wife write to me to tell me to stay away from you and your family. You couldn't even find the courage to tell me yourself." Bea was filled with years of hurt and she was letting it all out right now.

Albert was silent. Did she really believe everything she was saying? When he finally spoke, it was like he was speaking to her in the hotel room back in Niagara Falls, like no time had passed at all.

"Bea darling, I didn't know. I didn't know anything. Weeks went by and I realized I couldn't live without you. I told Roberta everything. She threw me out. When I went to the bank Agnes told me what happened but nothing about a baby. I wrote to you, but all the letters came back unopened. I thought you wanted nothing to do with me. It took me a year to get my life back on tract. I left the transportation department and became an electrician. When the war started, I tried to enlist but they wouldn't take me. They said I had a bad heart. I would do more for the war effort if I stayed home and worked for the hydro company. Bea, you must believe me."

Bea didn't want to believe him but somehow it all made sense. Her mother didn't want her to keep Mary Ellen so of course she wouldn't tell Albert about her. And Roberta was so bitter she wasn't going to let Bea have him if she couldn't.

"Oh Albert. What have I done?" All the time that they had lost. Could they start over with their daughter or was it too late.

"Bea, I really did love you. Please know that. If I had only known"

"Maybe it's not too late, maybe we can try again." She was almost crying now, and he took her hands in his.

"No Bea we can't. I'm married again. And I love her very much" The words hit her with the force of a freight train. How stupid! How stupid she was. I'm such a fool she thought. She had to gather herself and quickly.

"Oh of course" she said. "How foolish of me. Well, I really need to get back to work now, I'm a beautician and I have clients waiting." She was standing now, and he was trying to get out of the booth.

"Bea what about Mary Ellen?" He asked

"What about her" she looked perplexed.

"Well, I'd like to see her." Bea couldn't believe what she was hearing. He wanted Mary Ellen but not her, ha.

"Sure, we'll work something out I'll be in touch." And she was out the door. She wished she had been able to see his face when she walked out, but she didn't want to give him the satisfaction of watching her look back. After all this time, was this some kind of cruel joke? Fate had stepped in and kicked her in the teeth again. She almost fell for it. Not this time, she thought.

Chapter 16

The war was over, and the boys were coming home. Things were looking up. She was making a good living now because women cared about the way they looked again. She went with her mother to the train station to meet her brothers. Peter was nowhere to be found. The platform was packed. There were so many parents, wives, girlfriends and even children anxiously awaiting their loved ones it was hard to find a spot. Finally, they saw the train coming into view. The men inside were hanging out the windows. The excitement had reached a fever pitch as people cheered and cried waiting for a glimpse of their hero's.

As the train pulled into the station people began to push and shove. Bea held on to her mother for fear someone would knock her down. Then Ernie came into view and right behind him was Lewis. Ernie looked to his left and that's when Bea noticed a pretty, red head on his arm. Lewis passed Ernie and was headed straight for them. For a moment she lost sight of Ernie and then she heard a great whoop!

"Mother! Bea! Ah man, it's good to see you both." He had lifted their mother off the ground and spun her around. Bea's mother was yelling for him to put her down, but she had a big smile on her face. Ernie was a little more reserved but still gave his mother a long embrace.

Meanwhile Lewis now got a hold of Bea and was swinging her like a rag doll. They were all laughing.

"Mother this is Cora, she's, my wife." Ernie barely got the words out when a fellow soldier came running up to shake Ernie's hand.

"Thanks for everything Sarge, and don't forget look me up, my father has a job for you all lined up." With that he turned and headed back to his waiting family. Mrs. Ledoux was in a bit of shock, so Bea extended her hand to Cora and said,

"Well, welcome to the family Cora." Cora smiled a smile of relief. The four of them made their way to a waiting taxi and headed home.

Once inside, the house seemed to instantly come back to life. Louise was waiting in the front yard about to explode. She was eighteen now and her brothers barely recognized her. Roselyn was in the kitchen setting out the last of the silverware. Her husband Ben was in the living room making himself at home. Bea didn't like the way he was looking at Mary Ellen, but Mary Ellen was oblivious to it.

"Mary Ellen come here and see your uncles". Mary Ellen came over and gave them both a big hug "And this is your new Aunt Cora." Mary Ellen looked at her red hair and immediately fell in love.

Cora and Mary Ellen became fast friends. Mary Ellen wanted to go everywhere with Cora. And when Ernie and Cora found a place of their own Mary Ellen became very difficult. Mrs. Ledoux needed Bea to take Mary Ellen more and more and Bea was not very happy about it.

"If you're coming with me, you'll have to stay here because I have plans." Bea always had plans on the weekend and no kid was going to get in the way. Bea had found a one-bedroom apartment so at least Mary Ellen wasn't hanging around when she brought a date home. There were plenty of guys to choose from now that the war was over, and they were all willing to by a girl a drink. Bea wasn't the prettiest girl in the room anymore and she knew it, but she was the smartest. She knew who to talk to and who to stay away from. Some would call that experience, she just thought she was smart. Life was what you make it she decided, and she was going to have fun.

Chapter 17

Mary Ellen was 12 years old now and Bea's mother had met a man. From what everybody told her he was a nice man. A real French man. His name was Francis and he wanted to marry Bea's mother. The one thing he didn't want however was to raise someone's granddaughter. Mrs. Ledoux had to make an impossible decision. Mary Ellen had to go to her mother.

"No" was the response Bea gave her. "I can't take her, what would I do with her?"

In the end Mary Ellen would be shared amongst Bea's brothers and sisters so Mrs. Ledoux could have some happiness.

First, she went with Bea's brother Ernie and his wife Cora. Mary Ellen seemed happy there but then Cora got pregnant and wanted Mary Ellen's room for her baby. So, Mary Ellen went to stay with Lewis and his new wife Kathy. Kathy was not at all happy and made life for Mary Ellen hell.

"You have to take her Bea" Lewis pleaded with his sister. "She belongs to you and it's not fair to the rest of us.

"Let me talk to Roselyn first, okay?" Bea said

"Okay, but if she says no you have to come and get her, or Kathy will have my head." Roselyn had three children of her own but also had a large house and could use the help.

"You have to pick her up every other weekend Bea, promise me or there's no deal."

"Alright Rose whatever you say." Bea knew Roselyn hated to be called Rose so that's why Bea did it. Power, she thought. Roselyn reluctantly agreed. Mary Ellen had a home and Bea was a free woman.

Bea decided one day that the real fun was at the beach in the summer so that's where she needed to be. Now all she had to do was to come up with a way to make it happen. Capital, that's what I need. I need money to make money she thought. Bea had her grandmothers diamond ring hidden in her sock drawer. No one knew it was there. Bea worked out the details of her money-making venture but had to talk to the one person who could make it happen, her Aunt Mirna.

Aunt Mirna was happy to see Bea even after everything she had put her sister through.

"Come in Dear. It's so nice to see you" Bea got right to the point, she needed a loan, and she would give her aunt her grandmothers ring as collateral. She would pay back all the money at the end of the summer. If she didn't Aunt Mirna could keep the ring.

"Well, it sounds like you've got everything figured out." Aunt Mirna said a little impressed with her niece.

"Yes, I do, everyone heads to the beach in the summer. Leamington was thick with people vacationing and nobody wanted to cook." That's where Bea came in, she explained. She would open a seasonal diner that also sold staples like bread and milk. She couldn't lose.

"Okay Bea, I'll give you the money but if you don't pay me back by Labor Day the ring is mine." Mirna was stern.

"Great when can you give it to me?" Bea said anxiously.

"Meet me at the bank tomorrow I'll have the cash ready for you. Oh, and Bea, don't forget the ring."

When summer arrived, Bea was ready for it. She had lined up all her venders, rented the equipment she needed and told her clients she would be back in the fall. She packed a little bag and headed to Leamington. The plan was simple. Make money, have fun. Bea was busy setting up dishes on the shelves in the little diner when she heard and knock at the door.

"Hello, can I help you?"

"Well actually I was hoping I could help you. My name is Henry. Do you need a short order cook or maybe a dishwasher? I'm happy to do just about anything." He was bold and she liked that. Bea did need help, but she didn't have any money left.

"I'm not really ready to hire anyone."

"Look lady, let me help for a week, if I do a good job then keep me if not let me go." He wasn't begging but he obviously needed the work.

"Alright." Be here at six am tomorrow and we'll get started." Word traveled fast within the first week people were waiting for a seat. Breakfast was her busiest time. Kids were lining up for hot dogs and hamburgers at lunchtime because they could take them back to the beach and not miss any fun time with their friends. Henry was a God send. His cooking was great, and people loved his food. He kept his head down and things ran more smoothly than she could have imagined. Bea was busy up-front taking orders and working the cash. She cleaned tables, did dishes and loved it. At the end of the day Henry and Bea would lock the door and count the money. She would pour them a glass of whiskey and once she had taken out her expenses, she would give him one third of the profits. Henry was happy with the cut as it was more than he would get anywhere else.

Bea had a makeshift bed in the back room next to the rented freezer. So, she didn't have to pay for an apartment. One night after a long successful day Bea asked Henry where he was from.

"Here and there" he said. I came home from the war to find out my wife had started up with some guy who didn't have the guts to fight like the rest of us. He did have money though and I guess that's all that matters right?" He was stating a fact. Not asking a question.

"Well from what I can see it's her loss." Henry gave Bea a little grin.

"At least there were no kids so I can just forget it ever happened."

"Does she live around here." Bea didn't want to pry but she was curious.

"No." Was all he was willing to share.

"Want another drink?" She asked.

"Sure, fill it up."

Roselyn was faithful about bringing Mary Ellen to her sister every other weekend. There wasn't anywhere for Mary Ellen to sleep so Bea threw a couple blankets on the floor next to her and they made the best of it. Mary Ellen was a good little helper. Bea got her a stool, and she did dishes. It wasn't all work. Mary Ellen made a friend, and she was able to play at the beach. The weeks flew bye and the money had exceeded her wildest dreams. Fall was in the air and the patrons were packing up to return to their lives elsewhere. Business was slowing to a crawl. Bea knew it was time to shut down for the season, but she really hated to. Henry had lined up work for the winter but promised he would return the next spring. They really had become friends, just friends and Bea liked it. It was 1950 and times were changing quickly.

Bea and Henry had continued their friendship and partnership. Mary Ellen was fourteen now and looked more like a nineteen-year-old. Bea didn't really know her daughter. But she did see the way men looked at her.

Bea new that Mary Ellen was unhappy with Roselyn and Ben but what could she do. She was in no position to take on a teenager. Bea's mother was living a happy life with her new husband and didn't really have time for Mary Ellen either. It was late April when Bea got word that Ben had passed away suddenly. Roselyn was a mess. At a time like this Bea thought Mary Ellen would have been a great help but she thought wrong. Roselyn had gone into a deep depression and was no longer able to care for her own children let alone Mary Ellen. Ben's mother had come to stay with her, and Roselyn needed Mary Ellen's room. Bea was livid.

But Mary Ellen was standing at her door with a bag in hand and there was nothing she could do but let her in.

"Well, we need to get a couple things straight" she said with authority. "If you stay here you have to pull your weight. You can go to school, but you'll have to get a job afterward. I can't be expected to support you. Do, you hear me?"

"Yes, mother." Mary Ellen was like a broken dog. She simply did as she was told. Within a week Mary Ellen had a job as a waitress at a local diner. They were happy to have her and with the experience she had gotten working with her mother over the past few summers she was ready to start immediately. They never asked her age and she never told them. It wasn't long before Mary Ellen quit school. She was only in grade nine but and education wasn't a priority anymore. Getting away from her mother was.

Bea knew that Mary Ellen resented her but what was she supposed to do about it. Bea didn't have a clue how to deal with her daughter. As far as Bea could tell Mary Ellen wasn't interested in trying either. It was not really a surprise that only after a year of living together Mary Ellen announced she had met a man, and they were going to get married. The problem was she was too young. At fifteen she needed Bea's permission.

"Does he know how old you are?"

"We never really talked about it. Can't you just sign for me? I'll be out of your hair." Mary Ellen was almost pleading. Even though Bea knew she probably shouldn't do this it really was for the best. Mary Ellen would be cared for, and she would be off the hook. Bea insisted on buying a dress for her and taking them for lunch after the civil ceremony. They decided not to tell Bea's mother until after the fact. Just in case she tried to stop them.

Chapter 18

It was 1951, time was marching on and with Mary Ellen gone Bea could focus on her own life now. Times were tough for a single woman. But Bea was educated, and she would always get by. Her brother Peter wasn't so lucky. He did odd jobs with skills he picked up here and there. But alcoholism had taken him over. He was one of the many WWII vets that were never able to settle back into life. Homeless, he eventually died alone in an abandoned warehouse downtown. Bea received a call from the police telling her they thought they had found her brother. In his pocket he had a piece of paper and on it was her name and address and the note simply said my sister. Bea arrived at the police station and was redirected to the coroner's office where she could identify the body. The only other body Bea had ever seen was her father. Ronny's casket was closed for obvious reasons. How was she going to do this?

"Miss. Ledoux" Bea turned startled.

"Yes" she said

"I'm Dr. Elliot. Please come with me." Bea wished she had a drink. The coroner took her by the arm and led her through a set of double doors. There was a hum coming from the fluorescent lights that shone overhead. Everything was so sterile and there was a disinfectant smell that hung thick in the air. Laying on a metal table was a body draped in a white sheet.

"Miss. Ledoux take your time." Bea stepped close and he lifted the sheet from her brother's head. She simply nodded her head.

"Are you sure?" He asked

"Yes." She could barely get the words out. How was she going to tell her mother? Peter was the funny one. He was the one who could fix anything. How was he going to fix this?

Bea was walking towards a desk where a kind looking woman was seated.

"Please have a seat Miss. Ledoux. There is just a couple of things we need you to sign. This first one states that you have identified your loved one, and this gives us permission to send the body to the funeral home." Bea was signing her name through tears. When she finished, she got up and headed toward the door. There she was met by a taxi ready to take her wherever she wanted to go. Her mother's house was quiet. Bea had only been here once since her mother married Francis. They had made a nice home together. He was a gentle man but had no patience for Bea. She knocked gently on the door, and he answered.

"Bea what is it? Your mother is laying down and I don't want to upset her. If you've been drinking, please just turn and leave." His words were short and to the point.

"No, I haven't." Her words were little more than a whisper.

"I can see something's going on so just spit it out." Oh, she'd spit it out alright.

"Peter is dead." His face went ashen.

"Oh no, when?" But Bea wasn't interested in explaining anything to him.

"I need to see my mother" Bea said sternly. He led her into the living room and told her to wait. Bea could her the guttural scream coming from the bedroom. Why hadn't he let her tell her mother.

Bea waited for what seemed a very long time until her mother finally appeared. She looked so frail.

"What happened Bea?"

"They're not sure. They found him, ah alone in a warehouse mother." Tears were streaming down her mothers' cheeks. Mrs. Ledoux knew her son was a drunk. She knew that he chose to live on the streets. But she loved him non the less.

"Where is he?" She asked

"They are sending him to Osgood funeral home on Tecumseh Rd. You can see him tomorrow."

"Are they sure it's him?" She asked hopeful Bea would tell her no.

"Yes mother, I identified him." There was a look of shock on Mrs. Ledoux's face.

"Why" she asked

"He has a piece of paper with my name and address on it in his pocket. Just in case" she said. Francis was at her mothers' side and said,

"Thank you, Bea, I've got it from here." With that he led her to the door. As if she was nothing more than a currier. Bea was so angry she brushed him away and walked out the door she had just come through. Bea found herself at her favorite bar on her third glass of whiskey. She had felt alone before in her life, but this was different. Her beautiful brother was gone. And he had been alone. All alone. Was this going to be what her future was going to be.

"Kevin" she slurred "give me another.

The funeral was uneventful. The usual cast of characters. Her mother's church friends even though she didn't go to church anymore. Her sisters and brothers and their respective others. All doting on her mother. Even Mary Ellen and her funny looking husband were there. The one thing they all had in common was how they all tried not to make eye contact with her. Oh, how they forgot all the things she had done for each of them. The money she gave them when they were running short. How she co- signed for their loans when they didn't dare ask their mother. What about the clothes she bought their children?

"Ah who cares" she said out loud before she could stop herself. Everyone looked at her then. "Ha" and with that she left. Weeks had passed then months then years. In that time her mother's second husband had passed but her precious Mary Ellen had been with her. Both of her brothers and one sister were also gone. All that was left was herself and Roselyn. They barely could stand to be in the same room as one another. Bea was alone as she had always been, she had given up working because of her health. Really it was because she couldn't stay sober long enough. Lydia had finally taken all she could and asked her to leave. With all the new health regulations and licenses Bea couldn't continue her summer gig. The only good thing that came out of that was her friendship with Henry. He was faithful every summer. True to his word on April 30th he would show up like an angel, work all summer and at the end he would smile, and say, see ya next year. She hadn't seen him in five years now. And she really missed him. He was easy and he drank with her without judgement. Maybe she should look him up she thought. Oh, how?

Mary Ellen was back from Nova Scotia with five kids. What a hoot Bea thought I've got five grandchildren and I barely know any of them. Mary Ellen had been guarded with the kids but every now and then, Bea would guilt her into bringing them by. Where had the time gone, she thought. What happened to me. Bea was 69 years old and not in good health. Her heart, like that of her brothers was bad. She had been told that years ago.

"You really shouldn't drink" the doctor said and that's the last time she set foot in a doctor's office. Bea thought maybe she should go for a walk. It seemed like a good idea until she realized she had been walking for a long time and had no idea where she was. Panic washed over her. How did she get so turned around? It was getting dark when she saw a taxi coming down the street. She frantically waved her arms. To her surprise and relief, he pulled over.

"Oh, thank God" she said. Just then the driver turned and smiled it was Henry, her Henry.

"What in the world?" She squealed like a younger version of herself.

"Well, aren't you a sight for sore eyes?" He exclaimed.

This was her lucky day.

Mary Ellen

Chapter 19

Mary Ellen was fascinated with the way the ladybug tickled the back of her hand. It was so pretty. And she wasn't afraid of it. Not like those nasty grasshoppers. Every time she lay in the grass behind her meme's house, they would jump all over her. They were hard to catch; she would reach out to grab one and that darn grasshopper would always jump in the opposite direction. But this ladybug had been easy. She simply reached out her hand and it gladly landed right on her. They had a bond. She thought maybe she could keep it like her meme had kept her. But just as the idea came to her the ladybug flew away. Mary Ellen rolled over in the grass and sure enough a grasshopper jumped right over her.

"Mary Ellen! Come in for lunch." Her meme was calling to her. How she loved the sound of her meme's voice. She was a French-Canadian woman with short legs and a big heart. Mary Ellen hurried across the yard and skipped up the steps to the back door. Her meme had made her favorite vegetable soup. No surprise really, they ate a lot of soup. They had toast with lard, and potato's, a lot of potatoes. Life was simple here. Mary Ellen was able to be a kid. She mostly loved her best friend, Ilene.

Mary Ellen ran to Ilene's house after lunch to see if she could come out to play. No one had screens on their doors, and on a hot day they left their doors wide opened. Mary Ellen stood on the steps to the back door and was able to look right into the kitchen. Sitting on the table was a can of strawberry jam covered in flies. Mrs. Hunter peaked around the corner,

"Is that you Mary Ellen?"

"Yes, can Ilene come out to play?" The two children skipped and giggled and enjoyed the warm sunshine as they rolled around in the grass. Mary Ellen loved playing with Ilene, they were like sisters. And although Mary Ellen had her Aunt Louise the age difference stopped Louise from having fun. Summer quickly turned to fall and fall to winter. Mary Ellen was always cold and going to school was a terrible test of endurance. Later in life her own children would roll their eyes when she told them stories of how she had to walk a mile to school in the snow. What she didn't tell them was that she was only 6 years old. Because they would never have believed her.

Her Meme was doing the best she could, but she insisted that Mary Ellen go to a catholic school and the closest one was a mile away. Mary Ellen would bundle up and head out the door for her long, lonely trek to school. Her best friend Ilene got to go to the public school that was only a block away. There was no sense in complaining because her meme would hear none of it.

Once at school Mary Ellen would sit at her little desk and try to absorb as much as she could, she loved school. And her teacher loved her. Sister Thomas paid extra close attention to Mary Ellen, and it was paying off. Mary Ellen was coming out of her shell. She loved to learn and that was a dream of every teacher.

"Your mother is coming to get you this afternoon Mary Ellen and I want you to behave. Her Meme hated to let her go but knew she had to. Do you understand me?" Mary Ellen didn't want to go with her mother. She knew that her mother didn't like her. She tried but it was hard to be good. Mary Ellen was always left alone when she went with her mother. She was afraid. Really afraid.

Mary Ellen was six years old, and she wasn't sure why things were the way they were, but she knew that she shouldn't ask too many questions. Her Aunt Louise told her that her meme loved her and wanted her so much that her mother gave Mary Ellen to her as a gift. But when she told her mother that, she had gotten very angry, she said

"What! A gift ha! Your meme never wanted you, she wanted me to give you to strangers, but I made her take you. You remember that. Sooner or later, you'll see that I'm telling you the truth." Bea almost spat the words at her. Mary Ellen was a smart little girl, so she knew not to bring it up again.

When Bea came in the house to get her, Mary Ellen's meme left the room. There were no goodbyes. Mary Ellen lifted her little bag and with her head hanging she left trying to keep up with her mother's quick steps.

"Hurry up Mary Ellen or we'll miss the bus and I have things to do and places to be." She barked. Why did she want me to go with her if she hates me so much Mary Ellen thought? She hurried along to the bus stop only to have to wait. They sat in silence. Mary Ellen busied herself by counting the windows on all the houses on the street. First the big white house on the corner followed by the red brick then another white one. When she got to twelve, she would lose count and have to start over again.

"Come on Mary Ellen." Her mother was taking her hand roughly and pulling her onto the bus. Mary Ellen stumbled but quickly regained her footing and followed her mother down the aisle. Her mother pointed to a seat and Mary Ellen slid in first. She pushed her nose against the window and wished she was at home with her meme. When the bus came to a stop her mother was up and headed toward the door. Mary Ellen jumped to her feet and ran to catch up. They were standing on the sidewalk in front of a grocery store. Her mother put a key in a door next to the large window that had all kinds of meats on display. They headed up the stairs and then to another door.

The staircase was dark, and Mary Ellen couldn't see. Her mother opened the door and light illuminated the stairs. She entered and told Mary Ellen to put her things down on the bed. This was the first time Mary Ellen had seen her mother's new place. She already hated it. There was one bedroom and a small living room with a kitchen sink and a small bathtub and toilet separated only by a curtain.

Her mother fed her some canned meat on toast and hurried to put on some lipstick.

"So, I have to go out for a bit." Bea said. And Mary Ellen began to cry. "Okay settle down, you're a big girl now. Your six years old and there's no need to cry. Please stop crying Mary Ellen," she said. Mary Ellen sniffled and wiped her eyes on her sleeve. After she had put on her nightie, her mother put her in the bed and tucked the blankets around her. When Mary Ellen woke up the apartment was dark and quiet.

"Mommy?" She waited but no response came back. Mary Ellen had to pee but was too sacred to get out of the bed. She pulled the blankets up over her head and began to cry. When she woke a second time she was in a cold hard place, and she didn't recognize anything. She looked around and realized she was in the bathtub. This time however she could hear her mother's voice as well as a man's. Mary Ellen laid still and soon fell back to sleep. The urge to pee had overtaken her now so she climbed out of the bathtub which was conveniently next to the toilet. She hoisted herself onto the cold seat and found relief. When she was done Mary Ellen walked into the living room, but all was dark. She did, however, hear sounds coming from the bedroom.

She pushed the door opened a crack and what she saw scared and confused her. Their bodies were all tangled up and her mother was groaning in an odd way. They didn't even notice that Mary Ellen was standing there. She didn't like what she saw, it made her feel very uncomfortable. She was about to turn and leave when the man let out an awful grunt and then everything was quiet. Mary

Ellen thought he might be dead on top of her mother but then she heard her mother giggle.

She quickly ran back to the bathtub and pulled the towel over her head. In just a few minutes her mother was in the bathroom. Mary Ellen couldn't understand why her mother had giggled but when she tried to ask, she was quickly shushed and told to go back to sleep. Shortly after she heard the man leave.

Bea was mad at her in the morning. Mary Ellen didn't know why; it seemed her mother was always mad at her, she was ready to go home, and her mother was ready to take her. Back on the bus followed by a short walk back to her meme's.

Mary Ellen was so glad to be back in her safe place. Her room wasn't much, and she did have to share it with her Aunt Louise but at least she had her own bed. Her meme had made her a quilt out of old clothes that her uncles had left behind when they went to the war. Mary Ellen wasn't sure exactly what that meant but she knew it was bad and that her meme was very worried about them all the time.

"When are they coming home?" She would ask. And her Meme's response was always the same.

"Soon."

It was a Thursday afternoon in 1942 when Mary Ellen's mother dropped her off. Mary Ellen had been particularly difficult, so Bea was going to have a little chat with her meme. When they walked into the kitchen, they were stopped dead in their tracks. There at the kitchen table was her meme head in hands crying.

"Mother what is it, what's wrong." Her meme handed her the letter and then they embraced. Mary Ellen didn't understand what was going on, but she knew it was bad.

"Meme are you alright?" "Yes, yes. Your Uncle Peter is coming home," she said. Bea only stayed for a few more minutes and then was gone.

Mary Ellen was overjoyed. She loved her Uncle Peter. Well at least she thought she did. She really didn't remember him, but her meme talked so much about all her uncles it was like she knew him very well.

The day he came home was a hectic one. Meme was running all over the place trying to get everything ready. It was going to be funny having a man living here Mary Ellen thought. She didn't remember her Pepe. He passed away when she was still a baby. Her uncles left shortly after. So having Uncle Peter back was going to be exciting. Maybe he could build her a doll house. When meme saw him, she ran to him and threw her arms around his neck. He didn't look like he was all that happy to be home but that didn't stop them from having a big party. He didn't stay long before he and her mother left which really upset meme. Mary Ellen helped clean up and everyone went home. Aunt Louise had met a boy and was spending all her time with him these days. That was ok with Mary Ellen because she had her meme all to herself. Her uncle Peter didn't come home until the next day, and he didn't look so good. She hadn't noticed his limp the day before but today she couldn't see anything but the limp.

"Is your leg hurt?" She asked.

"Not anymore" he smiled and rubbed the top of her head.

"What happened". Her question was innocent enough, but her meme was displeased by it.

"Mary Ellen! Stop asking your uncle such things. Now go to your room." Mary Ellen didn't understand what she had done but she did as she was told anyway.

Uncle Peter stopped her and said, "Its ok kid I got shot is all. But I'm all better now." He smiled at her and rubbed the top of her head again. She liked him a lot. When she came out of her room for supper, she was told Uncle Peter was going to live downtown with a buddy from the army. Mary Ellen was so disappointed she missed him already.

Chapter 20

Life was full of adventures and Mary Ellen was happy to participate in all that she could. Her meme had lots of important men coming to their house at all hours of the day and night and Mary Ellen had learned to stay out of the way.

"Mary Ellen, you need to go outside and play." These were Mary Ellen's favorite words. She was done her chores and out the door to find her friend Ilene. Together they could let their imaginations run free. Today they were and old married couple with a baby. Later they would be cowboys and Indians. The sun was high in the sky and Mary Ellen knew that meant they had another hour or so to play before her meme would call her for supper.

Mary Ellen found the feather from a bird, which she of course imagined was an eagle and stuck it in her ponytail. She quickly transformed into a great Indian Chief. Poor Ilene was a lonely cowboy that stumbled onto Indian property and had to trade his way out of trouble. Lucky for Ilene she had marble that Mary Ellen had her eye on,

"Okay cowboy what will you give me for your life?" She asked in her deepest voice.

"Um I have a lucky marble, will that work? Ilene asked

"Well, I think that will do, now get on your horse and get off our land." Mary Ellen was tickled to have gotten this marble but when the game was over Ilene asked for it back.

"No, you gave it to me fair and square." Mary Ellen insisted. Before she knew what was happening Ilene was crying and said she was going to tell her mother. Ilene ran home as fast as she could.

Mary Ellen sat for a while in the dirt rolling her new marble and holding it up to the sun to see all it's beautiful colors. This would be a great marble to add to her collection. Her playtime was interrupted by the sound of her meme's voice.

"Mary Ellen time for supper!" It was like hearing a song. Could this day get any better? She thought. When Mary Ellen entered through the back door, she spotted Ilene sitting at the kitchen table with her mother.

"Do you have Ilene's marble?" Her meme was obviously annoyed.

"She gave it to me." Mary Ellen said trying to sound convincing.

"Give it back." Mrs. Ledoux demanded

"But it's mine, she gave it to me." Mary Ellen pleaded

"No, I didn't, you tricked me." Ilene started crying again.

"Now!" Mrs. Ledoux meant what she said, and Mary Ellen knew it. She handed Ilene her new treasure. Once in Ilene's hand the war was over.

"Now go and wash for supper." Mary Ellen shot Ilene a look and then left the kitchen. When she returned, they were gone.

September was here which only meant one thing Summer was over and school was about to begin. Mary Ellen dreaded this time of year because she would be alone again. Ilene was her best friend and not being able to go to the same school was heartbreaking. She would plead with her meme, but all her reasoning would fall on deaf ears. Her meme's mind was not something anyone could change. She was in grade three and she already knew who her teacher was.

Mary Ellen didn't like Mrs. Porter. She knew there was something different about her because of the way Mrs. Porter ignored her.

When Mary Ellen knew the answer to a question Mrs. Porter would call on anyone but her. It wasn't fair but she knew not to complain.

Mary Ellen's feeling of dread about school was only surpassed by her mother's visits. Mary Ellen always felt like she had to choose between her mother and her meme. Why was life so confusing? She had a teacher that didn't like her, a mother that didn't want her and no friends. Mary Ellen's grades were slipping, and no one seemed to care. Sometimes she would pretend to be sick so she wouldn't have to go to school. Her meme didn't have time to worry about her so she would just let her stay home.

On this particular day however, Mary Ellen wasn't making it up, she really didn't feel well. Her meme said she could stay home but she would have to stay in her room. For the first time she was happy to stay in her bed. Mary Ellen had slept most of the day away. Her meme had been busy canning vegetables for the long winter. She called for Mary Ellen at supper time, but Mary Ellen didn't feel like eating. Mrs. Ledoux insisted she try to eat something. Mary Ellen mostly pushed the food around on her plate.

The bootleg business was in full swing. Mrs. Ledoux was making good money selling alcohol to men who didn't want to go home to their own families. On this night Dr. Curtis stopped in for a drink as Mary Ellen was finishing her meal.

"Hey Cecile, is Mary Ellen, okay?" He asked calling her meme by her first name.

"She's fine, just a little cold I think." She answered,

"Come here Mary Ellen." He told her and she listened. He put his wrist to her head and then asked her to stick out her tongue. Again, Mary Ellen did as she was told.

"Cecile she's burning up. I have something here I want you to give her," he said. Mary Ellen was back in bed and her meme was shoving a horrible tasting medicine in her mouth.

"Yuk!" She blurted out. But her complaints were short lived, and she fell back to sleep. When she woke up, she was in an unfamiliar place. She was scared and it was dark. She sat up but her head hurt so she laid back down. Her meme came close to her bed taking her little hand in hers and Mary Ellen felt instant relief.

"Hi sweetheart, how do you feel?" Her meme was being so nice.

"I'm okay, I guess. Where are we?" She asked

"You're in the hospital honey. You really gave us a terrible scare." Mrs. Ledoux seemed genuinely concerned.

"My head hurts" Mary Ellen said as she pushed on her temples.

"It's okay it will go away now that your awake. You were asleep for a long time. Two days to be exact." She sounded relieved.

Mary Ellen stayed in the hospital for another week. They said she had rheumatic fever. It was a slow recovery but by Halloween she was back to old self. Dr. Curtis drank on the house for as long as her meme ran her bootleg business.

Halloween was going to be the best ever. Mary Ellen couldn't believe her luck this year. Her mother bought her a pumpkin costume. That meant she didn't have to dress like a hobo again this year. Every year she would have to listen to her friends talk about their store-bought costumes, but not this year. Made of paper the costume barely fit over her clothes let alone her coat. As usual the weather was cold in these parts. Mary Ellen knew she wasn't a little girl, but everyone told her how pretty she was, so it was okay.

When the day finally arrived Mary Ellen ran all the way home from school. Ilene was already and waiting for her. Ilene was dressed like a gypsy. Mary Ellen couldn't wait to show off her new costume. Mrs. Ledoux made her put her hat on and mittens as well as her coat but then the moment of truth. There she was in all her glory a big round pumpkin and her meme began to laugh and laugh. Not the reaction she expected but nothing could ruin this day. With a pillowcase in hand, she and Ilene began their mission to get the biggest bag of candy they could. Their first stop was a little disappointing not only did the people laugh at her they gave her an apple. Yuk! But she would not be deterred. The next house another apple, then the loot started to arrive. Gum drops and jellybeans.

Homemade cookies that she just had to taste. And on and on they went hurrying between houses.

With their pillowcases also most full they made their way back to their homes to empty and start again.

"Come on Mary Ellen, hurry" Ilene was yelling to her. Mary Ellen was trying to keep up, but she was so hot with all the layers of clothes and her size, she was falling further behind. That's when it came to her, she would take a short cut behind the houses and then meet Ilene back at her house. They set off. She was running as fast as her fat little legs would carry her, when suddenly, she was sprawled out like a giant eagle soaring in the sky. She was slipping and sliding as she tried to get to her feet and there was a God-awful smell. What had happened? She thought. And that's when it hit her someone had tipped over Ilene's outhouse. They were the last house on the street to have an outhouse and some hoodlums had decided to tip it over. Poor unexpecting Mary Ellen ran right through the spilled mess. When she was finally able to get to her feet she began to cry! She made her way through her own back yard and opened the back door to her house. Her Meme was at the front door handing out candy when Louise spotted her.

"Oh my God Mary Ellen, what did you do?" Louise was yelling at her, this only made Mary Ellen cry harder.

"What's going on in here? Oh, my what's that smell" Mrs. Ledoux then began to yell in French. Words that Mary Ellen knew were bad but knew better than to say so. "Take her in the bath and clean her up Louise." She ordered. Louise was so angry she didn't talk to Mary Ellen for days.

Her night had abruptly ended. Her beautiful pumpkin costume was completely ruined. Ilene was sent home and Mary Ellen was sent to bed. Gosh I don't know why everyone is so mad at me, it's not my fault. My Life is ruined my costume is ruined and all the kids are going to laugh at me. She thought. Unfortunately, she was right, word had spread even to her school. Kids who never spoke to her laughed at her when she walked past them. The only thing that made this worse was that her meme wouldn't let her eat any of her candy because the bag had also fallen in the slop from the outhouse. Could life get any worse!

Chapter 21

It was December 1944; Mary Ellen's mother was at the door. Mary Ellen really didn't want to go with her, but she had no choice. They got into a car her mother had borrowed and drove directly to her mother's favorite bar. Mary Ellen knew this place well and all the regulars met her mother by name. They walked straight to a booth and her mother promptly order whiskey. Mary Ellen knew that when her mother drank this, she became different, slower somehow and her words didn't sound the same. Her mother seemed sadder than usual and when a song came out, the juke box she began to sing and cry all at the same time.

Mary Ellen wanted to crawl into a hole. A nice man brought Mary Ellen a nice plate of food and a milk shake. Things were looking up. It was when a gust of wind came in the door that Mary Ellen noticed a man walking up to the table calling out to her mother by name. Not that it was unusual since her mother knew a lot of people, but this man was somehow different. Her mother was shocked Mary Ellen could see that but what she heard next stopped her in her tracks. This is your daughter! Her mother has spat the words out. And this man was now staring at her. Mary Ellen swallowed hard. She stopped asking about her father years ago. No one would answer her questions and now this man standing in front of her was her father? Mary Ellen had so many questions, but no one seemed to care. He had such nice eyes. He smelled good too. Now he was looking right at her saying how much she looked like his mother.

And just when Mary Ellen thought she was dreaming he stood up and walked out. She wanted to yell WAIT! But it was too late. What had just happened? She looked at her mother for answers but instead her mother barked at her and ordered another drink. Mary Ellen didn't sleep much that night or for many nights after. She tried to talk to her meme, but she was told her father didn't want her. That's why she was here with her meme. Something didn't sound right about this. The man she met seemed genuinely surprised about her and Mary Ellen could have sworn he said he wanted to see her again.

Mary Ellen stopped playing with Ilene and was losing weight, but no one even noticed. Mary Ellen didn't know who to believe or where she fit in. She wondered if she would ever see him again, did he love her? How could he she thought he didn't know her. When she did sleep, she would dream about a family full of love with brothers and sisters and a mother and father who laughed and cared about each other. She knew when she woke up that that would never be her life. No one ever spoke about her father and mother. Mary Ellen knew she was a bastard because she had overheard a girl at school tell another girl. She asked her Aunt Louise what it meant. Louise explained it was a name they called people who didn't have a father.

"But I have a father," she said.

"No, you don't." Louise insisted.

"Yes, I do! I met him!" Mary Ellen was crying now.

"What? When? Louise seemed shocked

"When I was with my mother. And he wants to see me again." Mary Ellen was sniffling.

"Did you tell mother?"

"No, my mother told me not to. Is meme going to be mad at me?" she asked

"No, no it's okay. I'll take care of it. Now stop crying and just ignore those girls." Louise took Mary Ellen in her arms and rocked like a baby. Mary Ellen didn't stop her because it really did feel nice. No one ever said a word to Mary Ellen about her father but for a while everyone seemed a little kinder to her.

It was 1946 Mary Ellen was ten years old and the war was over. Her meme was so excited that her uncles were finally coming home. The whole house was electric. Her Aunt Roselyn was helping in the kitchen and Uncle Ben was sitting in the living room with his feet up on the ottoman.

Mary Ellen always felt uneasy around him. She had to babysit for her Aunt Roselyn, and she hated it when Uncle Ben drove her home. He looked at her funny and talked about how she was becoming a beautiful young woman. He even said he liked the shape of her. When she tried to talk to her meme about it, she was told not to be silly he was just being nice. Mary Ellen was having a hard time remembering her uncles, but she was still excited to see them. Everyone set off to the train station, but Mary Ellen was told she had to stay home. Uncle Ben said he would wait at the house in case Mary Ellen needed help with anything.

"Oh, darling that's so nice of you" Roselyn said and then she gently kissed his cheek. Mary Ellen heard this and suddenly had a huge pit in her stomach. She thought she would just stay busy finishing the list her meme gave her. Everyone left and Mary Ellen found herself alone in the kitchen with Uncle Ben. She hurried to the sink to finish the last of the dishes when she felt him come up behind her. Before she knew it, he had reached around her and had is hand on her breast.

"Stop! What are you doing?" She yelled.

"Come here Mary Ellen." He said with a smile on his face. She had moved from the sink and was standing in the dining room.

What did he want? Why was he touching her? He slowly moved to the dining room.

"I'm sorry Mary Ellen, I was just going to help you with the dishes that's all." He was lying and she knew it. But she was shaken so she said it was okay. She turned and tried to sidestep around him to get back to the sink. But he stopped her and now had taken her hand in his.

"Please Uncle Ben, I have to do the dishes." She pleaded, but he was pulling her hand downward to his crotch. She was mortified. There was a large hard thing in his pants and when her hand touched it, he breathed hard and began to rub her hand on it. Mary Ellen felt sick to her stomach, and she began to cry.

"Shhh." He whispered. Then he seemed to snap out of whatever it was that had overtaken him. Then instead of apologizing he stormed off to the bathroom.

Mary Ellen stood in the same spot shaking when he emerged from the bathroom. He was flushed and angry. He grabbed her arm but this time her looked her straight in the eyes. He was hurting her arm. But she couldn't free herself from his grip.

"Don't you say a word. No one will ever believe you! Do you understand me. And if you do decide to tell anyone I will tell them you threw yourself at me and I had to stop you!" He was shaking almost as much as she was. Mary Ellen simply shook her head, and he loosened his grip.

It was over he went back to the living room and sat back down. She gathered herself and went back into the kitchen and busied herself with the rest of the list her meme left. Why did he do this? Who could she tell? Instead, she pushed aside what had just happened. She didn't understand it, but she knew it was wrong.

When they all arrived back at the house her Uncle Ernie had a beautiful red headed woman on his arm. Mary Ellen couldn't take her eyes off her. Her name was Aunt Cora. And she spoke funny. It was hard to understand her, but Mary Ellen was totally enthralled with everything she said. She told her about her home across the sea.

A place she called Scotland and how she met Uncle Ernie. How they fell in love while she aided the troops as a nurse.

Mary Ellen could listen to her forever. Uncle Lewis was quiet. He didn't really interact with anyone but his brother. Finally, Uncle Peter came in and all her uncles embraced. They slapped each other on the back and laughed and laughed. The stories came one after the other and the whiskey flowed. Her mother had joined in the fun and if she didn't know better it looked like one big happy family. But like everything else in Mary Ellen's life this to would end abruptly.

Soon the laughter ended, and the voices became louder. Her meme was not happy about the turn of events and of course everyone seemed to blame her mother. Aunt Cora took Mary Ellen by the hand and led her into the next room.

"Everything will be okay darlin" she said with sweetness.

"Why is everyone so mad?" She asked,

"They're not child, it's just the liquor talking." Her Aunt knew exactly what to say to calm Mary Ellen. The front door slammed, and the party ended. Uncle Ben and Aunt Roselyn took Aunt Cora and Uncle Ernie to stay at their house. Aunt Louise was cleaning the kitchen and her mother and Uncle Peter had taken the party to another location. Uncle Lewis was asleep on the couch. Mary Ellen was disappointed that Uncle Ernie and Aunt Cora had left but she had a feeling she would see them soon.

Chapter 22

Mary Ellen set off to Ilene's first thing in the morning the sun was shining, and summer was finally here, and nothing was going to stop her from having fun today. She was 10 years old, and all her chores were done. Ilene was waiting on the back porch. They took each other's hand and skipped off into the woods. This was one of Mary Ellen's favorite places. They played Robin Hood and climbed trees. The sun dappled ground was full of moss. They laid for what seemed like hours staring up at trees. They shared dreams about what they were going to be when they grew up. Everything was changing. Everyone seemed happier now that the war was over, and all the boys were coming home. Mary Ellen felt lucky all her uncles had returned. Some of the kids she knew weren't so lucky. A girl at Mary Ellen's school was one of them. When her father got off the train, he was missing one arm and one leg. Everybody treated her different now and Mary Ellen wondered if they had a funeral for his dead arm and leg but had no one to ask. She hoped so, because she wanted him to get to Heaven in one piece. She lit a candle in church and said a prayer for his arm and leg. Ilene shook Mary Ellen out of her day dreaming.

"Come on let's go to the park." Mary Ellen couldn't believe Ilene wanted to leave this heavenly place, but she reluctantly agreed. Hand in hand they ran out of the forest and back to civilization. Houses were being built everywhere. There were piles of dirt to climb and big sewer pipes to crawl through. There was fun to be had everywhere.

When Mary Ellen arrived home for dinner, she was shocked to see some man sitting at the table in her chair. She gave him the once over. He seemed okay. He had a nice smile and gray hair. He had a big belly, and it shook when he laughed. He caught her looking at him.

"Well, hello there, you must be Mary Ellen." Mary Ellen just stood there. How did he know her name? She had never seen him before.

"Mary Ellen, say hello." Her grandmother was beside her giving her a little push towards him.

"Hello" she said her face turning a deep shade of red.

"Mary Ellen this is my friend Mr. St. Pierre. We have some news. We are getting married." Her grandmother was smiling and looking sad all at the same time.

"Are you okay meme?" She asked.

"Yes darling, but." She shifted her eyes from Mary Ellen to Mr. St. Pierre and then back to her.

"Well, there's something else dear."

"What?" Why did she have a feeling of dread?

"Well, we have decided that it would be best if you went to live with your Aunt Roselyn for a while." What was she saying? Maybe there was a mistake. Why would she have to leave, this was her home. Didn't her meme love her anymore?

"Why" was all she could say before the tears began to fall. But there were no answers that made sense to her. This man came to her house and now there was no room for her. Two weeks later her meme had a new name and a new husband and Mary Ellen no longer fit into their life. Her little bag was packed and off she went.

Uncle Ben picked her up and Mary Ellen cried the whole way to their house. Aunt Roselyn was pregnant with her second child and was happy for the help. She showed Mary Ellen her room and put her things in a small dresser.

"It will be okay Mary Ellen. You can help me with your cousin, it will be fun you'll see." Her Aunt Roselyn was trying to sound convincing, but Mary Ellen knew better. This was the end of her childhood. There were no more summer days at the forest or running to the park. Mary Ellen was a live-in babysitter. It was trade for room and board Uncle Ben explained.

"You help with the household chores and take care of your cousin and you can stay with us." He told her. As if she had a choice. Her mother came every other weekend to get her and although Mary Ellen hated going with her mother, she was thankful for the break away from handsy Uncle Ben and dirty diapers. Most weekends she sat across a booth from her mother while her mother got drunk. It wasn't all bad though, lots of nice men bought her milkshakes and fed her anything she wanted. All she had to do was sit quietly while her mother entertained them. Whatever that meant. Mary Ellen had potty trained her little cousin. He followed her around wherever she went. He was a really good boy, one that Mary Ellen had grown very fond of.

Mary Ellen of course, had to start a new school in the fall and make new friends. She told her aunt everything was good, but the truth was she had no friends. She sat alone every day at lunch. Word had gotten out that her mother and father didn't want her and that's why she was living with her aunt and uncle.

The days were long, but the nights were longer. Mary Ellen was always on guard for her Uncle Ben. He had come into her room one night and lifted her night gown, when Mary Ellen protested, he put his hand over her mouth. "Shhh" he said, "you don't want to upset your Aunt Roselyn, do you?" Mary Ellen shook her head and laid still. She would remember the forest and the birds singing in the trees. The way the light crept across the forest floor. The first time was very painful, and she bled a little. Her Aunt then explained to her that every month girls had a visitor and that her time had come for that visitor. She showed Mary Ellen how to use a rag and told her she would have to wash one while another was in use it would dry and so on. Mary Ellen listened intently not wanting her Aunt Roselyn to know the real reason for her bleeding. When her visitor didn't come the next month Aunt Roselyn said there was nothing to worry about sometimes it's a false alarm. His visits came every few weeks and Mary Ellen would always go to the same forest in her mind and when he was done, he would clean himself and sneak out the same way he came in.

When Aunt Roselyn was in the hospital giving birth to their second child Meme came to stay with them so, Uncle Ben stayed clear of Mary Ellen. Oh, how she missed her Meme. The way she smelled, the way she made Mary Ellen tea and the way they sipped it from the saucer instead of the cup.

"Can I come home now" she asked. But the answer was always the same.

"I'm sorry Mary Ellen this is your home now"

Summer was always an adventure for Mary Ellen. This one was no exception. Her mother's cousin Betty had come for visit and wanted to take Mary Ellen to Chicago with her and her wonderful husband Phil. There was always a chance someone would say no, but it was very unlikely. And without fail there was no one to protest. Phil and Betty arrived on Wednesday at noon and Mary Ellen was packed and ready to go. When they pulled up in their brand new 1946 Ford V8 Mary Ellen was tickled pink. Phil jumped out and took her suitcase from her and opened the car door for her. She felt like a real grown-up lady.

After driving for what seemed an eternity the city came into view. All the tall buildings and fancy dressed people. The war was over, and people were happy again. Mary Ellen had her face pressed against the window watching all the excitement. Shops were open and ladies were carrying multiple bags. How exciting she thought, and she was in the heart of it. They pulled up to the Palmer Hotel where a finely dressed man opened the door for her. She couldn't believe when he reached in with an extended white gloved hand to help her out of the car. She shot a look at Betty who smiled and nodded. Mary Ellen took his hand and smiled at him. There was another man holding the door opened for them and he nodded at Phil as they walked by.

Once inside Mary Ellen was overtaken with the beautiful chandelier that was the centerpiece of the entire room. How grand she thought. Just like in the movies. Another man pushed a golden cart with their suitcases on it and they followed along. When they arrived at the door to their room this same man unlocked and held open the door for the three of them. The room was beautiful. And Mary Ellen had her own bed separate from theirs. It was like being in a dream. It was late so Phil called someone and before she knew it there was a knock on the door and someone was pushing a tray of food into the room. Mary Ellen giggled as Betty told her to come and eat. There was a hamburger and a chocolate milkshake waiting for her. Soon after eating Mary Ellen had washed her face and brushed her teeth and was tucked into her bed. Sleep came easy this night. And it was a sweet slumber to say the least.

The next day was filled with sightseeing and shopping. Betty was just like the ladies she had seen the day before carrying multiple bags. Mary Ellen couldn't help but wonder if someone was looking at her thinking that she was one of those beautiful people. The day rushed by quickly and they were back at the hotel. Betty had bought Mary Ellen a pretty dress. She protested but Betty said she could wear it to church on Sundays so then Mary Ellen knew it would be okay.

When they were rested and cleaned up, they put on their new clothes and headed down to the dining room. Reservation for Mr. Trumbull, Phil said to the man standing at a podium. He immediately smiled and said Mr. Trumbull party of three, follow me. They did as they were told. They were seated at an elegantly dressed table and a waiter came over and took Mary Ellen's cloth napkin and placed it on her lap. Which at first startled her but then made her giggle again. Phil ordered for Mary Ellen which was fine with her since she really didn't know what to eat. When her dinner arrived, Mary Ellen was perplexed. Wrapped around the leg as of her chicken was pink paper that curled at the end. Mary Ellen had never seen this before and wasn't sure if she was supposed to eat this or not, but she made up her mind that even if she was supposed to, she was going to have to decline. She began undoing the paper when Phil gently reached over and explained that the paper was there to keep her fingers from getting messy. Mary Ellen could feel her face turning red but then felt Betty put her hand on hers and smile. Mary Ellen felt like she was in Heaven, and she also hated that they had to leave the next day.

Betty's smile had turned to concern.

"Are you okay Mary Ellen?" She asked,

"Oh yes, I was just thinking I wish this would never end, that's all." She answered fighting the urge to cry.

"All good things must come to an end." Phil responded. Why she wondered. She was so grateful to them she didn't want to ruin their night. Just then two men playing a violin came right up to the table and played a beautiful song that Mary Ellen had never heard before. Maybe she had died, and this is Heaven she thought, and if it is, it's great.

Chapter 23

Mary Ellen had been with Aunt Roselyn for almost two years. It was no surprise when she announced she was pregnant with her third child. Mary Ellen was doing the dishes when she felt him behind her. His breath was putrid and the heat coming off his body made her skin crawl. He was grabbing her breast when suddenly there was a loud crash. They both jumped and turned to see Aunt Roselyn standing in the kitchen doorway with her hand to her mouth. Mary Ellen couldn't move, and the breath stopped entering her lungs. But Uncle Ben moved quickly toward Aunt Roselyn with a litany of excuses as to why he had his hands all over Mary Ellen. Get out was all she said to him. He looked at Mary Ellen and then stepped around his shocked wife.

Mary Ellen couldn't look at her Aunt Roselyn. But she did hear loud and clear that she was no longer welcome in their home.

"But I didn't, I'm sorry Aunt,". Her words were like feathers in a windstorm. They were being blown all around with nowhere to land. Her little bag was packed, and her Uncle Ernie was at the door waiting for her. Mary Ellen felt so ashamed, but she wasn't sure why. All she knew was that Uncle Ben had done something terrible and

Aunt Roselyn had forgiven him, and she had done nothing wrong, and she was being tossed aside.

The ride to Uncle Ernie's was a long quiet one. Just as they were pulling in the driveway, he looked at Mary Ellen and said,

"I never did like that guy." Mary Ellen felt the air flow back into her lungs and then began to cry. Aunt Cora couldn't have been kinder to her. She taught Mary Ellen to sew, and garden, not vegetables but flowers. They walked to the park pushing their new baby in the stroller. Aunt Cora seemed to understand Mary Ellen. She didn't judge her or ask her stupid questions she just talked to her like she was a real person. When Uncle Ernie came home from working in the factory all day Aunt Cora always had a cold beer waiting for him and a nice dinner. Mary Ellen loved to watch the way they interacted with each other. Someday I'm going to marry a man like Uncle Ernie.

Mary Ellen loved her Meme but on this she was wrong. Aunt Cora was a wonderful person. Mary Ellen absolutely knew this to be true. She had a pretty room in their house and so long as she kept it clean, they got along wonderfully.

Over the next year Mary Ellen thrived at school. She even made a new friend. Her name was Susie and Mary Ellen called her Sues for short and Susie loved it. They were twelve years old now and inseparable. They had both started their periods and could commiserate about how horrible it was. And they had discovered boys. Neither of them would ever have the nerve to act on their feelings of puppy love but they would giggle about how cute this one was or how strong that one was. Sues was going to marry a doctor but Mary Ellen had always known she was going to marry a movie star. So, she could ride around in a Rolls Royce and have people wave to her. They had sleep overs and listened to the radio every chance they got. They knew all the Dinah Shore songs and Nat King Cole was so dreamy. Life was everything she hoped it would be. Although she missed her Meme, she finally felt like she belonged.

The new school year had begun and Sues was in the same classroom. They managed to get desks right next to one another. They had a new teacher to. Mrs. Kenner. She was and older woman with kind eyes. Mary Ellen took an instant liking to her.

The two girls were soon called teacher's pets. And they were just fine with that. Especially Mary Ellen. She had never been a teacher's favorite before. She loved cleaning the brushes for Mrs. Kenner and so it was officially given to her and Sues as a job! Mary Ellen would rush home to do her homework and help with dinner. Aunt Cora was always happy to see her come in from school. Some days she would have cookies and milk waiting for her. Her little cousin was now one and a half. Mary Ellen loved playing with him. He had red hair just like his mother. So, they nicknamed him Red.

At night Mary Ellen would say her prayers and she always remembered to thank God for all her blessings, then she would pray for her Meme. She still ached for her. But life was good here. Christmas that year was one she'll never forget. They all gathered at her Meme and new Pepe's house. All the aunts, uncles, cousins and even her mother were in attendance. There was food as far as the eye could see. Boy things sure were looking up from the days when her Meme ran the bootleg. No one ever talked about those days. Leave the past in the past they would say. Even her Meme's sister was there, Aunt Mirna. She seemed to get along pretty good with Mary Ellen's mother. She was glad for that. Everyone seemed to look down on her mother.

When all the food was gone, and the dishes were done and the family started to break up and go their separate ways, her mother and Aunt Cora seemed to be in a very deep conversation. Uncle Ernie stepped between them and then Meme took Mary Ellen by the hand and led her into the living room.

"Sit down here Mary Ellen. How are you my dear?"

"I'm fine Meme, is everything alright?" She asked Just then her mother walked into the living room. Followed by Aunt Cora and Uncle Ernie. Then without warning her mother blurted out

"You're going to come live with me" It was happening again, she couldn't breathe.

"What? Why?" Aunt Cora came, sat next to Mary Ellen and took her hand.

"I'm sorry Mary Ellen but we're going to have another baby and my mother is coming from Scotland to live with us and we need the room." Her words were like daggers piercing Mary Ellen's heart. How could this be happening to her again! She wanted to scream but nothing would come out. It was clear Aunt Cora felt bad but not bad enough. Her mother lived on the other side of town which meant another school. No friends, no Sues, no Mrs. Kenner. Mary Ellen couldn't help herself; she burst into tears and ran out of the room. She found her old room and threw herself onto the bed. It was Uncle Ernie that came to her.

"Please try to understand Mary Ellen if there was another way. We love you very much but."

There it was the but. The but that she had heard her whole twelve and a half years on this earth. But you have no father, but I'm not your mother I'm your Meme Sorry but you can't stay here. Sorry was a word that Mary Ellen knew all too well. She also knew it was just a word, one used by adults far too often. Sorry and but.

They always brought Mary Ellen bad news. She had said goodbye to her friend and her teacher, all that was left was to make another move.

Life with her mother was terribly miserable. Mary Ellen was thirteen and was told she couldn't just sit around she would have to help during the summer at her mother's dinner. And after school she could get a job as well. The first summer she worked with her mother wasn't as bad as she thought. It was at a beach and after Mary Ellen was done scooping ice cream all day, she would go into the kitchen and her mother would feed her and then she was free to do whatever she wanted. It wasn't long before Mary Ellen met a group of kids who vacationed here every summer. At first, they were a little standoffish but once they realized Mary Ellen could get them booze everyone wanted to become her friend. It was easy. Mary Ellen had been around booze her whole life. She would simply take a little here a little there and keep it in a mason jar under her bed. She only took it after her mother had passed out, so she didn't notice.

Cynthia was her best pal. Mary Ellen didn't drink but Cynthia never gave her a hard time. They would share the contraband with a couple of boys who were really cute and in no time the four of them were inseparable. They walked the beach late into the night and swam in the lake long after dark. One night Clark thought it would be a good idea to skinny dip.

"Come on you guys, don't be chickens!" He slurred after having a few too many sips from the mason jar. His pal Kurt laughed and began to strip down. Mary Ellen looked at Cynthia with panic written all over her face. But Cynthia to was feeling a little tipsy.

"Come on Mary Ellen don't be a prude." Cynthia to was stripping. There was a big splash, and the boys were jumping up and down yelling. Cynthia was naked in front of her laughing saying

"Come on! Hurry up." Without thinking Mary Ellen stripped and joined the fun. The four of them splashed each other and bobbed up and down in the water until their skin was wrinkled. Having sobered a little from the cold water they were all a little shy about getting out. The boys finally said they would get out first Mary Ellen couldn't believe her eyes. She tried not to look but found it almost impossible to look away. She found them beautiful. Not like her uncle who was ugly, disgusting really.

Clark told Mary Ellen to stay put he would run and get her a towel. Mary Ellen did as she was told. Cynthia stayed close. In just a couple minutes both boys returned with towels for them.

"Turn around please" Mary Ellen asked, and Clark immediately complied. She hurried out of the water, and he turned and handed her the towel but not until he got an eye full. Mary Ellen was blushing so terribly she couldn't find words. He smiled devilishly and then turned away. Mary Ellen dried as quickly as she could and dressed in the clothes that she had left piled on the beach. The four of them laughed all the way down the beach until they were back in the park.

Mary Ellen had a hard time sleeping that night all she saw was the beauty of Clark and how he looked at her. They hadn't asked her how old she was, she guessed they thought she was their age. Mary Ellen was thirteen and these kids were all sixteen. She decided if they asked, she would say that she was sixteen too. Everyone told her how pretty she was, and no one ever believed her when she said her real age so what harm could there be in a little lie.

That first summer flew by and all the families were packing up their belongings in preparation of heading home. Mary Ellen had grown so close to Cynthia and Kurt, but Clark was a different story. She just knew she was in love with him. She was pretty sure he was to. They did everything together since the night they skinny dipped together, but he never made any advances toward her. She was glad. Even though she loved him she was still afraid of getting too close.

"Hey Mar." he said with his head down.

"Hey" she said trying to read his feelings

"Will you write to me?" He asked

"Sure." But before she could say anything else, he bent down and kissed her hard on the lips and slipped a piece of paper in her hand. Mary Ellen was flushed and looked at her hand. When she looked up, he was walking away.

She opened the paper and written on it was an address. Mary Ellen didn't know whether to laugh or cry. Instead, she headed to Cynthia's to say goodbye.

Summer had turned to Fall and that meant yet another school. This time Mary Ellen didn't even try to make friends. She knew how this worked; all the kids had their own clicks if she just stayed out of the way, almost invisible, she would get through this school year. It was easier than she thought. No one noticed her. Not even the teachers. She didn't even care about her grades mainly because no one else did. She got herself to school, got herself to work afterward and then home late at night and then to bed. Her mother barley spoke to her except of course on pay day. Mary Ellen could count on her showing up at the dinner on pay day with her hand out. Mary Ellen was allowed to keep her tips but her pay went to her mother. She was told it was expensive supporting her. Funny Mary Ellen thought she was never home to eat and did her own laundry at the laundry mat. What expenses was her mother talking about. They slept under the same roof but that was the extent of their relationship.

Mary Ellen wrote Clark every day at first and then with less to say she wrote once a week. She made up friends and adventures to tell him about. In the beginning it was fun but as time passed, she had less and less to say. When Christmas came, they all gathered at her Meme's house. Mary Ellen didn't want to be there but when she saw her Meme, she suddenly felt horribly home sick. Her Meme greeted her with a big hug, but Mary Ellen had a hard time reciprocating.

"Are you alright honey?" Meme asked with a look of concern.

"Oh, sure Meme, I'm just tired I guess." She replied.

"Well why don't you go sit with your cousins and catch up." Mary Ellen looked in the living room where all her little cousins were playing and laughing. She didn't belong with them. She looked for her Aunt Louise, but she was with her new husband and not really interested with talking to Mary Ellen. Feeling overwhelmed with loss Mary Ellen grabbed her coat and went outside. Sitting on the back porch was Uncle Peter.

"Well, if it isn't my little Mary Ellen all grown up!" He had obviously been drinking but that wasn't anything new. "How are you beautiful?" He genuinely wanted to know.

"Fine I guess." she said.

"Well, that's not very convincing." He stated.

"I don't fit in, anywhere." She said sadly.

"I understand." Was all he said, and he handed her a cigarette. Mary Ellen had never smoked but she felt like this was a good time to start. He pulled out a match and with his fingernail lit it. Mary Ellen put the cigarette in her mouth and sucked in. It was lit and she felt lightheaded. But after a bit of a cough, it passed, and she enjoyed it. They sat without speaking. Mary Ellen knew in that moment that he felt the same way she did. Like a misfit. It was her mother who came out and broke the silence.

"There you are." she said. Well at least her mother noticed she wasn't in the house.

"I'm just visiting with Uncle Peter." she said

"Well, that's good but I need to talk to my brother." she said

"Awe let her stay, she's alright." He insisted Her mother took a bottle out of her bag and the three of them sat on the porch. Uncle Peter and her mother passed the bottle between themselves until they were called in for dinner. Mary Ellen was shivering with the cold, but her mother and Uncle were totally oblivious.

Mary Ellen used her tip money to buy cigarettes. She would sneak in the bathroom at school and have a few puffs. A lot of kids did it, but they were all older than her. Again, she was invisible. Onetime a teacher came in and everyone got in trouble but her. It never occurred to anyone that she smoked because she was the youngest of the bunch. She was just instructed to return to class.

By early spring the letters that had been exchanged between Clark and herself had become less and less. Eventually they just stopped writing. Really Mary Ellen had expected this. After all nothing lasts forever. Besides she might not even go back to the lake this summer. Mary Ellen's grades were suffering but she didn't really care. She liked having her independence. She worked and kept to herself. She didn't really see her Meme much anymore. She had her life and Mary Ellen tried to respect that. It didn't really hurt that much anymore. She got a card in the mail from her for her birthday but that was over a month ago.

Loneliness was something Mary Ellen tried hard not to think about. Weekends were the worst. If she could pick up extra shifts, she would. The diner was opened twenty-four hours and she could count on at least a twelve-hour day. The older waitresses were always warning her that she was on her feet to long. Your young they'd say. You better take care of your feet or when your older you'll have trouble. Mary Ellen tried but her shoes wore out way faster than she could afford to replace them. Winter was the worst because a lot of time she would arrive at work with wet feet and have to work like that all night.

Some nights Mary Ellen would come home, and her mother would be entertaining some man. Sometimes her Uncle Peter would be dead asleep in her bed and Mary Ellen would have to sleep on the couch. The only thing that was constant in her life was that she was alone.

Chapter 24

Much to Mary Ellen's surprise her mother asked her if she would be willing to come back to the lake for the summer to help her out. She spoke with the owner of the diner, and he said her job would be waiting for her when she came back in the Fall. This was the first hurdle, the second would be facing Clark if he came back this summer. Mary Ellen agreed to help her mother again but this time she expected to get paid. Again, her mother surprised her and said yes. Business was slow for the first week and then like someone flipped a switch they were so busy they could barely restock the supplies.

Her mother had made friends with a man named Henry. At first Mary Ellen didn't like him. He didn't even speak to her, and he acted like he owned the place. But her mother and he had been working together for a while before Mary Ellen joined them, so she thought maybe he felt she was intruding. Now, however Mary Ellen liked him. He was a hard worker, and he kept the kitchen running smoothly.

Mary Ellen oversaw the ice cream counter and waiting tables when she could. Her mother did everything, from cooking to waiting tables to cleaning to stocking. This was a side of her mother Mary Ellen liked. Here she treated Mary Ellen like an equal. Mary Ellen was always getting hit on. Mostly by older men. It was her mother that would scare them off when she would tell them how old she was. Mary Ellen was scooping ice cream when she heard a familiar voice.

"Hey Mar." Mary Ellen swallowed hard and looked up. There he was. Was it possible that he had grown almost a foot and gotten even better looking?

"Hi there." She said as calmly as she could muster. Her heart was beating so fast, and she could feel the heat in her cheeks rising.

"What's new?" But before he could answer a tall brunette came up behind him and grabbed his arm.

"There you are!" She squealed. "I thought I lost you. Oh, ice cream, how lovely. I'll have a strawberry single cone please." Mary Ellen tried to regain her composure and then looked directly into Clark eyes and said, "And for you?" Clark took a deep breath and said,

"Nothing for me thanks." Mary Ellen watched them walk away arm in arm. And wanted to disappear. Thankfully Cynthia arrived the next day. And then Kurt. Cynthia and Kurt had stayed in touch over the winter and now were an item. They had both been accepted to the same college in the Fall and were excited about the next chapter of their life.

"What about you, ya going to college?" They asked.

"Umm I think I'm going to take a year to travel. That's why I'm helping here so I can make some extra spending money." It was a little lie but one she had to tell. She couldn't bear the thought of them knowing the truth about her age and living situation. They bought her story and then prattled on about themselves.

"Hey, have you seen Clark yet?" Kurt asked

"Ya, and his new girlfriend." She answered

"What?" Cynthia sounded surprised

"They were in yesterday, she's a real beauty". That was the best Mary Ellen could come up with. She was still so hurt and embarrassed.

"But he told me he was crazy about you." Kurt interjected

"Well, you could have fooled me. Besides I'm too busy to bother with a boyfriend." She lied and hoped they bought it.

"His loss. There's lots of guys here. A girl as pretty as you won't have any trouble." Kurt said with a smile.

"Hey, hey there mister, keep your eyes over here." Cynthia was grabbing his arm. They all broke out in laughter. "What time do you think you'll be done here?" Mary Ellen wasn't sure but guessed about eight. "Okay meet us at the band stand." Cynthia gave her a quick hug and they were off.

It was quarter to nine by the time Mary Ellen was able to get away. She didn't think they would still be there, but she thought she'd take a chance. Sure, enough they were there. But so were Clark and his new girl. She thought of turning and running but it was too late Cynthia was calling out to her.

"Hey sorry, I had to help out a little longer." She could feel Clark eyes on her, but she didn't want to look his way.

"Hello, my name is Bridget." Her hand was extended, and Mary Ellen had to shake it.

"Mary Ellen. Nice to meet you." She was regaining her composure.

"Clark has told me so much about you. I was hoping I'd get to meet you." She said.

"Funny he hadn't mentioned you." She regretted saying it as soon as she heard herself. "But I'm sure it's because I haven't talked to him since Christmas." She smiled and tried to smooth over her misstep. Bridget just smiled and cozied up to Clark.

The Band was starting at nine o'clock and it was five minutes till. They moved to a picnic table and suddenly Mary Ellen felt like a third wheel.

The music was hopping, and people were getting up to dance. Bridget pleaded with Clark to dance with her, and he finally gave in. Mary Ellen watched as the moved into the crowd and then she lost sight of them.

"Aren't you going to dance? She asked,

"We don't want to leave you alone." Cynthia said.

"Don't be foolish, go I'll be fine." Mary Ellen insisted. Kurt took Cynthia's hand and led her to the dance floor. Mary Ellen felt so foolish. Why had she come back here? She felt more alone now than she did at home. When no one returned to the table when the next song began Mary Ellen decided she just couldn't stay. But just as she stood a tall blonde-haired boy walked up to the table and asked her to dance. Mary Ellen didn't really feel like it but said yes anyway. When they got on the dance floor the song ended and a slow song began.

"Well, were here" he said and took her in his arms. He moved expertly and she was actually enjoying it, but he was holding her awfully close. When she tried to pull away a bit, he pulled her closer. Mary Ellen was inexperienced, and he had misread her intention. She began to squirm, and he gave her a tug. Before Mary Ellen knew what was happening Clark had her by the arm and gave her a quick pull.

"Hey are you alright?" He asked. "No not really." She said. The blonde guy loosened his grip and looked a little confused.

"Hey I thought." But Clark didn't want to hear it.

"Take a walk friend" To Mary Ellen's surprise he did. Bridget was back at Clark side asking what was going on.

"Nothing just some guy was getting a little handsy." He explained. Bridget took Mary Ellen by the arm and led her back to the table.

"Are you okay?" She asked.

"What's going on?" Cynthia was back at the table at Mary Ellen's side.

"Oh, some guy was getting handsy with Mary Ellen, but Clark took care of it." Bridget explained. Mary Ellen just wanted this day to end.

"If you will excuse me, I think I'm going to call it a night." Mary Ellen hoped they wouldn't protest. Instead, Bridget insisted Clark walk her home so Mary Ellen wouldn't be alone. Mary Ellen tried to convince them she could take care of herself, but Bridget wouldn't hear another word. Mary Ellen and Clark walked in silence most of the way then suddenly he took her arm and said,

"Can we talk?"

"About what" she said. "Mary Ellen I'm sorry. It's not what you think. Bridget is my moms' friend's niece. She's staying with my family for the summer, and she has the wrong idea about me." He was almost pleading.

"It looks like you and her are perfect for each other. Really, I'm happy for you." She lied.

"I've missed you Mar. I was hoping you'd be here this summer. Really. I'll straighten things out with Bridget, I promise." He pleaded for Mary Ellen to give him a chance. She started walking again and he joined her. They stayed in silence until they arrived at the diner. She turned to thank him, and he took her by the shoulders and kissed her.

"Please" he said. The next week flew by, she saw Cynthia and Kurt when they stopped by the diner but other than that Mary Ellen had stayed close to home. It was late and Mary Ellen was taking the last bag of trash around back to the dumpster when she heard a strange sound.

"Mar, it's just me. I hope I didn't startle you." Clark was standing by the side of the building. When she turned, she could barely believe her eyes. Clark was standing under the humming light holding a bouquet of flowers.

"Your mom told me you were out here."

"Are those for me?" She asked. Clark handed them to her, and she gladly took them.

"I'm sorry Mar, Bridget left today to go home. I told her that I cared for someone else and that I didn't want to hurt her and that nothing was going to happen with her and I." The words came out in a rush. Mary Ellen was overwhelmed. He bent down and kissed her, and she kissed him back. For the next month they were inseparable. Cynthia and Kurt, Clark and Mary Ellen were the best of friends.

Mary Ellen still had to work but on busy days Cynthia would come to the diner and help. Mary Ellen had never felt so cared for. Henry kept her mother busy drinking most nights after the diner closed which meant Mary Ellen was on her own.

It was late into July when the four of them decided to leave the park. Kurt had a car and a plan. Clark and Kurt were eighteen now and Cynthia was going to be eighteen in two weeks. Mary Ellen had secured enough whiskey to get the party started. They headed out of town. The dirt road seemed never ending. When Kurt pulled over, they knew they were lost. There wasn't another car in sight. It was hot and still.

The cicadas were loudly singing in the trees. They set off on foot and stumbled on a large field covered in fireflies. Mary Ellen stopped and took it all in. It was the most beautiful thing she had ever seen. Clark took her hand and led her into the field. She didn't even notice that he had a blanket. He laid it down and sat with his hand extended to her. Mary Ellen took his hand in hers and sat down next to him. Cynthia and Kurt had move on into the field and out of sight.

They laid on their backs looking up at the night sky with the fireflies dancing all around them.

"Are you afraid to leave your family to go to college?" She asked

"No, I'm looking forward to it. Maybe you can come and visit some weekends." He asked. Mary Ellen didn't know how to answer him, so she just nodded. He rolled over onto one elbow and was looking down at her.

"You're so beautiful Mar." And he bent to kiss her. She lifted her back and he slipped his arm under her shoulders. He was so gentle and kind. Not at all like Uncle Ben. Oh God why was she thinking about him? Not now she thought. She tried to push those awful memories out of her mind, but Clark stopped and asked if she was okay.

"I'm sorry Mar, am I going to fast?" He looked so concerned. Mary Ellen was nervous but assured him she was ok.

"I'll be careful" he said. Mary Ellen was only fourteen, but she felt like a woman. Just then a light flashed on them, and a man was yelling at them to get off his land. Clark and Mary Ellen jumped up and ran but before they could get to the car Cynthia and Kurt were yelling their names. Clark took Mary Ellen's hand and turned only to be stopped dead in his track by a farmer with a shot gun. Mary Ellen froze, and Clark began to talk.

"Hey mister, we're really sorry we didn't mean any harm." Kurt and Cynthia were at their side now and Kurt was apologizing to.

The farmer pointed to the road and yelled "Get" and the four of them turned and ran as fast as they could. When they got to the car they jumped in and sped off. Only when they were sure they were out of the farmers sight did they all start laughing. Clark was in the backseat with Mary Ellen. He put his arm around her and pulled her close.

When they got back to the diner the sun was coming up. Bea was standing out front with a policeman. Mary Ellen couldn't believe her eyes.

"Shit" Kurt said, and Clark lost all the color in his face. They thought about driving on, but it was too late the Policeman had seen them. When the car came to a stop Mary Ellen slowly got out. Clark followed her knowing he would have a lot of explaining to do.

Bea grabbed Mary Ellen by the arm.

"Do you know how worried I've been?" Was Mary Ellen hearing this right? Surely her mother must be drunk.

"To think my fourteen-year-old daughter was out all night with these boys." Mary Ellen looked at Clark who looked like he had seen a ghost.

"What!"

"That's right young man this girl is fourteen. You are in a lot of trouble." The policeman was looking at Clark with steely eyes. Clark looked at Mary Ellen in total disbelief.

"Is that true?" He asked and Mary Ellen wanted to die.

"Yes." She said she couldn't even look at him. The police officer looked at Bea and asked if she wanted to press charges.

"Oh no mother. It was my fault. He didn't know. I swear. Please Mother. Please." Mary Ellen was crying and begging all at the same time. Kurt and Cynthia were standing next to Clark now unable to process what they had just heard.

"Fine. Let them go. But don't you come near my daughter again. Do you hear me?" Her mother had obviously been drinking but only Mary Ellen could tell.

"Yes Mam." Clark looked at Mary Ellen one more time and then got back in the car followed by Kurt and Cynthia. Mary Ellen watched as they drove off. Mary Ellen hated her mother more than she thought possible. She knew about the age difference and had never cared.

Later Mary Ellen found out that it was Henry who was worried about Mary Ellen and told her mother to call the police. Bea didn't want to look like a bad mother to Henry, so she called. It was just an act. One that had ruined Mary Ellen's life.

Chapter 25

Mary Ellen didn't see Clark after that night. Cynthia came to the diner a couple of days later only to tell Mary Ellen that Clark had left to go home. When Cynthia explained that Clark could have lost his scholarship to school if he had been arrested Mary Ellen felt horrible. She hadn't understood the consequences of her deceit. She explained everything to Cynthia. The truth was. it was the first time she had ever been honest with anyone. Cynthia was understanding but told her they could no longer be friends. Mary Ellen was devastated. The rest of the summer dragged on. When September finally arrived Mary Ellen couldn't pack fast enough.

The drive home was endless. Bea and Mary Ellen drove in total silence. Only when they stopped for gas did they exchange words.

"Do you want something to eat?" Bea asked but Mary Ellen's response was short

"No." Although Mary Ellen was starving, she wouldn't give her mother the satisfaction of eating with her. When Bea stepped out of the car Mary Ellen went in the gas station and asked for the key to the lady's room. A kind looking older man handed her the keys Mary Ellen couldn't help but notice he had a wooden leg. She knew better than to ask. She knew the effects of the war. When she got back to the car. Bea handed her a bag of red licorice. Mary Ellen took the bag thankfully. It was long after dark when they returned to the apartment her mother had rented. Mary Ellen went straight to her room without a word. And went to bed. The next morning to Mary Ellen's surprise, her mother was at the kitchen table drinking coffee.

"Would you like a cup?" She asked.

"Sure" Mary Ellen said

"Look, I know I'm not perfect and I know your still mad at me, but we are going to have to talk eventually." Her mother said matter of fact. Mary Ellen knew she was right but didn't know what to say.

"So, I was thinking, your pretty well grown up so how about if we ack like roommates?" Mary Ellen could see that her mother was trying. Funny that's all Mary Ellen thought they were anyway.

"Ok" she said. But I smoke, and if I have to work, I'm not going back to school. And I will pay rent, but you can't have my paychecks anymore." Mary Ellen couldn't believe she had just said all that, but she did and now she had to wait for her mother's response.

"Okay." And with that her mother got up from the table and got dressed. Mary Ellen knew she had to find a way out of this life. She prayed every night and worked hard every day. But she could never seem to get ahead.

Her mother didn't take her check anymore but charged her rent and on top of that Mary Ellen still had to eat and pay for the bus. She tried to cut back on smoking but that seemed impossible. She was fifteen now and she had only seen her Meme twice since returning from the lake. Their family was growing, and Mary Ellen was called on frequently to baby sit. She didn't mind though because despite everything she really did love all her little cousins.

It was a Wednesday after the lunch rush when two girls came into the diner looking for her. Mary Ellen didn't recognize either of them but somehow, she felt she knew them.

"Hi, Mary Ellen. My name is Samantha, and this is my sister Angela. This might come as a shock to you but we're you sisters." Mary Ellen couldn't believe what she was hearing.

"Who, how?" She asked

"Well, we have the same father." Samantha said. Mary Ellen didn't know what to say. They were older than she was, but she had no idea they existed. Where had they been?

"I'm sure you have a lot of questions, so we were wondering if you would like to come home with us and maybe we could answer them." Angela said. Mary Ellen felt faint. She could feel the blood leaving her face.

"I think I need to sit down" she said, "Will my, our, father be there?" She asked

"No, I'm afraid mother and daddy have divorced but mother knows all about you and would love to meet you. I'm sure daddy would love to see you to." Samantha sounded kind and reassuring.

"When?" Mary Ellen asked

"Now if you want. We will wait until your done work." Angela said. Mary Ellen's boss walked up and told Mary Ellen to go on, he had overheard the conversation and was happy to help the situation. Mary Ellen couldn't stop staring at them. It was uncanny how much they all looked alike. They all had strawberry blonde hair and blue eyes. Her mother had big brown eyes. But she did remember meeting her father once and the impact his blue eyes had on her. It was the first time she felt like she looked like somebody.

When they arrived at their house Mary Ellen suddenly felt out of place. They lived in a modest house but a house none the less. It has a pretty yard, and the trees were all turning the shades of fall. Samantha took Mary Ellen's hand in hers and smiled. Angela went through the front door first.

"Mother we're home." They followed and as Mary Ellen's eyes were adjusting to the light a woman came into the living room. She was a small woman with graying hair. She was rather plain but still pretty.

"Mother this is Mary Ellen" Angela took care of the introduction. Mary Ellen was trembling. What must this woman think of her? She thought. The bastard child of her husband.

"Well Mary Ellen, your just as beautiful as your sisters." Their mother's name was Roberta and she insisted Mary Ellen call her that. "Thank you" was all Mary Ellen could manage to say.

"Are you hungry dear? Would you like a drink?" Mary Ellen didn't know if Roberta was being sincere or not but thought she better just say no thank you. Just then Samantha took Mary Ellen by the hand and said,

"Come on I want to show you something." Mary Ellen followed along. Samantha took Mary Ellen to her bedroom and pulled out two photo albums.

"Would you like to see some pictures of daddy?" She asked. Mary Ellen shook her head in response. They sat on the bed close to each other. It felt like she had found the other half of herself. Samantha was eighteen and Angela was twenty. Mary Ellen was only fifteen, but she was as mature as both her sisters. Samantha flipped the album open to a beautiful picture of Roberta and her father on their wedding day.

"Mother gave me this after the divorce, I hope seeing it doesn't hurt." She was already thinking it was a bad idea.

"No, it's fine" Mary Ellen tried to sound convincing, but it did hurt. She wasn't sure why since no one ever really explained what happened between her mother and father. It was just a reminder of what could have been. Next Samantha was showing Mary Ellen pictures of their childhood. Shots of life as a family. Posed pictures in the beginning then fun pictures like birthdays parties and family vacations. It was making Mary Ellen sad, and she wasn't sure if she could look at another.

It was then that Angela must have seen the hurt in Mary Ellen because she took the album from Samantha and said,

"I think that's enough for today Sam I'm sure we don't want to bore Mary Ellen." Mary Ellen was grateful but tried to protest a little.

"Oh no I'm not bored really. I think I'm just a little overwhelmed that's all."

"I'm sorry." Samantha said. "That was probably a little insensitive of me. Let's go sit in the kitchen and have something to eat. I'm sure mother has something prepared for us." Roberta had been busy; they were served a feast. There was chicken and dumplings, homemade biscuits, beets and coleslaw. None of these things went together but it didn't matter to Mary Ellen it was just so nice to sit at the table and share a meal with her sisters.

Roberta was a little quiet at first, but she finally asked Mary Ellen if she would like to see her father.

"Oh yes I would, very much." She tried not to sound too anxious but was unsuccessful.

"Good because I told him the girls were going to get you and he is going to come by. If it's too soon I'll call and let him know."

"No, no that's fine." Mary Ellen was trembling inside. Samantha took her hand and said,

"It will be okay Mary Ellen he really wants to see you. He told us all about you." Why hadn't anyone told her about him she wondered. She only had a brief memory of a chance meeting in a bar. And his blue eyes. She suddenly wished she looked better. She was painfully aware that she still had on her work uniform. And she wanted to fix her hair and put on some lipstick. Without thinking she smoothed her hair and straighten her uniform. Angela looked at her and said.

"Mary Ellen, you look beautiful" Mary Ellen got big tears in her eyes. She suddenly felt the loss of a big sister. A loss she didn't know she could feel.

"Thank you, Angela," she said.

When the doorbell rang Mary Ellen almost jumped out of her skin. She took a deep breath and Roberta went to the door.

"Albert, come on in." Mary Ellen could feel the heat rise in her face and was rethinking her decision. But it was too late. Her father walked into the kitchen. Samantha was on her feet.

"Hi daddy." She was hugging him. Mary Ellen stood with Angela. She watched as Angela moved to her father and kissed his cheek.

"Hi, look who we found." She said as she took Mary Ellen's arm. He stepped close to her not sure exactly what to do next. He put his hand out to her and Mary Ellen took it.

"Hi Mary Ellen, I'm so glad to see you." She was surprised that his had was a little moist. He is as nervous as me she thought.

"Come on girls let's leave them alone for a bit." Roberta was leading her girls out of the room. Albert looked at his ex-wife and said,

"Thank you, girls." "Please sit-down Mary Ellen. How are you?" He asked Mary Ellen sat back down and wasn't sure how to answer him. So, she said

"Fine thanks." "I don't know what your mother might have told you, but I'd like to explain if that's alright." Mary Ellen didn't know how to explain that she really didn't know anything about him.

"Okay" she said. Albert proceeded to tell Mary Ellen the whole story. From start to finish. Mary Ellen sat quietly unable to process everything, he was telling her.

"Do you have any questions for me?" He asked.

Was he kidding questions she had a whole laundry list of questions? Where should she begin.

"If you knew about me, why didn't you come and get me?" She felt this was the most important question that needed to be answered.

"Things were different Mary Ellen. I was married to Roberta and although we both knew our marriage was over it was important for the girls that we kept a stable home. I know that doesn't make it right, but I want you to know I always thought about you." He tried to answer but instead he added fuel to the fire that was burning inside her.

"What about my mother, did you love her? Or was I just a mistake." Her question was more of a statement, but it had to be said. Mary Ellen had been told her whole life that she wasn't wanted. First by her mother than her father. Then it was her Meme and her aunt and uncle. Then Uncle Ernie and Aunt Cora. What he said next was the most important thing Mary Ellen would hear in her life.

"Yes" he said. "I loved your mother and when I found out about you, I wanted you to, but." And there it was "but". The word that defined her life. It really didn't matter what he said next. It wouldn't matter. Those three little letters explained everything. Mary Ellen stood and extended her hand.

"Thank you for telling me the truth. I think I've heard enough. I'd like to go home now." She was fighting back tears but didn't want him to see. She quickly turned away from him.

"Mary Ellen, I'm sorry did I say something wrong? I don't want you to leave I just found you." He pleaded.

"I've been right here my whole life." She said and headed for the door. Angela went after her.

"Wait Mary Ellen, wait." Mary Ellen stopped for her but only for a moment.

"I'm sorry Angela, I don't belong here." She was overwhelmed and wasn't trying to hide it anymore.

"Please Mary Ellen. Can I see you again?" She asked

"You know how to find me. Please tell your mother thank you for me. I just need to go home."

"Okay, I'm sorry, really, I am. Please remember we're sisters and we will always be here for you." Mary Ellen believed her; she just wasn't ready for a new family. She walked to the bus stop in a bit of a daze. She still had so many unanswered questions. She wasn't sure she would ever find the truth, but she was going to try.

Chapter 26

It had been a week since her sisters had walked into the diner. Her boss must have sensed thing didn't go well because he didn't ask when Mary Ellen showed up the next day with big circles under her eyes and a chip on her shoulder. She knew if she asked her mother, she couldn't trust what she might tell her, so she was going to see her Meme. When she arrived at her Meme's house, she was awash in sadness. Would she ever feel whole? she Wondered?

"Hi child." Her Meme was the most beautiful woman Mary Ellen had ever seen. She knew her Meme loved her even though she had given her away.

"Meme, I need to talk to you. Can we sit?" As usual her Meme was busy in the kitchen. She wiped her hands on her apron and sat down at the table.

"Of course, what's going on?" Mary Ellen told her Meme how her sisters came to the diner. How she went home with them and how her father showed up. Mary Ellen began to cry, and her Meme took her hand across the table.

"Oh Mary Ellen, I'm so sorry. We tried to protect you from all that terrible business."

"So, it's true?" She looked at her Meme with a broken heart.

"Yes, I'm afraid so. I lied to your mother when she told us about you. We said your father didn't want her or you. We thought it best for your mother to give you up for adoption. You must understand what your mother had done brought this family such shame. We didn't want you to be raised amid that. But your mother had other plans. You must know Mary Ellen, when she put you in my arms at the train station that day, I knew I would love you for the rest of my life."

"But you gave me away to." Her words we little more than a whisper. With that her Meme was on her feet and taking her into her arms.

"I'm sorry child, it was for the best."

"The best for who? Not me." She took a deep breath and then apologized. "I'm sorry Meme, I know you did the best you could. Thank you for telling me the truth." Mary Ellen left the kitchen and all its wonderful smells knowing it would never feel the same again.

With fall turning colder by the day so to was Mary Ellen's mood. She told her mother about the meeting with her father and sisters and got the response she expected. First shock then lies then her mother went on a bender. Mary Ellen swore she would never drink. It changed people. Not only their personality but it changed the way they looked. Their skin became softer but not in a good way and their eyes changed. Her mothers' eyes were dark brown but when she drank, they became lighter somehow, like they were drowning.

No, she had made up her mind that life wasn't going to be kind to her so she would have to take control of it for herself. Whatever that meant. The diner was unusually busy today and Mary Ellen was in no mood for flirtatious men. She was still only fifteen, but she looked and acted like she was twenty. Men found her almost irresistible. On this day a tall man walked into the diner in uniform and sat alone at the counter. Mary Ellen approached him with a chip on her shoulder.

"What can I get you?" she barked. He barely looked up and said,

"Black coffee and a piece of pie, you pick." She walked away and quickly returned with a hot black coffee and a piece of rhubarb pie.

"Anything else?" He shook his head, so she left the bill. When she returned, he was gone. He left the amount of the bill plus a hefty tip. She scooped up the money and the dirty dishes and the next person sat down. It was going on seven that night and the rush had finally ended. Mary Ellen was refilling the sugar jars when the same man pulled the door opened which set the little bell hanging on the door ringing. This time she looked at him and he looked right back at her. It was a little unnerving.

"Hi your back?" She said this time with a tired smile on her face.

"Ya I really liked that pie" he said with a smile.

"How she remembered which pie she gave him she'll never know but she did.

"Unfortunately, we're out of rhubarb. But we still have two pieces of apple." She offered

"Sounds like apple it is." He had a kind way about him. He wasn't all that handsome but looks weren't everything. He was the last to leave that night.

"Can I drive you home?" He asked.

"No thank you" she said. He was there for the next three nights in a row. And each night he asked her if he could give her a ride home. On the third night though, it was pouring down rain and she was dead on her feet. The thought of walking home in the rain held no appeal. This time when he asked, she said yes. He held the door for her, and she slid into the front seat. She had to admit it was nice to have a ride home.

"Would you like to go somewhere for a drink? He asked.

"I don't drink." She said but she really didn't feel like going home to that drab apartment.

"But I wouldn't mind going for a soda."

"Great, I know the perfect place." They closed the diner and then drove to a sightseeing spot at the river. They talked all night. More like he spoke, and she listened. That was okay because she really didn't want to get into anything about her life anyway. He told her how he had been in the navy and toured the entire world. He was originally from Nova Scotia and was terribly homesick. He explained how he had been engaged to a girl in Detroit name Kathrine but how it didn't work out. She was fascinated with his honesty. It was like he had been waiting for the right person to come along and listen.

The sun stared to come up and they snapped out of it.

"I guess I should get you home."

"Yes, I think it's past my bedtime." They laughed and she liked the way it felt. When he pulled up in front of the apartment, she shared with her mother he looked a little shy all of a sudden.

"Can I see you again?" He asked,

"I'd like that." She said without thinking. It was obvious he was much older than she was but maybe that was exactly what she needed.

"I still don't know your name" he said. Then he laughed and said, "My name is Andrew." She giggled and replied, mine is Mary Ellen, nice to meet you, Andrew." Andrew picked Mary Ellen up after work every night and on her days off he made a point of planning a day out together. It was never anything fancy, but they enjoyed each other's company, so it didn't matter if he didn't spend a lot of money. He had a job working for customs and although the work was considered good it didn't pay a lot.

Christmas was less than a week away and since he had no family here, she invited him to her Meme's house for Christmas dinner. The closer the day came the more nervous she became. She liked him enough, but she didn't feel like she did when she had been with Clark. But look how that turned out she thought. Christmas Day 1951 started like every other Christmas Day with her mother. Mary Ellen was alone. Not literally her mother was still sleeping. Mary Ellen had long ago stopped looking for a gift from her. However, she always got her mother something regardless. This year it was a bottle of Chanel. Her mothers' favorite perfume. Mary Ellen wrapped it and put it on the table next to a cup of coffee she had made for her.

Her mother came into the kitchen and to Mary Ellen surprise she was holding a box.

"Merry Christmas Mary Ellen."

"Merry Christmas mother." Bea sat down across from Mary Ellen.

"Is this for me?" She asked.

"Yes, I think you'll like it."

"Here this is for you." Bea handed Mary Ellen the box. Mary Ellen opened the box slowly. Inside was a music box that played Amazing Grace. Mary Ellen didn't think of her mother as religious, so this came as a real surprise. She was seeing a side of her mother that she didn't think existed.

"Thank you, Mother. I love it." And she meant it.

"Oh Mary Ellen, I love it. Thank you so much." Her mother was truly happy with the gift.

"Is your friend meeting you at mother's or is he picking you up?" She asked,

"He's picking me up."

"Would you mind if I came with you?" She asked. "Ah, no that would be fine." They sat at the table in silence for what seemed like a long time when her mother asked her "Do you like him?"

"Well kind of. He's a lot older than me. He thinks I'm twenty. I haven't told him any different." She admitted.

"How old is he?"

"Twenty-eight." Mary Ellen had a hard time saying it out loud.

"Don't tell him he'll find out soon enough." With that she stood and went back to her bedroom, perfume in hand. Mary Ellen sat at the table for a while longer. Maybe she should listen to her mother. He would find out soon enough. Look what happened with Clark when he found out. Yes, she would just keep it too herself for the time being.

Chapter 27

She saw him pull up from the window in the kitchen.

"He's here mother, hurry!" She yelled as she headed out the door. The last thing she wanted was for him to see her apartment.

"Merry Christmas" she said as she jumped in the car. He looked a little annoyed that he hadn't opened the door for her, but she didn't mind doing it herself.

"My mother is coming with us if that's okay?"

"Yes of course." This time he was out of the car holding the door for her mother. It took Bea a couple of minutes but when she came out of the building, she looked beautiful.

"Well hello Andrew, or should I say Merry Christmas." She said in her best mother voice. Mary Ellen had seen her mother in action before, but this was good.

"Mary Ellen has told me so much about you. Thank you for picking us up today. I really hate to drive in the winter." She smiled as she slid into the back seat behind Mary Ellen. Mary Ellen couldn't believe how smooth her mother was. She really could charm anyone.

"My pleasure Mrs. Ledoux." He said as he closed her door. He told her how much he enjoyed Mary Ellen's company and was excited to meet the family. Windsor was starting to feel like home now that he had Mary Ellen in his life. Suddenly Mary Ellen felt like she was a third wheel. They talked about her as though she wasn't even there. When they arrived her Meme's house, she was rethinking her decision to invite him again. She felt sorry for him and didn't want him to be alone, but it was becoming obvious he was thinking this was more. A lot more.

Everyone seemed to like Andrew. Her mother was introducing him to everyone. The only one who seemed to have any objections was her Meme. Mary Ellen helped her Meme in the kitchen like she did every year. She loved her Meme so much. She was the one person in her life she would do anything for.

"How old is he?" Her Meme asked without looking at Mary Ellen.

"Um, twenty-eight." Mary Ellen could feel the heat rising and in her cheeks.

"Does he know how old you are?" Now her Meme was looking right into her eyes. It was hard for Mary Ellen to return her gaze.

"No not yet Meme, but I'm going to tell him tonight." She lied.

"Do you like him?"

"Yes, I think so." She replied,

"You better know." It was a statement that hung in the air as her Meme left the kitchen. The usual cast of characters were there and in full display. Uncle Peter and her mother had left right after dinner. Uncle Ben and Aunt Roselyn had four children now and they were playing with their cousins. Aunt Cora and Uncle Ernie brought her mother and Meme was trying to be polite but kept talking to Uncle Ernie in French so Aunt Cora couldn't understand. Uncle Lewis and his new wife were there, and they were arguing as always, she couldn't understand why they always had to spend Christmas with his family.

Mary Ellen asked Andrew if he had had enough. He smiled and said,

"Ready when you are." They said their goodbyes and thanked her Meme for a wonderful meal and were on their way. When they reached the car, he opened the door, and she was taken with what a gentleman he was.

"Are you tired?" he asked.

"No not really. Why?" "I was wondering if you would like to come to my place, I have your gift there," he said. Although she was nervous, she said yes. His apartment was small but clean and neat. Everything was perfect she thought. She was glad she hadn't invited him into her apartment.

"Can I get you a drink Mary Ellen. Pop or tea?" He had never bothered her about not drinking.

"Tea would be nice," she said. It took him a few minutes but when he returned, he had everything on a tray.

"I wasn't sure if you wanted milk or lemon, sugar or honey. So, I brought everything." He looked nervous.

"Milk and sugar" she said and gave him a warm smile. He sat next to her and took her hand.

"Mary Ellen, I know we haven't known each other very long but in that short time I've grown very fond of you." He took a deep breath and reached into his pocket and took out a little box. Mary Ellen felt the blood drain from her face."

Mary Ellen, I think we could make a good life together. Will you marry me." It was like time stood still. Her life was laid out in front of her. She could say yes and escape her life with her mother. He would take care of her. No more worrying about what would become of her. She would be his wife, free!

"If you need time to think about it?"

"Yes" she said

"Yes?" He looked shocked

"Yes" He took her in his arms and kissed her. Then he took her hand put the ring on her finger and although it wasn't what she had dreamed of it was just what she needed. She looked down at her hand and when she looked up, he had his hand extended, and she took it. He led her to the bedroom where he undressed her and then himself. He laid her down on his bed and took her virginity, well so he thought. She laid awake afterward and watched him sleep. I can do this she thought, I have to do this.

The next morning, they looked at each other uncomfortably.

"I'm sorry I fell asleep Mary Ellen," he said.

"That's okay, but I do need to get home."

"Of course, we can leave right after I have a coffee." He was already on his way to the bathroom when he looked back and said, "You don't mind do you darling?" And he was gone. Did he want her to make it for him? She went into the kitchen and found what she needed. She made his coffee and sat at the table patiently waiting for him. She needed to use the bathroom, but he was in there. And she wished she had her toothbrush. She went to the sink and rinsed her mouth. About ten minutes had passed when he emerged from the bathroom. Mary Ellen almost knocked him down to get to the bathroom. When she was done, she fixed her hair and walked back into the kitchen.

"The coffee is perfect darling. I love that you cooled it for ten minutes for me" he said. Was he serious? Did he really think she had done that on purpose? Well good start she thought, lucky for me it worked out to her advantage.

"Should I come up with you?" He asked

"No, I want to tell her myself. Will I see you later?" She was looking at his brown eyes unable to read what he was thinking.

"Yes, I'll Pick you up at eight, we'll get something to eat and make plans." He smiled, leaned over her, kissed her and pushed the door opened.

When she opened the door to the apartment the smell of alcohol and cigarettes hit her like a wall. Her Uncle Peter was asleep on the couch and her mother was passed out in her bed. Mary Ellen went into the bathroom and ran a hot bath. She was soaking when there was a knock on the door.

"Hey, I have to go!" It was her mother.

"Mom I'm in the tub." She yelled

"Come on I have to go!" Mary Ellen got out of the tub, wrapped a towel around her and unlocked the door. Her mother came in and lifted her night gown and began to pee.

"Where were you last night?" She asked

"I was with Andrew" she said. She showed her mother her ring finger.

"He asked you to marry him. Does he know how old you are?"

"No mother and I'm not going to tell him until after we're married." Mary Ellen said matter of fact.

"You'll need my permission you know." Bea said

"Can't you just do this for me Mother? I'll be out of your hair." She pleaded. Bea took care of everything. She had a nice luncheon for them after the ceremony at the justice of the peace. Bea even bought Mary Ellen a pretty dress to wear. Andrew was fine with the speed in which the whole thing handled. He was just happy to be married. When they were alone that first night Mary Ellen broke the news about her age. Andrew was surprised but not really shocked.

"Would you have married me if you would have known? She asked. It took him a long time to answer and when he did it was Mary Ellen who was shocked.

"No" he said.

Telling her Meme wasn't easy. Mary Ellen hated to disappoint her, and she had.

"Why Mary Ellen, what kind of man marries a child?" She's said with disgust.

"Meme, he didn't know." Mary Ellen was trying to protect him.

"And now?" Meme demanded.

"Now it's too late, but he loves me." She lied. It occurred to her that they had not told each other. He said he was fond of her, and they made love, but they hadn't said the words. Her Meme sat down and let out a deep breath.

"I'm sorry Mary Ellen. I should have been there for you. This never would have happened if I would have insisted you stay with us. Your Pepe didn't understand." Tears streamed down her Meme's cheeks. Mary Ellen had never seen this side of her Meme. She had always been so strong. What had she done?

"It will be okay Meme, please don't worry. He's a good man and we will make a good life." She bent over and hugged her. She hadn't noticed until this very moment just how small her grandmother really was.

Chapter 28

Life wasn't exactly how she thought it would be. Mary Ellen still had to work at the diner and then she had to come home and take care of Andrew. He was very particular, and Mary Ellen was having a hard time keeping all his request straight. Coffee had to be cooled ten minutes, eggs had to be over easy, but not slimy. Toast had to be buttered right to the edges but could not be allowed to get cold. But the thing that bothered her the most was his hygiene. He wouldn't bathe. He shaved every day, but he had terrible body odor. And on and on. It had only been a couple of months and Mary Ellen was already planning a way out. That's when everything changed.

Mary Ellen was sixteen and wanted to get her driver's license, but Andrew told her no, he would drive her wherever she needed to go. He was the man, and he would be the only one with a car. They had a terrible fight and Mary Ellen stormed out of the house. It was early spring, but it was still cold, and she had left without a coat. At first, she was so angry she didn't notice how cold it was but as she cooled down so did her skin.

"Damn it!" She said out loud. She knew she had to go home and that made her even madder. The door was locked, and he had left for work. Mary Ellen didn't know what to do so she began to cry. She buzzed the apartment Manager and explained she had locked herself out. He buzzed her in and met her at her apartment.

"Is everything okay Mary Ellen" he asked.

"Oh yes" she lied. "I wasn't thinking when I left. Thank you so much."

The apartment was dark. She sat alone on the couch that they were given by a lady she worked with at the diner. Andrew took her paycheck every week, but she only gave him half her tips. She was smoking a lot more these days and if there was anything left, she hid it in a can that she kept in the back of the closet. She was working the early shift at the diner, so she was up and gone before Andrew woke up. She was glad. She didn't want to get into it again.

They had been married four months when Mary Ellen realized she hadn't had a period for a second time. She thought she might be pregnant and was overjoyed. This would change everything. They hadn't really talked about children, but Andrew was always telling her how when his father died, he was the oldest and had to care for his younger siblings. She thought he'd be a natural. When she missed her third period, she made an appointment at the doctor. Mary Ellen was very nervous. She had never had and examination like this before. This man was between her legs with no regard for how she felt.

"Well Mrs. Allen, you are pregnant. I would say sixteen weeks. I'd like to see you in a month. Just make an appointment with Linda on your way out." He snapped off his rubber gloves and walked out the door.

Mary Ellen laid there for a moment trying to wrap her head around what he had just said. She must have gotten pregnant the first time they had sex. She was going to be a mother. She made up her mind in that very moment she would never abandon her child. She would do anything it took to protect it. She stood up, got dressed and hurried home to tell Andrew. Mary Ellen sat patiently in the apartment alone waiting for Andrew to come home. As light faded and da turned to night there was still no sign of him. Mary Ellen's excitement was waning. Feeling unusually tired Mary Ellen put her nightgown and housecoat on and curled up on the couch.

When Mary Ellen awoke, the apartment was thick with darkness. At first, she wasn't sure where she was but quickly, she regained her bearings. Sitting up she reached for the lamp that sat on the end table. When her eyes adjusted, she focused on the clock it was two forty-five. Panic heightened all her senses. Where was he? What if something happened to him? What would she do? Barely sixteen and pregnant. Just then the door opened and in came Andrew. He was feeling a bit wobbly from the wine he had shared with her but that wouldn't stop him from doing what had to be done.

"Andrew, I've been worried. Where were you?" She asked.

"Sit down Mary Ellen we need to talk." He was summoning all his nerve.

"I have something to tell you as well." She answered. But obviously his news must be very important.

"I was with Kathleen tonight" he said. "I love her, and I want to be with her." Mary Ellen could feel her blood going cold.

"What do you mean? We're married." She stated an obvious fact.

"Marrying you was a mistake. I didn't know how old you were. I should never have gone through with it." He was holding his head in his hands. Sitting on the couch now and Mary Ellen was standing.

"You mean you didn't want to know! You didn't think twice when we had sex or when my mother paid for everything. Well, that's fine but you won't get my baby! She was eerily calm.

"What? What baby?"

"Our baby! Or should I say my baby."

"Oh my God, your pregnant!" She had his full attention now. Mary Ellen began to cry and ran to the bedroom. She couldn't believe what had just happened. She knew there wasn't some great love between them, but she hadn't seen this coming.

"Mary Ellen! Open the door! Please Mary Ellen, I'm sorry." But his pleads fell on deaf ears. When Mary Ellen opened the door a few hours later she found him on the floor asleep.

"Andrew, wake up. Get off the floor and go to bed." She was fully dressed and ready for her workday.

"Mary Ellen please wait." He was scrambling to his feet. "I had too much to drink last night I'm sorry. I'll fix it" he said.

"Fix it? You said I was a mistake." Tears were welling up in her eyes. "I don't know what I said. I'm a mess. Please let me fix this. You're going to have my baby. That changes everything."

"I have to go to work." She grabbed her purse and headed for the door.

"I'll fix this, he said. Please just give me a chance" he said.

She looked at him for a long moment. It was in that moment she realized that she didn't love him at all and probably never would. She walked out the door and it slowly closed behind her. She was more determined to find a way to give this baby the life it deserved. If that meant she had to do it on her own, so be it.

It had been a long day on her feet. There was a lot of construction in the area which meant a lot of construction workers. The lunch rush spilled over into supper. At six p.m. Mary Ellen found herself sitting alone at the bus stop. She looked at her hands and realized they looked like the hands of a much older woman. She was lost in thought when the bus pulled up. She was about to get on when she heard her name. It was Andrew.

"Want a ride?" He asked. The bus driver said

"On or off Miss." Mary Ellen took a step back and the bus doors closed. Mary Ellen walked toward Andrew.

"Hungry?" He asked

"Starved" she answered. He took her by the hand and led her to the car. When they got back to the apartment, he had dinner waiting. They sat down and before she could get the fork to her mouth. He began to apologize again.

"I talked to Kathleen today and it's over. I told her everything and that my place is with you." Mary Ellen put her fork down, looked him straight in the eye and said,

"If you ever do this to me again, I'll leave and take this baby."

"I understand" he said. But she didn't think he did.

It was 1951, the phone rang.

"Hello" she said. It was her mother with the news that her uncle Peter had died. Her mother was shakier than Mary Ellen had ever heard.

"What happened?" Mary Ellen knew her Uncle had been homeless. The war had left so many men broken. And although Uncle Peter showed her nothing but love he fought many demons. Mary Ellen was heartbroken when her mother explained everything to her. She had nightmares for days. She felt so ashamed that he died alone in a warehouse. He had been such a good man and had given so much for his country. It wasn't fair. Just another casualty of a war that took so much from so many.

November came much quicker that Mary Ellen expected. Her pregnancy was easy compared to what everyone had told her. And the delivery was just a memory now that she was holding her beautiful baby boy in her arms. He was fat and full of color. His hair was blonde. And he had a great set of lungs. The nurse had brought him in so Mary Ellen could begin nursing. It was times like this that she wished she had a mother that cared about her.

The nurse directed Mary Ellen and in no time the baby had taken to her breast. When he was full the nurse returned and took him away. Andrew came into the room after the baby was safely back in the nursery. She was exhausted.

"He's really something isn't he?" He beamed. She smiled and said,

"He's beautiful." And tears streamed down her cheeks.

"I'd like to name him Steven" he said. She wanted Matthew but she settled on Steven Matthew. And then fell fast asleep. Baby Steven was everything she could have asked for. He smiled and laughed and cooed. He ate and slept and brought her total joy.

Mary Ellen was back to work in just a matter of weeks. She had a new job at a dry cleaner. She needed better hours than she was getting at the diner now that she had Steve to think about. Andrew was working nights at customs, so she had Steve all to herself.

She would fall into bed at night exhausted but that didn't stop Andrew. When he came in after midnight, he had no trouble waking her to be sure his needs were met. Mary Ellen was pregnant again almost immediately.

"Again? Already but Steve's just a baby." He yelled. She was shocked by his response. After all he was the one who wouldn't follow Dr's. orders when it came to having sex too soon. Mary Ellen was doing the best she could at the cleaners but as the summer went on the heat was almost unbearable. She felt faint and could barely eat.

"You eat like a bird" Mr. Rossini would say. Her new boss was like a worried father, and she appreciated it.

"You must keep up your strength for the baby" Steve was eight months old and sleeping through the night thank goodness. He was a big boy with pink cheeks and a happy disposition. The only time she saw Andrew smile was when he was playing with Steve. If she wasn't feeling so bad all the time, she would be glad to join in. But when Andrew played with him, she took that as an opportunity to rest.

"I'm worried about you Mary Ellen" her Meme voiced concern when she stopped in for a visit. "Are you eating?"

"I'm fine Meme, I'm just a little tired." Mary Ellen tried to sound convincing. Her Meme, however, wasn't buying it.

"What does the Doctor say?" she asked

"Meme, he said I should be gaining a little more weight, but I just can't. I'm tired and hot and when I get home there's things that need be done and Steve needs me" and she began to cry.

"Okay, okay come here and sit down." Her Meme took charge. Mary Ellen fell fast asleep. When she woke Steve was bathed and in his crib. Dinner was in the oven and her house was clean.

"Oh Meme. How can I ever thank you?" She hugged this little woman that she loved so much.

"Now, there child." She said as she patted Mary Ellen's back. "I'm just a call away don't you ever forget that."

"I love you, Meme." Mary Ellen couldn't remember the last time she said that. Or heard it said back to her. With that Mrs. Ledoux picked up her purse and headed for the door.

"Your Pepe is on his way to get me." She turned when she opened the door and looked Mary Ellen in the eyes and said,

"I love you to child." Then closed the door behind her.

Mary Ellen was so grateful for the help. With everything done she sat at the table and enjoyed the dinner her Meme had prepared and then after cleaning up her mess crawled into bed. The summer heat was fading, and the cool fall temperatures were taking hold. This was her favorite time of year. She loaded Steve into a stroller that was given to her by one of the girls she had worked with at the diner and headed to the park. Steve would be year old soon and she was crazy about him.

She was still too thin according to everyone but at least she was feeling a little better. Andrew seemed to always be gone. If he wasn't working, he was out with the guys from work. To be honest she didn't mind all that much. She would never get used to his poor hygiene and being pregnant seemed to heighten her sense of smell. She could hardly stand it when he came to bed at night.

Steve's first birthday was a big deal. He was her Meme's first great grandchild and she adored him. They had a little birthday party at the apartment and her mother made a beautiful cake. Meme brought cold cuts and homemade bread. Mary Ellen put out all the condiments and they had a big time. Steve was as always, the star of the show. He laughed and showed off his new skills walking, although he was pretty wobbly everyone made a big deal about his abilities at such a young age. Andrew beamed with pride. They opened presents which Mary Ellen was thrilled with. Money was so tight. It was always so tight. She really had no idea what he was doing with all of it. And it worried her especially with another baby coming in a few months.

When everyone left that night, Mary Ellen was putting away the last of the dishes. Andrew came into the kitchen in a foul mood.

"Well how much did that cost me?" He demanded.

"Nothing Andrew. My family brought everything." She answered him without turning around.

"Sure, that's what you tell me, but your damn family is always hanging around here." What was he talking about? No one ever came here. Mainly because no one liked him.

"No, they don't Andrew." He was putting his jacket on.

"Where are you going?" She asked.

"Out!" He shot her a look at he was gone. She picked Steve up and put him on her skinny hip. Even being seven months pregnant didn't change her shape. She was a little worn looking these days, but she still turned a head or two. Steve stared to cry which was very unusual. So, Mary Ellen heated some pablum and after feeding him put him to bed. Sitting in the quiet living room alone was becoming a normal was to spend her evenings. She was lonely but so thankful for Steve. She made up her mind that things would change after the new baby came. Unfortunately, she didn't have any idea how much.

It was December 23rd and Mary Ellen was busy getting Steve dressed when the first pain hit her. She wasn't due for another month. She finished getting Steve ready for the day when the second one came and almost took her to her knees.

"Andrew!" She yelled. He was still in bed. He had been out late the night before and wasn't happy to be awoken to her yelling.

"Andrew Hurry!" He came into the living room where Mary Ellen had just finished her third contraction.

"What's going on?" He asked.

"I think I'm in labor, but it's too soon!" Just then her water broke. They bundled Steve up and headed down the stairs to the car. Andrew opened the door and Mary Ellen holding Steve in her arms got in.

They sped all the way to the hospital. When they got there, she handed Steve to his father, and they took her away. She could hear Steve crying and wished this wasn't happening.

"Mrs. Allen it looks like your baby has decided to come early." The doctor had a look of concern on his face, but his voice didn't match. It was calm and level sounding.

"Is my baby going to be okay?" She couldn't and wouldn't hide her fear.

"We will do everything we can." He tried to reassure her, but it wasn't working. A nurse came in and said this might hurt a little and put a needle in her arm. Then everything went black. When Mary Ellen woke, she was told she had given birth to a baby girl. She was very premature but God willing would survive.

"Can I see her?" She asked

"Tomorrow, right now you need to rest." Then he walked out of the room. Andrew came in looking like a ghost.

"What is it?" She asked, "What's the matter?"

"She's so little Mary Ellen. I don't know how she'll make it." He wasn't holding back.

"Don't say that she's going to be fine." She was willing it to be so. Sleep didn't come easy that night. She shared the room with two other women who had given birth and the nurses kept coming in and waking them up to feed their babies. Mary Ellen prayed and prayed for God to hold her baby in his arms for the night. She promised that if he did that, she would take care of her the rest of her life no matter what happened.

In the morning the doctor said she could be taken in a wheelchair to the nursery to see her baby. Andrew hadn't returned from the night before, so she was going to face this on her own. When she reached the nursery, the nurse opened another door and pushed

Mary Ellen into a room that was filled with beeps and humming sounds. There is a little glass box was her baby. The nurse put her hand on Mary Ellen's shoulder and said,

"She's tiny but she's a fighter. Now you need to be strong." With that Mary Ellen stood up and walked around the incubator to see her baby. Nothing anyone said could have prepared Mary Ellen for what she saw. The baby was only twelve inches long and weighed four pounds and 11 ounces. Her skin was wrinkled, like an old lady, and there were tubes everywhere. She felt faint. The nurse must have seen the color drain from Mary Ellen's face because in an instant the wheelchair was hitting the back of her knees.

"Sit down Mrs. Allen." She can hear you if you want to talk to her." Mary Ellen didn't know what she was supposed to say. So, she just stared and prayed. Steve was the opposite of this baby. He was full of life when he was born. Fat and happy. She had to name her daughter, and, in that moment, it came to her Claire she thought, Claire Mary. Then she touched the glass and said,

"Hello Claire, I'm your mommy."

Chapter 29

Mary Ellen was missing Steve's first Christmas because she was in the hospital. He was almost fourteen months old now and wanted to know where his little sister was. Mary Ellen smothered him with as much attention as she could. Andrew fell back into his old ways within days of her return home. He would leave for work early and return home late. Mary Ellen was left to take a bus back and forth to the hospital with Steve every day to visit Claire. She was getting stronger and stronger every day.

After three long months the doctor told Mary Ellen Claire was now five pounds, so she was finally able to take her home. Andrew was kind enough to drive to the hospital to pick his daughter up but didn't stick around for long when they got home. Mary Ellen's Mother had dropped in to meet her new granddaughter but didn't stay long. It was her Meme who came to help Mary Ellen. Steve was a going concern, and it was hard for Mary Ellen to keep up with him and care for Claire at the same time.

Unlike Steve, Claire didn't sleep and cried all the time. Tension in the apartment grew as each day passed.

"Can't you shut her up! I have to work you know." Andrew barked at Mary Ellen. She tried everything but nothing worked. Claire had the lungs of an opera singer. And she hit every note. Mary Ellen finally took Claire and Steve to her Meme's house.

"She won't stop crying Meme, I've done everything I know to do." Mary Ellen said.

"She has colic." Meme answered. Her Meme put a drop of whiskey on a cloth and let Claire suckle it. In no time she settled down.

"Go to the doctor he will give you something to calm her down." Mary Ellen did as she was told but nothing the doctor gave her worked. Finally, she gave up and just learned to deal with it. Unfortunately, Andrew didn't share Mary Ellen's patience.

"I can't take it!" Andrew yelled as he headed out the door. Nothing new there she thought. He had such a short fuse. It was truly better when he was gone. Claire ate like a bird and Mary Ellen was growing more and more weary with each passing day. Claire wasn't developing like Steve had and it worried her, not that she could share those fears with her husband. He had absolutely nothing to do with Claire.

Mary Ellen was asleep on the couch with the bassinet next to her when Andrew finally came home. She woke to his groping her."

Stop it Andrew" she pushed him away, but he just pushed her back into the couch. "Your drunk."

"It's been long enough" he said. Mary Ellen knew there was no sense in trying to reason with him, so she just gave in. When he was done, he simply rolled over, and she was forced off the couch. Mary Ellen picked up Claire and the bassinet and went to bed. Claire was three months old when Mary Ellen discovered she was pregnant again. Oh no, she thought, God I can't go through this again. Not yet. Mary Ellen always knew she wanted children, but this was too much. Steve was such a good baby, but he still needed a lot of attention and Claire took every bit of energy she could muster.

Another baby would surely be the end of her. That night when Andrew came home from work, she broke the news to him.

"What? Is this some kind of joke? Mary Ellen what are you trying to do kill me?" He was furious.

"Well, it's not like I planned it. But we wanted a big family so" But before she could finish, he pounded his hands on the table spilling his glass of water.

"We can't afford this, damn it!" He stormed out of the room leaving Steve and Claire crying and Mary Ellen shaken. Mary Ellen was having a terrible time keeping things down. Everything she ate immediately shot itself out of her like a missile. Andrew didn't even notice. So long as she took care of the babies all day and had dinner waiting for him when he came home there was peace.

Mary Ellen got a job as a car hop at the local Big Boy at night so childcare wasn't an issue. She hated leaving he babies but she really didn't have an option. On her way to work she would daydream about being out on a shopping spree buying nothing but the best for her children. Or maybe they would be going to the zoo. Anything to take her mind off the dreadful reality her life had become. She was only eighteen years old, and she felt like she was forty. When the bus approached her stop, she pulled the cord alerting the driver that she wanted to get off. It was another busy night and her legs ached. Mary Ellen was not feeling well but wouldn't dream of going home early.

Mr. Morris was her boss. He was a kind man with a big family. Mrs. Morris would come to work with him sometimes and the two of them would laugh and carry on like a couple of kids. Tonight, was one of those nights. Every time Mary Ellen came through the door to pick up her next order, they were laughing about something. How she envied them. She turned, order in hand and it hit her like a knife being driven through her abdomen. She let out a loud scream and the place fell silent. Mary Ellen was doubled over and could feel blood running down her leg. Mrs. Morris was at her side.

"Mary Ellen what is it dear?" But another contraction hit. Mrs. Morris yelled to call an ambulance.

"No, no, I'm okay." Mary Ellen tried to reassure them. Mrs. Morris had her by the arm and was leading her into the bathroom.

"Mary Ellen are you pregnant?" she asked.

"Yes."

"I think you're having a miscarriage" Mrs. Morris was trying to be as gentle as she could. Fear gripped Mary Ellen. Mr. Morris drove Mary Ellen home. By morning Mary Ellen had lost the baby. Andrew took care of the babies. He also asked her Meme to come and stay while he went to work. Which was a great relief to Mary Ellen. She stayed in bed for two days. She cried and slept. Then slept and cried. Meme came into the bedroom only to give Claire to her for feeding. After two days she was back to work. She was pale and weak but also strong. Losing her baby was the hardest thing she had ever gone through. Worse than what she had endured at the hands of her uncle. She knew if she could get through this, she could get through anything.

Weeks passed and life was back to normal. They never really spoke about the miscarriage, but she knew in her heart he was grateful it had happened. It was a Thursday afternoon Andrew was at work and Mary Ellen was in the kitchen feeding Steve lunch when she heard what sounded like rushing water. She looked toward the sink, but she had turned the taps off. She hurried into the bathroom fearing she might have forgot the tub running but when she entered the bathroom she was met with a great rush of water. The water heater had burst, and water was flowing into the hallway of their apartment. She ran to the phone to call the super. She hurried back into the bathroom trying to locate a water shut off but wasn't having any luck. The super was pounding on the door which of course frightened the babies. Mary Ellen hurried to let him in.

By the time he was able to stop the water, it had leaked into the store below their apartment. She had no choice but to try to get word to Andrew at work, something she dreaded.

When he came home, he was like a bear.

"What the hell happened here" he yelled. It seemed like that's all he ever did these days. Mary Ellen could feel her skin crawl. She was still mopping up the floors and squeezing the rag mop into the bucket she had borrowed from the super.

"Andrew the water heater burst, and I tried to shut the water off but." Before she could finish there was a knock on the door. The owner of the building was standing there with a scowl on his face.

"Ah Mr. Willet, we're in a bit of a mess here. What can I do for you?" Andrew asked,

"Look Andrew we've seem to have a problem here" he said.

"Yes, we do. I just got home from work and Mary Ellen is going to have to miss work." Andrew was prepping to plead his case for a rent discount when suddenly the tables turned.

"There's been a lot of damage to the ceiling downstairs, and I've lost a lot of inventory. Someone is going to have to make that up to me." Mary Ellen had been listening and couldn't believe what she was hearing.

"Excuse me" she interrupted "what about the damages to our apartment?

"Well, I would say that's your problem now isn't it." He was looking right through her. His intense look shifted from her to Andrew.

"Mary Ellen, go into the kitchen. I'll take care of this." Andrew was obviously frustrated with her. They walked into the bathroom and then out of the apartment and down to the store downstairs. Mary Ellen continued to mop all the time worrying about what she would make for dinner. She saved all the money she could to buy groceries. But things had been slow at work and now she'd miss more work. Steve and Claire were waking up from their afternoon nap when Andrew came back into the apartment. He began swearing and kicking things. Mary Ellen had seen his temper before, but this was a bit much.

"Andrew! What are you doing?"

"Son of a bitch. Can't you do anything right?" His anger was directed at her.

"What are you talking about?" She couldn't believe that he would blame this on her. "How was I to know the water heater was going to burst?" Before she knew it, he was standing over her with his hand raised over her. She immediately coward. "You stupid bitch!" He spat the words at her. She moved away from him and into the kitchen. She grabbed the frying pan she had taken out to use for dinner.

"What's wrong with you?" She asked

"I had to sign a two-year lease and now we have to pay an extra sixty dollars a month. All because you were too stupid to turn the water off." He was furious.

"What? You signed a lease? Are you crazy? It's his water heater. He's responsible not us!" She was livid.

"Shut up! You don't know anything!" He grabbed his hat and stormed out the door. Mary Ellen sat down at the table realizing she still had the frying pan in her hand. What had just happened? She thought. Was he really that stupid? She put her head in her hands and began to cry.

"Mommy" she looked up and Steve was standing next to her. He was so adorable. She reached down and picked him up.

"Are you hungry? She asked. And he smiled.

Chapter 30

When Andrew came home later that night, he had a man with him.

"This is it" he said pointing to the couch and chair in the living room. The man sat down and said,

"Okay I'll take it." With that he handed Andrew some cash and said he'd be back tomorrow to pick it up. Andrew walked him to the door and shot her a look as he turned and went into the bedroom.

"Andrew, what was that all about?" She asked. He was taking his shoes off and then his socks.

"What did it look like?"

"It looked like you sold our couch and chair."

"That's right. We need to pay the first sixty dollars tomorrow." He stood unbuttoned his shirt and then his belt and told her to get undressed.

Mary Ellen got the children ready for church and quietly closed the door behind them. Andrew liked to sleep in on Sunday and she was happy to have the time to herself. With Claire in her arms and Steve walking beside her they walked to church. Mary Ellen loved coming here. She hated it when she was young but now it brought her peace. She took her seat in the pew nearest to the door in case Claire woke in a fuss. The hymns were sung, and communion handed out. When the basket was passed Mary Ellen reached into her handbag and found a quarter. Please Lord use this to help someone who needs it. Then she dropped it into the basket.

When Mass was over, she made her way out the grand doors at the front of the church. Father Brant was shaking hands with everyone and when Mary Ellen tried to sneak passed him, he called her by name.

"Hello Father. Very nice sermon this morning."

"Well thank you. I was thinking I haven't seen your husband lately."

"He's been working so much lately Father I'm sure he would be here if he could." She lied.

"Well tell him we miss him" he said.

"Yes, thank you Father I will." Claire was getting restless in her arms and Steve was starting to move farther away from her. She smiled and moved away as the next person anxiously waited to have their turn with Father Brant.

Claire wasn't developing the way Steve had and Mary Ellen was becoming increasingly concerned. She was two years old and still couldn't say mommy or daddy. She grunted and did a lot of screaming. When Mary Ellen asked the doctor questions she was told because Claire was a premature baby, she would develop more slowly than usual. But as time went on Mary Ellen just knew there was something else going on.

It was 1955 and Mary Ellen was pregnant again. The debt from the flooded apartment was almost paid. And Mary Ellen had taken in ironing to make some extra income. Andrew didn't have much to say when Mary Ellen told him the news of her pregnancy, but she hadn't really expected much. He babysat while she was at work but other than that he really didn't have much to do with them. Mary Ellen was overjoyed. She loved being a mother. She felt like it was the one thing she was meant to be. When May rolled around, Mary Ellen was more than ready to have this baby. Steve was four and Claire was three. Her back hurt all the time and Claire was becoming a real handful. The sooner this baby got here the better. But the baby decided to wait until the last day of the month. May 31, 1956 was the day Sara Marie arrived. She was so beautiful. She had a head full of dark hair and full round cheeks. She was the opposite of her big sister who was so tiny she looked like a China doll. When Andrew came to pick them up at the hospital, he took Sara in his arms and immediately bonded with her. It was obvious to Mary Ellen she would be his favorite. Mary Ellen couldn't imagine loving one child more than another. Her heart was full of love for each one of her children.

Houses were springing up everywhere and the government was giving veterans an opportunity to own their own home. Andrew was still working for customs and took advantage of this opportunity. When Mary Ellen stepped into the house for the first time she could have cried.

"Where are the cupboards." She asked.

"Look Mary everything costs money you know." She hated it when he called her Mary but lately, she hated everything about him. The floors were plywood. It was six rooms counting the bathroom and for the first time in her life she had a real home of her own. Young couples were moving in all around them. All the houses were the same and all the couples were trying to make theirs a home to raise their young families. Right next door was a young couple with three children to.

Mary Ellen and Pearl became fast friends. They would meet in the back yards daily after the husbands went to work.

"Coffee Mary Ellen?" Pearl asked

"Sure, cream and one sugar please."

"Okay I'll be right back." They stood in the back yard and enjoyed every sip of the steaming hot energy boost. Pearl's mother owned a restaurant in Detroit and spoiled her daughter and her grandchildren. Mary Ellen had to admit she envied Pearl and her life. Pearl was always complaining about her husband Ken.

"I only married him because I was pregnant." She told Mary Ellen in confidence. "He's been in jail you know." She said it like she was proud of him.

"Why?" Mary Ellen asked shocked.

"Oh, he was caught stealing something or other, I don't know. It was before I met him. He wouldn't do anything like that now." She said with confidence. Mary Ellen had secretly wished Andrew was more like Ken. Ken had built Pearl cupboards for her kitchen and tiled their bathroom. Mary Ellen was using crates for cupboards and sweeping plywood floors.

Cynthia lived on the other side of them and was constantly yelling Mary Ellen's children. Cynthia and her husband put up a fence and dug a trench at the back of their yard to use the soil to fill in their yard for a garden. Mary Ellen had complained that the trench was unsafe, but her complaints fell on deaf ears. Across the street was another young couple Chris and Dan. Mary Ellen and Chris got along famously. They were always helping each other with something.

Chris came over and helped Mary Ellen paint with leftover paint her father had given her. She would give Mary Ellen clothes her kids had outgrown. Life was going along just fine. Claire was forming words because Mary Ellen was relentless. Claire was smart but if she couldn't talk how was she going to start school.

Mary Ellen heard about a teacher at St. Charles school who dealt with deaf children and was told she should take Claire to her so she could be evaluated. Mary Ellen had tried everything, so she thought, why not?

When they walked into the school office Claire must have sensed something was going on because she began to act out. Steve and Sara were at Chris's so at least she didn't have to worry about them. She took Claire's hand firmly and sat her down with a stern look.

"Mrs. Allen, Mrs. Prince will see you now." Mary Ellen squeezed Claire's hand a little more firmly and stepped into Mrs. Prince's office.

"Good morning. I'm Mrs. Prince please have a seat." Mary Ellen did as she was instructed. "What can I do for you?" She asked. "This is my daughter Claire." Mary Ellen didn't know why she was nervous, but she was.

"She was born premature and has some developmental problems. Because she's not talking in sentences, yet I was told she might be deaf." When Mrs. Prince approached Claire, she recoiled. Then began to yell. Mary Ellen did everything to try to calm her down, but Mrs. Prince had already made up her mind.

"I'm afraid she's retarded. I'm sure it's from her premature birth." Mrs. Prince said with a dismissive tone.

"I assure you she's not. She interacts with her sister and brother and responds to me with understanding." Mary Ellen said.

"You did come here for my opinion, didn't you?" It was more of a statement than a question. She stood and opened the door. Mary Ellen knew their meeting was over.

"Thank you for your time." She took Claire's hand and left. Andrew had gone to work, and Mary Ellen was cleaning the kitchen it had rained for the past two days and the kids were climbing the walls.

Chris had given Claire a coat that she had sewn by hand. Mary Ellen couldn't believe how kind Chris was. She was the only person that understood how much Claire meant to Mary Ellen.

The sun was shining and although it was cool out, it was Saturday, and it was time to go outside and play. Mary Ellen dressed the kids and sent them out to discover the day.

"Don't go far. Be home for lunch. Steve, watch your sister." Sara would stick close to her brother and sister. But Mary Ellen knew that in about twenty minutes Steve would bring her back into the house. For now, however, she could get a lot done in twenty minutes.

Five minutes passed when she heard Steve yelling and Claire screaming. What on earth she thought. She ran to the back door and to her shock Steve was holding Michelle and Claire was dripping in mud and water.

"She fell in the hole" he said, "I had to pull her out Mom." He was visibly shaken. Claire was crying uncontrollably. Mary Ellen took her into her arms and brought her into the kitchen.

"What the hell happened?" She asked. Steve was catching his breath and taking off his wet clothes as Mary Ellen stripped Claire. Little Sara stood close watching the activity unaware of the turmoil. Steve explained how Claire stepped backward and lost her footing, tumbling into the neighbor's trench. Something snapped in Mary Ellen, and she flew out the door. Before she knew it, she was pounding on Cynthia's front door. She could hear Cynthia's husband playing the piano, so she ponded harder. When she looked around, she saw Ken sitting on the front porch.

"What's going on?" He asked

"Claire fell in the hole!" She yelled

"Ya, I saw her" he said. Just then the door opened.

"Where's Cynthia?" She demanded. She could see her walking in the kitchen. "Hey! Claire fell in that damn hole in the back! She could have drowned and I'm not going to put up with it anymore! I told you to fill it or someone was going to get hurt." She stopped to catch her breath when she realized Cynthia had a smirk on her face. "Do you think that's funny?" Mary Ellen was furious.

"Well, if you would keep that animal locked up maybe bad things wouldn't happen!"

"What did you say!" Mary Ellen could feel her blood boil.

"You heard me she's nothing but a retard and you should lock her up somewhere!"

"Get out here you bitch! You can't talk about my daughter like that!" The door slammed shut on her.

When she caught her breath, she looked over and saw Ken laughing.

"What are you laughing at?" She yelled

"I didn't know you had it in you." He said and then went into his house.

When Andrew came home from work Mary Ellen tried to explain what had happened thinking he would immediately go next door and give them a piece of his mind. Instead, he told Mary Ellen she should keep a better eye on the children. She was so upset she wouldn't speak to him for two days.

Sunday morning, she was up bright and early getting the children ready for church. The church was two blocks away, so it wasn't a bad walk if the weather was nice and thankfully it was today. Chris walked with Mary Ellen and their children. Dan was a policeman, with hours that were crazy and most Sundays he worked. Mary Ellen was grateful for the company. As they walked together Mary Ellen told Chris what happened to Claire the day before and Chris shared Mary Ellen's anger.

"She could have drowned after all the rain we've had." Chris was visibly upset.

"That's what I said to that witch." Mary Ellen wanted to say something else but not in front of the children, that was Andrew's department.

When they arrived at church Cynthia was already sitting in her favorite pew with her husband and perfect boys. They were far from perfect. They were known throughout the neighborhood as bullies but anytime anyone tried to complain Cynthia found a way to turn it around to make her children the victims.

Father Henry gave a sermon on loving thy neighbor. How appropriate Mary Ellen thought. I wonder what God would do if he had a neighbor like Cynthia.

After mass was done and everyone made their way to the exit Mary Ellen couldn't help but notice Cynthia talking to Father Henry. By the time she and Chris got to him Cynthia was long gone.

"Good morning, Father."

"Mrs. Allen, I hope you got something from my sermon this morning."

"Ah well as a matter of fact I did. I was hoping someone else might have as well." She replied

"Well to be honest Mrs. Kemp came to see me yesterday and well, I hope you can find it in your heart to apologize for you behavior. She was very upset." Chris must have seen the look on Mary Ellen's face because before she could say anything Chris had pulled her away saying

"Thank you, father. Have a nice week."

"Can you believe the nerve of that woman! She told him it was my fault!" Mary Ellen was furious.

"Don't let her bother you. She'll get what's coming to her." Chris tried to calm Mary Ellen.

When they got close to the house, they were just beginning their goodbyes when a police car pulled up in front of Mary Ellen's house.

"What on earth" she exclaimed. Chris took the children while Mary Ellen approached the police as he got out of the car.

"Hi Chris." He said as he waved to her.

"Hi Bill, is everything okay?" She asked, but he didn't answer her.

"Are you Mary Ellen Allen?"

"Yes sir, I am. Is everything ok?" She was shaking.

"Yes ma'am. This is a summons."

"What?" She took the paper he handed her.

"Have a nice day. See ya Chris." And he got back into the car. Chris was at her side reading the summons over her shoulder.

"Well that bitch!" She said without thinking.

"Okay kids go in the house and change for lunch. And make sure you help your sister Steve." Chris had instructed her kids to do the same thing Ken was on the porch smoking a cigarette waiting for Pearl and the kids to get home from church.

"What's going on?" He asked

"Cynthia is pressing charges." she said unable to believe this was happening.

"Ken, you saw what happened, will you come with me?"

"Oh, shit Mary Ellen I can't the cops have got it out for me. They wouldn't believe me." He said with a wry smile.

"But Ken you saw everything. Claire could have drowned." She pleaded

"Sorry Kid, I can't." And he got up and went into the house.

"Don't worry Mary Ellen I'll go with you" Chris said.

"But you didn't see what happened."

"They don't know that. She can't get away with this." Chris hugged her and headed home.

Chapter 31

The day had arrived, and Mary Ellen was a ball of nerves. Her Meme and Pepe were with her and even her mother had come. Chris was at her side, but Andrew said he had to work.

He told her someone had to be the adult here." She shouldn't be surprised he was such a coward. They walked into court along with the lawyer her Meme paid for. Mary Ellen took her seat next to him and the judge walked in. Everyone stood and then were told to take their seats. Mary Ellen was a nervous wreck. But Chris was fearless. When she was called, she stood without hesitation and took the stand. Mary Ellen was so thankful for her.

"Mrs. Yates you say you witness the altercation between my client and Mrs. Allen is that correct? He asked.

"Yes sir, I did." She answered,

"Can you tell me which way the front door opened?"

"Ah, I don't understand." She had no idea which way the door opened.

"It's a simple question. Does it open left to right or right to left?" It was all downhill from there. Cynthia painted Mary Ellen as a crazy woman who had an out-of-control child that she couldn't or wouldn't care for. Mary Ellen did her best to explain the situation but was so nervous everything was coming out wrong. Finally, the Judge said

"I've heard just about enough of this. You" he said pointing his finger at Cynthia. "You need to be a better neighbor. It's obvious Mrs. Allen is doing the best she can. And you" he said now pointing at Mary Ellen. You need to respect Mrs. Kemp's property. Your neighbors. Now go home and find a way to get along!" He slammed his gavel and said court dismissed.

Mary Ellen sat down hard. Meme was the one who shook her back to reality.

"Come on dear let's get out of here."

The mail came early every morning and, Mary Ellen hated getting the mail. She hated answering the phone too. It was always bad news. Today it was both. There was letter from Andrew's sister. She was getting married and wanted her big brother to walk her down the aisle. He was overjoyed. He immediately began to make plans. Mary Ellen of course was worried how they would pay for the trip. But they had six months to worry about it. When they were done reading the letter the phone rang. Andrew had long ago stopped answering the phone it was up to her to fend off bill collectors. She really did hate him.

Mary Ellen found out she was pregnant three weeks before the big trip east. The pregnancy was a difficult one. Dr. Rocker told her that she would most likely lose this baby. She was devastated.

"What about traveling." she asked.

"Well, I don't recommend it" he answered.

"But my husband's giving his sister away in Nova Scotia. We have to go." She was so torn.

"Well, I suggest you pack a large quantity of Kotex pads and be prepared."

The drive was long and uncomfortable. Steve, Claire and Sara were as good as gold. She was so thankful. When I get home, I will find answers for Claire she thought. It was a promise to herself she would keep one way or another.

They drove five hundred miles the first day. Andrew had a plan, five hundred miles a day for three days. He was impossible. Who in their right mind would put three children and a pregnant wife about to miscarry through this? He would that's who.

They stopped the second night at a motel that had a diner attached to it. They were all too tired to sit down and eat so Andrew left them in the room and went by himself. He ate his dinner and then brought them sandwiches to share. Mary Ellen had the kids all bathed and, in their pajamas, when he finally returned. The kids ate and were fast asleep.

"Aren't you going to eat?" He asked

"I really don't think I can Andrew."

"Still not feeling good?"

"I'm going to lose our baby. Or have you forgot?" Mary Ellen looked at him to see if there was any remorse. Unfortunately, there wasn't. She put on her night gown and went to bed. Mary Ellen tried to be quiet as she slipped out of bed. The cramps had kept her up most of the night and she dreaded getting back in the car. But they were in New Brunswick so one more day and they would be there. Mary Ellen felt the cold floor under her feet, and she looked in the mirror and she looked so tired. She had dark circles under her eyes. What had happened to her? Why was this happening again? She loved her children and would have loved this one. She took her seat on the toilet and a great pressure hit her. Suddenly there was a whoosh and she felt weak. She stood still looking into the toilet and there in a mass was what would have been her fourth child. She screamed and passed out.

Andrew woke to a horrible scream. "Mary Ellen", he looked next to him, but she was gone. He jumped out of bed and found her on the floor. There was blood everywhere.

"Mary Ellen!" She was out. He ran to the phone and told the office he needed an ambulance.

Mary Ellen woke as they were transporting her. "My children?"

"Their fine Mrs. Allen. They're with your husband. Following us to the hospital." Then she was out again. Mary Ellen woke up in the hospital. Andrew and the kids were waiting in the room. Steve looked scared to death.

"Come here Steve" she said. "I'm okay honey." Steve began to cry. The doctor came into the room and asked everyone to leave. Andrew picked up Sara and Steve took Claire by the hand.

"Mrs. Allen I'm sorry but you've lost the baby. I had to do a D and C and I also have to say you were a real mess. You've had another miscarriage haven't you." He wasn't asking.

"Yes".

"Well, you'll have to stay here for a few days. You lost a lot of blood. We had to do a transfusion. I'll explain everything to your husband." He turned and left. When he opened the door, the kids came running in. A few minutes later Andrew followed.

"So now that I'm sure you're okay we have to get going or we won't make it." He was fidgeting.

"Andrew, you can't just leave me here." She was fighting back tears.

"Look Mary Ellen, we knew you were going to lose the baby but if I don't leave now my sister's wedding will be ruined." He almost looked annoyed with her. "Okay kids give mommy a kiss, we have to go now." Andrew turned and waited at the door.

"I'll be back in a few days I promise." Mary Ellen cried until there were no more tears to cry. It was then she realized she was in a strange place alone and it was Mother's Day.

Mary Ellen was twenty-three years old and the mother of three. She had had two miscarriages and found herself pregnant yet again. This time she wouldn't say anything to Andrew, why bother. If she was able to carry this baby past four months, she would say something. Unfortunately, she didn't. She lost her baby after three months. Maybe she couldn't have more children.

She needed to get back to work. Andrew was on days now so she could go back to Big Boy on nights. Work was exactly what she needed.

Claire was six years old and after one failed year in school for hearing children, the teachers recommended Claire attend school for the mentally handicapped. Andrew was all for it, but Mary Ellen knew in her heart Claire was not retarded. She could speak now and seemed to understand almost everything. Aside from her behavior she seemed normal. After one week of school with the mentally handicapped Claire started acting retarded. Mary Ellen complained but no one would listen. There was one teacher at Claire's school who suggested Mary Ellen take Claire to Detroit's children's hospital. Andrew was furious.

"There's nothing wrong Mary Ellen, she's retarded and she's right where she's supposed to be." But that wasn't good enough for Mary Ellen. She made the appointment and took the bus across the border into Detroit. Once at the hospital her hopes ran high. This was a beautiful place, and everyone was being so nice. But when the doctor tried to examine Claire, she threw a fit. She was screaming, yelling, fighting and kicking. Finally, the doctor told Mary Ellen they would have to reschedule so they could give her a sedative. Mary Ellen couldn't hide her disappointment. Let alone the cost. How would she make Andrew understand?

That was easier said than done. Andrew didn't understand at all. "Why can't you leave it alone?"

"Well, I won't Andrew, she's my daughter and she's not retarded." She wasn't going to argue with him anymore. She was in this alone and she knew it. Mary Ellen brought Sara to Chris's house and packed Steve's lunch for school then caught the bus to take Claire back to Detroit.

When they arrived, the nurse gave Claire a sedative. They waited the appropriate amount of time and then tried to examine her again. She was the strongest little girl Mary Ellen had ever seen. She fought and fought until the doctor gave up again. Mary Ellen couldn't believe it. With no answers Mary Ellen paid the bill and left. When Claire and Mary Ellen reached the stairs that led to the exit Claire finally gave in and passed out. Mary Ellen was holding her little hand and down she went. Mary Ellen picked up her daughter and headed home.

When they got back to Windsor, they had to change busses. Their connection was late, so they walked down the street to look in the store windows. One of the stores sold hearing aids. Mary Ellen knew it was a long shot, but she was willing to take it. She pushed the door opened and entered with her child.

"Hi, can I help you?" The man behind the counter looked up when they came in.

"I see you sell hearing aids. I was wondering if you could check my daughters hearing?" Mary Ellen was almost pleading.

"Sure, bring her back here." He smiled. Claire willingly went and Mary Ellen could have cried.

"Yes, your daughter is deaf."

"What?" Mary Ellen couldn't be sure she had heard him correctly.

"She is deaf. She has ninety percent loss in her right ear and ninety five percent loss in her left ear. Take this hearing aid home and see how she does. If it works for her bring it back and we'll make her special ear molds." Mary Ellen could have kissed him. Claire was like a scared bird. Life would never be the same. She now had to learn how to understand sounds. Andrew was in disbelief. Mary Ellen was elated.

Chapter 32

It was September 1959. Claire was enrolled in a special class for deaf children, Steve was excelling in sports and Sara was the light of her life. At three and a half she could light up a room. Meme was smitten with her and so was everybody else who met her. Mary Ellen found out she was pregnant and was overjoyed. Work was ok and Andrew seemed to be in a better mood these days. He started bowling. Mary Ellen had no idea where he got the money for that since she could barely scrape up enough money to feed them, but rather than argue with him, she was just thankful he was out of her hair. Mary Ellen worked out her schedule so she could be off on the nights he bowled. On this night she was extremely tired, she fed the kids and got them all in bed. Then she ate her dinner and put Andrew's in the oven to keep it warm. She curled up on the couch and watched a movie. When he came in, she was enthralled in the last half hour of the movie.

"Mary Ellen, where's my dinner?" he yelled.

"It's in the oven, I'll be right there." she said.

"Hey! Get off your ass. I'm hungry." Did he really just say that?

"Andrew this is almost done, I'll be right there." Before she knew what was happening, he had her up on her feet and was shaking her. "Get my damn dinner!" Her was furious. She pushed him and to her surprise he pushed her right back. She lost her footing and began to stumble. But when she straightened up, he pushed he again. This time she went through the front storm door. Blood was everywhere. The cut on her arm was bad. She ran across the street to Chris's thankfully she opened the door. Dan was home and he put Mary Ellen in his patrol car and rushed her to the hospital. They stitched her up and sent her back home. The police were called in and after talking with Andrew, they came back to Chris's to talk with Mary Ellen. Chris insisted she stay with her until the police talked to Andrew.

"Well Mrs. Allen it's our understanding that your husband maybe got a little upset with you because you refused to make him dinner." The office was serious. "He says he'll forgive you if you just go home." Mary Ellen couldn't believe her ears.

"He was bowling, and his dinner was in the oven. He pushed me through the front door. And he forgives me?" Now she was furious.

"Look Mrs. Allen why don't you just go home get your husband some dinner and call it a night." The officer looked tired. Mary Ellen looked to Don who turned his head.

"Okay" she said. I'm sorry Chris, thanks Don. She slowly made her way home to Andrew who was sitting at the table eating his dinner. She just wanted to scream. Instead, she went to bed. Mary Ellen was twenty-four and was holding her new baby girl. Diane had blue eyes and was happy and healthy. Mary Ellen had gone back to work almost immediately because they needed the money desperately.

It was Andrew's bowling night and Mary Ellen was in the back yard with the new baby watching Steve and Sara tell Claire what the sounds were when a fire truck went screaming down the road behind their house. Claire covered her ears. Then an ambulance followed. Mary Ellen smiled and explained what the sounds were.

"It's okay Claire they're going to help someone. Steve and Sara covered their ears to. Claire laughed.

Later that night Mary Ellen got a phone call from Angela.

"Hello" "Mary Ellen?"

"Yes, this is Mary Ellen." "This is Angela, I have some bad news." Mary Ellen sat down. "Yes, what is it?"

"It's Father Mary Ellen. He was killed today working on Jefferson Street. He was electrocuted."

"Oh my God, I'm sorry Angela." Then it hit her. The sirens she had heard that afternoon had been for her own father. "How are you?" Angela began to cry. Mary Ellen didn't know what to say. How could she cry for a man she didn't know but how could she not? "Is there anything I can do for you or Samantha?" She asked. Angela had two boys and one girl and Samantha had four boys. They tried to get together periodically but it was too difficult. They're lives were all so different. Angela married a farmer and lived in the country and Samantha married a Bar tender and she never worked. Since they kept such late hours, they slept the day away.

"We'll be in touch with the funeral arrangements."

"Okay, thanks for calling." And she hung up. How was she supposed to mourn the loss of a father she didn't know? And a funeral oh how she dreaded the thought of it. The looks, the questions. To her surprise Andrew agreed to go with her. Roberta was there with her new husband and their two children, which made them Angela and Samantha's siblings. What a mess Mary Ellen thought.

Angela greeted her with a hug and Samantha came over with tears streaming down her cheeks.

"I'm really sorry for your loss" she said.

"Thank You Mary Ellen. I know this must be hard for you, but daddy would be happy you came." Samantha was being sincere, but it really didn't mean anything to Mary Ellen.

When she told her mother what had happened, her mother began to sob. Mary Ellen realized in that moment that her mother never stopped loving him. She wished her mother would have told her what happened. Mary Ellen knew her mother would never talk about it. After the funeral Mary Ellen and Andrew were driving home and he broke the news to her.

"Mary Ellen, we have to move."

"What? Why? Did you get another job?" She asked

"No, we've lost it."

"Lost what?" She didn't understand what he was saying.

"The house and everything in it." He was barley speaking above a whisper.

"What are you talking about Andrew? How? What did you do with our money?" She was shaking. Where would they go. She started to cry, and he got angry.

"Stop it. We're going to move in with Bob and Diane. Just until I get on my feet."

"Who the hell are Bob and Diane?"

"I work with Bob, he said we could stay with them for a while."

"Oh my God Andrew how could you do this to us." They didn't speak the rest of the way home.

Mary Ellen spent the next week working crying and worrying. She walked across the street to tell Chris what was happening, and they cried together.

"Why don't you leave him Mary Ellen?" Chris was pleading.

"Where would I go Chris? He lost everything. I'm stuck." She was broken.

Andrew loaded the car and Mary Ellen carried Diane and led the kids to their seats. Andrew as usual insisted that no one touch the doors only he could open and close them. One thing was for sure, if it ever came down to her or his car, she knew she'd lose.

They arrived at Bob and Diane's and Mary Ellen wanted to die. Diane was very nice, but it was all so embarrassing. The only good thing in this awful experience was that it was summer. The children would start a new school in the fall. Until then they were oblivious. They settled in and Mary Ellen wasn't sure what was expected of her. Should she cook and if she did, should she cook for them to.

Two women in a kitchen is a bad thing. Oh Lord please help me through this.

Diane couldn't have been nicer. She told Mary Ellen to help herself to the kitchen. Bob and Diane didn't have any children, so she was tickled to have mouths to feed. Everyone called Baby Diane just that, Baby Diane. The children were so good, Mary Ellen couldn't have been prouder.

They had been there three weeks when Andrew announced he had found them a place in Amherstburg. Mary Ellen was glad to be getting into their own place, but Amherstburg. She didn't know anything about that part of Essex County. They stayed with Bob and Diane for one more week and then loaded the car again. Ten years of marriage and four children and everything they owned fit into this car. She was sick to her stomach. When they pulled up to their rented house Mary Ellen took a deep breath and said a quick prayer. The breath was so she would have the strength to move, and the prayer was so she would have the strength to stay.

The house was empty. Completely empty. Not one piece of furniture. The kids ran from room to room leaving an echo from their footsteps. Mary Ellen looked at Andrew and then around the house.

"They said they'd be here" he assured her. But she wasn't sure of anything anymore. Especially if he said it. They were sitting on the floor in the living room when they heard a honking horn. Andrews pals from the knights of Columbus had finally arrived. There were four men and a truck full of furniture. They had gone to Good Will and purchased all the necessities. Beds and a kitchen table. Even a crib. Andrew thought this was great. Mary Ellen however was mortified. To think she had worked her whole life and they were a charity case. Nothing in Mary Ellen's life had longevity and this was no exception.

They had only been there for a few months when Andrew came in and announced he had had enough with his damn job and the people here. "We're moving" he said

"What are you talking about? Where would we go Andrew." Mary Ellen was working at the dry cleaners and had the hours she wanted. She found a babysitter for Diane and the other kids were starting their new school.

"Look Mary Ellen there's nothing for us here. I'm sick and tired of being everyone's charity case." He looked defeated. "I want to go home"

"Are you talking about Nova Scotia?" She couldn't believe what she was hearing.

"Yes, we're leaving. I've given my notice at work, and you need to do the same. We will leave in two weeks." He got up and left the room. Mary Ellen's head was swimming. How could she leave her Meme? Mary Ellen didn't even like his mother. Oh, dear God help me.

Mary Ellen walked into her Meme's house and headed straight into the kitchen. As expected, her Meme was at the sink working on the something or other. "Hi Meme." Mrs. Ledoux turned around with a big smile on her face.

"Well, hello there. Give me that baby." She walked directly over to Mary Ellen drying her hands on her apron and took Diane from Mary Ellen. "What brings you by this morning? Would you like a cup of tea?"

"Sure Meme, I'll get it. Sit down here." Her Meme was playing with Diane singing something in French to her. Most of it, Mary Ellen still understood. Her Meme would talk to her in a mix of French and English. Mary Ellen wanted to teach her children French, but Andrew wouldn't have it. He couldn't speak French, so his children weren't allowed to speak French either.

"Meme Andrew wants to move."

"Again! What's wrong with him? What is he running from?" Her questions were coming faster than Mary Ellen could answer. Finally, there was a pause. Then her Meme looked her straight in the eyes. "He's your husband and if that's what he wants you have to do it."

"But he wants to move to Nova Scotia." Saying to her Meme made it more real and she began to cry. Her Meme reached across the table and took her hand.

"You have to go child."

put the figure to move to Nova Scotia with their three

children once rid of us," began to cry. Her Mattie settled first

the taxes and your husband

"You have a child..."

Chapter 33

All the goodbyes were said, and the tears were dried, and she was embarking on the next part of her life. Mary Ellen was scared to death. The car was loaded with children and pillows and food for the trip. They would be there in three days.

Behind them they were pulling a small trailer Andrew had bought from a farmer in Amherstburg. In it were all their possessions. Clothes, toys, pictures. Anything of value.

On day two, they were finally through Montreal and looking forward to the second half of the trip. Mary Ellen had made her mind up to begin anew. Her daydreaming was interrupted by horn honking.

"What's the matter with them." She asked. She turned to look back at the car that was honking when she saw the flames.

"Andrew!" She was screaming and the children began to yell. Andrew pulled over and unhooked the trailer as fast as he could. Mary Ellen took the kids and stood on the side of the road and watched their life go up in smoke. Cars stopped but there was nothing anyone could do. Andrew was cursing and swearing such profanities that a man who stopped to help took him aside and tried to calm him down. That's when Mary Ellen saw Claire running away screaming. Steve was running after her. Thankfully he caught her, but it took everything Mary Ellen had to calm her down.

They had to leave the burned trailer on the side of the road as it was a total loss. Mary Ellen put her crying kids back in car and lowered herself into the passenger side. All the doors were left open as they were all aware of Andrew's need to control his world. One by one the doors slammed. Then he plopped down into the drivers' seat and began to cry. Mary Ellen didn't know what to do so she just sat there silently and so did the kids. When he regained his composure, he started the engine and put the car in drive, and they were off again. Finally, they pulled up to his mother's house. Mary Ellen was exhausted. Diane had been restless for the last three hours and the kids were getting antsy. It took everything she had to keep them all quiet so Andrew wouldn't completely lose his mind. Mrs. Allen came to the door. She was a short woman with a limp and a glass eye. Although she was happy to see her son it was obvious, she wasn't happy that she had to share her home with his family.

"Kids this is your grandmother." Andrew seemed so proud. Steve was the first to approach her she shook his hand. Mary Ellen gave Claire a little push and she too got a handshake. Sara was going to have none of that she ran right up to her and wrapped her arms around this little woman. And Mrs. Allen broke out in a large smile. Mary Ellen let out a long slow breath that she hadn't realized she was holding in. They settled into the basement bedrooms and the family began to arrive.

His brother and sisters were a little standoffish. Mary Ellen knew that Andrew was the oldest and was in the navy by the time his brother and sisters were old enough to miss him. But she did think they would be a little happier about his return. Everyone had questions about Claire

"What exactly is wrong with her?" His sister Gale asked.

"There's nothing wrong with her, she's deaf. That's all." The hair on the back of Mary Ellen's neck was standing on end.

"Does she talk?" Asked his other sister Margaret.

"Yes, of course she does." Mary Ellen couldn't believe the nerve of these people. When Andrew came to bed that night, he was feeling proud of himself.

"See I told you, you'd love them" he said.

"Well, I don't think they like me very much. It was the same felling she had when she last came to Nova Scotia. When Andrew and his brother Danny came back to New Brunswick to get her after her miscarriage, the family let her know how bad they felt for Andrew having to drive all the way back to get her. And how hard it was for him to care for the children especially Claire she was so bad. They didn't know then that Claire was deaf, and it was very apparent to Mary Ellen they didn't want to believe that someone in their family could have offspring that weren't perfect.

"They sure loved Sara, didn't they?" He asked.

"Yes, they did." Steve was such a good big brother he never left Claire's side. Mary Ellen was so grateful for him. She was sure he would always look out for her.

"We won't be here long Mary Ellen. Those were the words that hung in the air as he dropped off to sleep. Mary Ellen said her prayers and fell into a deep sleep. Andrew set off early to get a job, leaving Mary Ellen alone with Mrs. Allen.

"Good morning." Mary Ellen was standing in the kitchen not really sure what to do with herself.

"Morning? You upper Canadian's." She didn't even try to hide her feelings now that Andrew was gone.

"Can I help you with anything?" She asked.

"Well, you could get your kids out of bed and feed them." She snapped.

"I thought since they had such a long hard trip, I would let them sleep in a little." Mary Ellen answered.

"What about my son? Didn't he have a hard trip, but he's up and out looking for a job."

"Okay." She said and went back downstairs into the basement to wake her sleeping babies.

The relationship between the two women only got worse but the straw that broke the camel's back was the day Mrs. Allen called Claire an animal.

"How can you say that about your own grandchild?" Mary Ellen was furious.

"How do I know she's my grandchild, you trapped my son into marriage. For all I know none of them are my grandchildren." She was small but she was the meanest woman Mary Ellen had ever encountered.

"I didn't trap your son. He asked me to marry him all on his own!" And if he was any kind of a man, we wouldn't be living with his mother!"

"Well, I can fix that. Take your kids and get out!" Andrew came by his temper honestly, she thought. Mary Ellen was packed when Andrew got home.

"What the hell is going on here?"

"Your mother told us to get out." Mary Ellen said matter of factly.

"What the hell did you do Mary Ellen." He was livid.

"She called your daughter and animal."

"Is that all?" He asked

"No but shouldn't that be enough! I won't stay here for another night Andrew." He stormed out of the room. When he returned, he told Mary Ellen to go wait in the car with the kids. When he joined them, he told Mary Ellen they were going to stay with his sister Gale and husband Tim.

Andrew wouldn't talk to Mary Ellen and barely said a word to the kids. She didn't know what went on between his mother and him and to be honest she didn't care. It was a long drive to his sister's house but at least when they got there they were welcomed with a hot meal.

"You will have to keep the kids in line Mary Ellen." He said, "I got a job driving taxi and I'm going to work as many hours as I can." He wasn't asking her; he was telling her.

Gayle and Tim had one child and he was in their eyes perfect. Young Tim. Mary Ellen had his number almost immediately. Steve and Tim were about the same age, and she hoped Tim wouldn't be a bad influence on Steve.

"Okay Andrew, I'll do my best." Things were going along smoothly. They had been there for the summer, but they had to think about the kids starting school. It was August. Mary Ellen stayed out of Gayle's way and almost never spoke except to correct her children. They were all a bag of nerves. Andrew was gone from morning to night. The only thing that was keeping her sane were letters from home. Surprisingly she got the most letters from her mother. Today her letter arrived with a shocking revelation. Her mother was coming for a visit. Unfortunately, the letter took a lot longer to arrive than her mother. According to the date she would be here in just a few days.

"Andrew what am I supposed to do? I just got the letter." She said when she saw his reaction.

"Call her, tell her no!"

"No, I can't Andrew, please I need her here. I could get a job and she could help with the kids." She knew that would get him. And she was right.

"Alright, I'll tell Gayle, but she won't be happy."

"We can start looking for a place, okay?" She begged.

"Okay."

Her mother looked pretty good. And Mary Ellen had to admit it was nice to have someone from home here. She was so lonely.

"Mother, you look good." She said with a smile.

"Well, you don't. What have you been eating? Nothing?" She meant it.

"I'm fine mom,". But before she could finish her mother was snatching Diane out of her arms.

"Oh, she's getting so big. And look at Sara. Come here and give your grandma a kiss. Claire, come here. Steve you're getting to be a young man."

When they got back to the house, Gayle and Bea took an immediate dislike to each other. Great, Mary Ellen thought. It's one thing for Gayle to not like me but my mother will never put up with her. A week had passed, and Mary Ellen had found a job at a bakery in a large grocery chain. Andrew was so happy he began to look for a place of their own. And within two weeks he found a house in a brand-new neighborhood. He told her it would be a fresh start. Oh, she hoped it would be.

Mary Ellen worked at the bakery and loved it. When she got home her mother had been drinking. Gayle barely let Mary Ellen in the door before she began to berate her. Telling her how horrible her kids were, and her mother was nothing more than a drunk. Mary Ellen didn't know what to say. But that wasn't a problem for Bea.

"Who are you calling a drunk? Your nothing but a jealous little housewife with a spoiled rotten brat for a kid and a husband who'd rather be anywhere but here with you!" Bea was pretty proud of herself. And then it happened.

"Get out! Get out and take your drunk of a mother!" Gayle was almost hysterical.

"Now wait a minute, you can't just throw us out where will we go?" Mary Ellen was still trying to process what had just happened.

"I don't care where you go just get out of my house." She spat. Bea grabbed Diane and yelled for Steve Sara and Claire and headed for the door.

"I won't let my daughter stay here another minute." The door slammed behind her.

"Mother wait." Mary Ellen was trying to catch up, her whole body was shaking with frustration.

"What on earth were you thinking mother! Where are we supposed to go?" What about our things?" She couldn't remember ever being so upset.

"You don't have to put up with that Mary Ellen you were raised better than that."

"What would you know about the way I was raised?" How could you mother. Andrew is going to be livid." Mary Ellen was trying to make her mother understand.

"I'll explain everything" she said. They walked about a mile when Andrew stopped.

"What are you doing?" He asked. Before Mary Ellen could say anything, Bea stepped to the window of the car and said,

"I won't let my daughter and grandchildren stay in that house one more minute." Her tone was filled with authority. Mary Ellen and Bea began walking down the long dirt road with the kids following behind. Andrew looked at Mary Ellen and pushed the car door opened and said,

"Get in." They all piled into the car and headed back to the house. Andrew went in alone. He was in the house for a long time but when he came out, he told Mary Ellen and Bea they would stay one more night and in the morning they would leave. Andrew had lined up a house to rent, he called the owner and asked if there was any way they could get in early. To his surprise the house was empty so although they would have to pay extra, they could move the next day if they wanted.

It was a long night and when morning came Mary Ellen had almost everything packed. They loaded the car and never looked back. Mary Ellen was pregnant again. Her mother was overjoyed.

"I'll stay till you have the baby." She announced. Mary Ellen had to admit it would be nice to have the help. The house was probably the nicest house she had ever lived in and in her twenty-six years she had lived in a lot of houses. It wasn't long before Bea wore out her welcome. Andrew and Bea, we're constantly arguing. Bea wasn't afraid to tell him what she thought, of course it was always after she drank too much, so no matter how right she was he always used her drinking against Mary Ellen.

Mary Ellen was seven months pregnant when her mother boarded a plane back to Ontario. Mary Ellen really had mixed feelings about her leaving. Life would be harder on her now, but there would be less fighting.

Chapter 34

Clark Christopher Allen was a beautiful baby boy and Diane was completely taken with him. Steve was ten years old now and was always looking out for his sisters. Now he finally had a baby brother. Unfortunately, there was ten years between them. Claire continued to go to hearing classes. With her hearing aids at least, she was making her way. It was a nun at the school who took Mary Ellen aside at a parent teacher meeting and told her about a school for the deaf in Amherst, Nova Scotia.

"It's not my business" she said "but is there a reason Claire can't attend that school? I think she would do a lot better." "Mary Ellen had no idea there was a school for deaf children.

"Thank you, Sister. What do I have to do so Claire can go there?" Sister Vincent took care of everything for them. Mary Ellen was a nervous wreck. Andrew kept telling her it was for the best. How would she explain to Claire that she was going away to school that it would be better for her? She would never understand.

They had a list of all the things Claire would need and although it meant the other kids would have to go without, but what choice did they have? It was mandatory that she have sneakers as well as dress shoes. Shirts and blouses, underpants and socks. Undershirts, raincoat and a winter coat. Mittens and boots. The list went on and on. She would be able to come home for holidays and the summer. Although Mary Ellen knew this was the best thing for Claire, she was having second thoughts. How could she send her daughter away? Would she even understand?

When they pulled up to the school Andrew insisted, they make it as painless as possible.

"Just like pulling off a bandage" he said. There was a teacher waiting at the curb and a man with a dolly. Andrew got out of the car and loaded her little trunk onto the dolly and Mary Ellen took her by the hand and led her to the teacher.

"You're going to love it here Claire I promise. And we'll see you at Christmas." Andrew called her name. She shot him a look and turned her attention back to Claire. She gave her a hug and hurried to the car. She was sick to her stomach and heartbroken all at the same time.

Mary Ellen cried for most of the trip home. To her surprise even Andrew got a little misty. Steve was lost, he was so used to taking care of his sister he didn't know what to do with himself. Sara managed to take care of that she was a tomboy and anything he could do she insisted she could do better. Diane was so taken with her baby brother she thought he belonged to only her. Mary Ellen had to admit life was a little easier with Claire away at school. They managed to stay in the house for two years before Andrew got into trouble with debt collectors. Mary Ellen still worked every day and had no idea where the money was going. Mary Ellen had made one friend in the two years they lived on Primrose Ave., and she was a real good friend. Her name was Betty. Mary Ellen confided everything in her. And she did the same.

Although Mary Ellen had two half sisters, Betty felt like a real sister to her. When Mary Ellen told her they had to move Betty was beside herself. "Oh no, don't tell me."

"We found a place in Fairview Betty. It's not that far. We can write and maybe you can meet me at work." They promised each other they would always be friends. The car was loaded again, and they were on their way. This time Sara cried.

The kids were already tired of starting over and they were still so young. Andrew would tell Mary Ellen he was doing the best he could. She knew his best was far worse than most men. She was so stuck. Lord, help me please was her prayer every night. She made up her mind a long time ago that her children would always come first.

It was a four-unit apartment complex. One of six on the street. Andrew had secured the lower left unit. The upper levels had two floors, unlike the lower that were on one floor. Mary Ellen didn't care she just need some stability for her kids. It was much closer for her to go to work and from here her kids could walk to school. Life went on without too much upset here. Andrew went to work at night and Mary Ellen worked days. The kids were extremely resilient, thank goodness.

"Mary Ellen, come to bed." Andrew wasn't asking. Would it ever end she thought? He never bathed and she couldn't stand the smell of him. So, letting him have his way with her was a real chore. He had been a good lover in the beginning, but that was a long time ago. He used to care about her feelings. Now it was just routine like everything else in her life.

Andrew's temper was worse these days and Mary Ellen was getting tired of being a buffer between him and the kids. It seemed every day was a new complaint from him. Sara wouldn't eat, Diane cried, or Clark fell again. Why couldn't she just come home to a smile she thought. Andrew had just left for work when there was a knock on the door.

"Damn it" she said under her breath. Always afraid it would be a bill collector she approached the door tentatively. Oh crap, it was the landlord. Steve opened the door before she could stop him.

"Hello" she said trying not to look apprehensive.

"Hi Mrs. Allen. Sorry for just dropping by but I was here to see the people upstairs. I'm afraid their moving. I remember your husband saying he would like the bigger space, so I thought I would check with you before I rent it out."

"Well, I'll have to speak with my husband, when are they leaving?" She asked

"Immediately." He didn't elaborate but she knew they had probably been evicted. She had lived that enough to feel bad for them.

"I can call you in the morning if that's okay?"

"That will be fine." He turned and left. Mary Ellen was already thinking about what she could do with the extra space. Andrew was all for it. He didn't even ask about the extra rent.

"Well, it's about time those losers get thrown out."

"Andrew, how can you say that? We've been in that same spot." He shot her a look that sent a chill down her spine.

"Why don't you take the kids to see mother?" He asked.

"Andrew, she hates me and everything I say is wrong." She complained.

"Why do you always have to make everything about you! You're going and I don't want to hear anything else about it." He rolled over and began to snore.

The week flew by. She busied herself with packing at night when he was at work. It was better that way. Steve was fourteen now and was her rock. He ran to the store if she needed something he took care of his siblings when she had to work late. Sara was only nine but was so helpful in the kitchen. Mary Ellen could count on her to get the potatoes peeled and the table set. They were settling into the upper unit and Andrew seemed to be working more and more, unfortunately, he wasn't brining in any more money. He stopped answering the phone all together.

"Just more people wanting money" he'd yell, like it was her fault. Sometimes they would just let it ring. Everyone sat quietly, as if they might know somehow, they were ignoring it.

"I'm going to be late tomorrow" he said.

"Working again?" She questioned.

"What else would I be doing?" He snapped

"I didn't mean"

"Mean what?" Oh, why had she asked. His tirade went on for five more minutes. All the kids sat like little statues. Scared to move until he was done.

"Steve, I got you a babysitting job" he announced.

"Where? She asked

"It's a fare I had today, she needs a sitter after school for a couple hours. Three times a week."

"Who's going to look after the little ones when I have to work?" She asked,

"Sara is old enough!" He barked Mary Ellen didn't want to get into it with him again, so she let it go.

Steve was given five dollars a week, four of which his father took. He let him keep one dollar but then stopped giving him an allowance.

"He doesn't need it now that he's making his own money!" He said when Mary Ellen tried to protest.

It was early in 1969 when Mary Ellen suspected Andrew was having an affair. There was never any money, and he was never home. She thought it was the Mrs. Kelley who lived down the hill. Steve had been babysitting for her for about six months now. He would tell Mary Ellen that dad dropped her off sometimes but left before Steve could get a ride home. Mary Ellen asked Andrew about it, but he said it was just a coincidence that his cab was the one who got the fare. Things didn't add up, but she wondered if it wasn't for the money would she really care?

Andrew complained of headaches all the time and when he did it was up to Mary Ellen to keep the kids as far away as possible. Diane had fallen off her bike and came into the house crying and Andrew completely lost it. He jumped up from his chair like a man possessed. Mary Ellen was able to block the blow that was meant for Diane with the back of her arm. Although he had come close to hitting Mary Ellen before he never actually did. Something always stopped him. But he wasn't afraid to hit his children. Not this time she thought.

"What the hell are you doing?" He yelled. Causing the pain in his head to increase.

"Don't you lay a hand on her! I swear Andrew you'll be sorry." She was standing between him and Diane.

"I've had enough! Do you hear me? Don't you ever touch my children again!" Andrew decided to back down. Mary Ellen had awoken a sleeping bear. She didn't know she had such strength. This was something she felt in her soul. Maybe the Lord had indeed answered all those late-night prayers. What she didn't understand was that the newfound power she felt was going to be matched by a devil that was rising in her husband. It only took a few days, but it happened.

Mary Ellen was standing at the sink watching Sara show Diane something in the grass. Clark had come in for a drink of water. They had just got home from school but since it was a rare spring day the kids headed outside immediately. The front door slammed bringing Mary Ellen to attention.

"Steve don't slam the door!" She yelled

"Where is he? Steve, get down here!" He was furious.

"Andrew? What's the matter?" She hadn't expected him and now something was terribly wrong.

"Where the hell is he?" His anger was palpable. Just then the door swung open. Steve was out of breath and running up the stairs as quickly as his legs would take him. Andrew was screaming. "Where the hell were you? Your supposed to be babysitting!"

"Andrew calm down."

"Sorry Dad I had to help Mr. Rightman put away the football equipment." Steve was trying to explain but Andrew took that as talking back and ran up the stairs after him. What happened next still haunts Mary Ellen. She saw the body of her son rolling down the stairs and her husband following screaming profanities. The back door opened, and Sara and Diane were coming into the living room. Clark was hiding behind his father's favorite chair. Before she could get to her son laying on the floor Andrew began kicking him over and over again. She began to scream his name and was pulling at Andrew with all her strength. When she managed to get him to stop, she threw herself on Steve laying on the floor in a fetal position.

"Your nothing but a son of a bitch!" He spat and walked out the front door.

"It's over Steve, I'm right here." She was trying to hold it together for her children but was having a tough time of it. Steve sat up and Clark was at his mother's side crying. Sara was comforting Diane who was shaking uncontrollably.

"Steve, can you get up?" She asked.

"Ya, mom I think so."

"Oh, Steve I'm sorry." She said as she checked his body. Although nothing was broken, he would be bruised and sore for a while. But the emotional scars would probably always stay with him.

Once Mary Ellen got the kids calmed down, she fed them and called work. She would not leave her children tonight. The kids were in bed and Mary Ellen sat alone in the living room waiting for the devil to return. She felt a calmness come over her. When she saw the headlights turn into the driveway, she stood. He came into the house like a mouse. Then he saw her.

"Look Mary Ellen I don't want to get into it" he said.

"Is she worth it Andrew?" She calmly asked.

"What are you talking about?" He looked at her like she was crazy. Maybe she was crazy. Why else would she have stayed with this man?

"It doesn't matter. I'm leaving you." Now she was looking at him.

"You're not going anywhere." He laughed. "Now get your ass upstairs." He moved towards her, and she turned the knife in her hand, so the light caught the blade just enough to draw his attention.

"What the hell?"

"You'll not touch me or the kids again. Do you hear me?"

"Now calm down Mar, I'm sorry maybe I over reacted."

"Go to bed Andrew." And she sat back down not letting go of the knife.

Chapter 35

Mary Ellen had been up all night planning her escape. Nothing would stop her. It might take a few days, but she could do it with a little help. When he got up in the morning, she was in the kitchen. "Morning" he said. She didn't respond. "I'm going into to work today, and I'll probably work a double shift. He poured a coffee, drank it down and headed out the door. She walked to the living room window and watched him pull away. Without realizing she had been holding her breath. She let it out slowly.

Her first phone call was to her grandmother. She hated to ask but she had only saved enough money to feed them for a week or so but that was it. As she hoped her Meme was happy to make arrangements to fly her and her five children home to Windsor. Her next call was to her best friend Betty. Betty would leave immediately to drive to Amherst to get Claire. She assured Mary Ellen they could stay with them until they had to fly home. She also told Mary Ellen she could store everything at her house until she could afford to send for it. Next movers were contacted. They would be there first thing Monday morning. Lastly, she called work and told them she wouldn't be back. She just had to get through Sunday. She hadn't said anything to anyone except Steve. He would have to stay clear of Andrew, but she didn't want his last memory of his father to be a merciless beating. Steve just hugged Mary Ellen and she realized what she had put him through.

Sunday was like any other. She got up got the kids ready and headed down the road for church. With every step she took the stronger she felt. She would go to confession so that when she left, she would have a clear conscience. She sat the kids in a pew and headed to the confessional.

"Forgive me Father for I have sinned." When she finished confessing her intentions to leave her husband, she felt a great relief. But the priest had other plans.

"You need to go home and ask your husband to forgive you. You must keep the vows you made to this man and promise to be a better wife." Mary Ellen sat in total disbelief. How could he profess to be a man of God and tell her to ask her husband's forgiveness? Well, she wouldn't. As he told her what her penance would be, she left, leaving him talking to an empty confessional. When mass was done, she took her children and exited through the front door not stopping to talk to the priest. They made their way home and Andrew was gone. Good she thought. One less thing to deal with. The kids played and Mary Ellen busied herself with preparing supper. She was replaying what the priest had said and she began to wonder if she was making a mistake. When she looked in the living room and saw Steve holding his side, she knew she was doing what she had to do.

It was Monday morning and Andrew got up early for work. They still weren't talking so it wasn't hard to watch him walk out the door. As soon as he left, she began packing. Steve got his brother and sister up and told them they had to pack anything they could and to make it fast. Mary Ellen got as much done as she could before the movers arrived.

"Take everything in these rooms. Leave the rest." She told them. She handed them a piece of paper with the address to Betty's. As promised, Betty arrived at noon with Claire. Mary Ellen gathered her children and a few suitcases and hurried out the door locking it behind her. She placed the key in the mailbox and quickly made her way to her waiting friend.

"Thank you, Betty. I don't know how I would have been able to do this without you." Betty took her hand and said,

"I don't know how you stayed as long as you did Mary Ellen," They drove the rest of the way to Betty's in silence. Even the kids were quiet. Claire looked confused so Steve took her hand and said it would be okay. They were all a little shaky when they arrived at Betty's. Steve, Betty's husband was showing the movers where to put Mary Ellen's things. He had cleaned out a space in the garage. Betty began to make sandwiches and the kids sat like little soldiers waiting to receive their next orders.

"Come on time for lunch!" Betty yelled but it wasn't until Mary Ellen told them it was alright that they moved.

"They're the best kids I've ever seen" Betty was in awe of her friends parenting. Five kids in her house and they were as good as gold. When they were done eating Mary Ellen told them to stay at the table because she needed to talk to them.

"We're going to stay here for a couple days and then we're going to fly on a plane to go to see Meme and Pepe." She tried to make it sound like they were going on a big adventure. It was Sara that wasn't sure they should be doing this.

"What about Daddy?" She asked,

"Your father isn't coming with us."

"But we didn't say goodbye." And with that she began to cry.

"It's okay" she said, "he knows." She lied. The phone rang and Steve answered it. "Yes, they're here Andrew. No, she doesn't want to talk to you. She told you if you ever touched any of her kids again, she would leave, did you think she wouldn't? Just let her go Andrew. Face it it's over. I'll ask her." He looked at Mary Ellen who was so grateful for Steve but knew she'd have to talk to him. She took the phone.

"Why are you doing this to me?" He asked

"Andrew, you did this. I've put up with you for years, but I won't put my kids though it anymore."

"You can't take my kids, you bitch, I won't let you!" He was yelling now. Mary Ellen Hung up. She was shaking like a leaf. Betty was at her side.

"You did the right thing Mary Ellen. It will be okay. You'll see."

It was the next afternoon that Mary Ellen would get the call that would change her life.

"Yes, she is, just a minute please." Betty had a look of concern on her face when she handed the phone to Mary Ellen. Mary Ellen held the receiver to her chest long enough for Betty to tell her it was the Halifax Hospital. Mary Ellen gripped the receiver a little tighter and said,

"Hello. Yes, this is Mrs. Allen. I see, yes, okay. Tomorrow then, yes Doctor, I'll see you then." She handed the receiver back to Betty and sat down. "He checked himself in."

"What?" Betty couldn't believe it."

"The doctor said he was in the throes of a nervous breakdown. Oh my God Betty what have I done?" She asked

"What have you done? You haven't done a thing. He's having a breakdown because he's a son of a bitch. And that's not going to change. Don't let him do this to you Mary Ellen." Betty drove her to the hospital the next day and waited in the cafeteria.

Mary Ellen approached the admissions desk with great apprehension. Was she doing the right thing? Could she be strong enough to do this?

"I'm looking for Andrew Allen." The kind looking woman searched her book and said,

"Oh yes, and who are you?"

"I'm his wife." She answered.

"He's on the fifth-floor, room 518." Mary Ellen made her way to the elevator and began to pray for strength. She stepped off the elevator and headed to the nurse's station.

"I'm here to see Andrew Allen." she said. The busy nurse looked up and seemed a little surprised to see Mary Ellen standing there.

"Mrs. Allen Dr. Owen will be right with you." Mary Ellen stood at the desk feeling quite out of place. Dr. Owen approached from the left and Mary Ellen was looking to the right.

"Mrs. Allen?" Mary Ellen turned with a start. "I'm sorry I didn't mean to frighten you." Dr. Owen was a middle- aged woman with a warm smile and ease that helped to calm Mary Ellen instantly.

"Hello" was the only thing Mary Ellen could think of to say.

"Your husband is resting but I'm sure he will be happy to see you. He has been having a difficult time with your leaving." She said with compassion.

"I have to." Mary Ellen said. "I don't know what he's told you but I'm sure he's been on his best behavior."

"Well, follow me. If you don't mind, I'll stay in the room with you.

"I would appreciate that" she said. Mary Ellen followed Dr. Owen into the room. Andrew was one of four men in this large drab room. They walked to his bed, and he sat up immediately.

"Mary Ellen, you came." He was on his best behavior she thought.

"Andrew, we're leaving in the morning for Meme's." She blurted it out without thinking.

"You bitch, you can't do this!" The tirade began. Dr. Owen tried to intervene, but things escalated even too fast for her. The river of profanities spewed from his mouth in a torrent. Mary Ellen backed away from him as the orderlies rushed into the room. Andrew grabbed the cup that was on his night table and hurled it at her. Dr. Owen took Mary Ellen's arm and led her out of the room.

"I'm sorry Mrs. Allen, I had no idea he would react like this."

"I did." Mary Ellen said in a voice that sounded completely defeated.

"Please leave me your forwarding address and I'll be in touch. And Mrs. Allen, I think you're doing the right thing. Good luck to you and your children."

Mary Ellen thanked her and turned to walk down the hall to the elevator. The stream of profanities getting louder and louder with every step she took. The elevator doors opened, and she stepped in. When the doors closed the noise stopped. She would never again have to listen to him.

Chapter 36

When Mary Ellen arrived in Toronto, she was exhausted and scared but waiting for her was her Meme and Pepe. She was home she thought. The kids had been so good on the plane the pilot thanked her for being such a great mom. Mary Ellen only hoped she could live up to his compliment. They boarded the train for Windsor and Mary Ellen fell asleep almost immediately.

Mary Ellen quickly found a job and began saving for a place of her own. She was able to take her experience at the bakery to the same grocery chain. She could start immediately. The kids were all back in school and she was given information about a school for the deaf near Toronto by the administrator of Amherst. Mary Ellen was starting to feel like she was in control for the first time in her life.

Summer was beautiful that year, breezes coming off the lake and the smell of roses in the garden made everyone a little happier.

"There's a letter for you dear." Her meme had set the mail on the kitchen table.

"For me?" Betty, she thought. She was still trying to get enough money to get all their things shipped. It was a professional envelope. Mary Ellen grabbed a kitchen knife and slit it open.

Dear Mrs. Allen, I hope this letter finds you and your children well. I'm writing this because I feel you deserve some peace. After intense treatment with Mr. Allen, it is my belief that you made the best and only decision possible in your situation. His issues run deep and since his treatment has ended, I felt you had a right to know. Good luck in the future. If there is ever anything, I can do for you please don't hesitate to ask.

Sincerely yours, Marsha Owen M.D.

Mary Ellen handed the letter to her Meme and sat down.

"I can't believe she wrote me."

"Well, I think she knew you probably needed some closure." Meme took Mary Ellen's hand in hers. "You are not responsible for that man anymore."

Before the school year started Mary Ellen found a basement apartment in Windsor. She also found a second job. With no help financially from Andrew, the cost of raising five children fell solely on her shoulders. She was thirty-three years old and for the first time in her life she had no one to answer to. It was going to be hard on her and the kids, but it was the right thing to do. She would get the kids up then take the bus to the bakery. After her shift there she would take the bus home. Make sure the kids were alright and then get back on another bus to work her night shift at the factory. Somehow, she would make this work.

It was working, thanks to Steve and Sara. They looked out for the two little ones and never complained.

Mary Ellen made a new friend at the factory. Kathy was a fiery red head who was absolutely fearless. Mary Ellen had never met anyone like her before.

"Come on Mary Ellen we're all going out after work." She pleaded

"I really can't, my kids are alone."

"A couple more hours won't hurt, come on you deserve this."

"Okay, but only for an hour." she said.

"Great, I'll drive." Kathy was going to show her new friend a good time. When the whistle blew alerting everyone the shift was done Kathy and Mary Ellen made their way to the time clocks.

"Where are you two off to?" It was Kathy's boss Brad. He was a tall blonde hair blue eyed dreamboat.

"Wouldn't you like to know?" she said, as she took Mary Ellen's arm and hurried past him. Then suddenly she turned around and yelled "The Ambassador Hotel!"

Mary Ellen and Kathy were enjoying their drink when their conversation was interrupted by Brad.

"Can I buy you ladies a drink?" he asked, never taking his eyes off Mary Ellen.

"Oh no, I'm fine, thanks." Mary Ellen barely had the words out when she felt Kathy kick her under the table.

"Yes of course you can." Kathy interjected. They sat and talked until the place closed.

"Can I drive you home Mary Ellen?" He shyly asked.

"Thanks Brad but I came with Kathy."

"Actually, I was thinking I might go to Larry's place tonight, so be a dear and let Brad take you home just this once." Kathy was winking at Mary Ellen. With no other way to get home Mary Ellen reluctantly agreed.

The ride home was very informative. She found out Brad had one child, a son that he was very proud of. He was in the middle of a messy divorce but was hopeful it would be over soon. Mary Ellen had barely said a word when they pulled up in front of her place. Her hand was on the door handle when he blurted out

"I'd really like to see you again."

"Well, I'll be at work on Monday" she said. He chuckled and said,

"Although I'm looking forward to that I was thinking maybe I could take you out for dinner sometime." Mary Ellen could feel the heat rise in her cheeks.

"Brad, I have five children and I'm just starting over." Brad smiled and said,

"See we already have something in common, I'm starting over too." Brad did take her out, and she was having a wonderful time getting to know him. He was athletic and loved being outdoors. The opposite of Andrew. He loved hunting and fishing and he even took her kids snowmobiling. The best part was that he made her feel like she was the only woman in the world. He met her family, and she met his. Brad's mother was a kind gentle woman who lost her husband years earlier. Brad was her world. Although she was worried about Mary Ellen and her five children, she had to admit she admired her strength. Mary Ellen was only thirty-three years old and working two jobs to give her children a better life. She wondered if she would have been able to do that when she was that age.

Brad's Aunt lived right across the street from Mary Ellen's Meme. Aunt Trina. Mary Ellen took an instant liking to her. She was a tough broad that didn't take anything from anyone, but still had a soft side. She was married to Uncle Percy. Well at least that's what they told everybody. They met after their divorces and decided they just wanted to live together. The first time Mary Ellen and Brad spent the night together, Kathy had arranged everything. She stayed at Mary Ellen's house with the kids. Mary Ellen had been a nervous wreck.

"You'll be fine." Kathy assured her. "He's crazy about you."

"Kathy, I haven't been with anyone but Andrew" she said. "And to be honest I don't know if I can do this again."

"Trust me Mary Ellen I have a good feeling about this."

Brad had kissed her many times but tonight his kisses we filled with passion. He was a tall man and Mary Ellen felt so small in his arms.

"Are you alright?" He asked when her knees went weak. She smiled and said,

"Fine," He picked her up and carried her to bed. He made love to her the way she had only dreamed of. Brad was showing Mary Ellen a side of life she didn't know existed. A life she didn't think she deserved, which was mind boggling to Brad. He tried to convince Mary Ellen that not only did she deserves a good life but that he would make sure she and her children would have just that.

"Are you asking me to marry you?" She said shocked.

"Well, if you have to ask, I guess I didn't do a very good job asking, did I?" He chuckled. Mary Ellen wasn't sure if she could commit to another man. At least not yet.

"Can we live together first? I need to be sure the kids will be okay." She hoped he wouldn't run screaming, but she had to be sure.

They rented a nice little house in the same town as her Meme. The boys would have their own room and so would the girls. She wasn't sure what she was going to do with Steve, he was struggling with life and having a new man around wasn't going to help matters.

The move couldn't have gone any smoother. The kids were settling in and so were they. It was like the family she always wanted.

"I have to go to Kim's house this afternoon she needs to talk to me about something."

"Brad, you don't have to explain to me. Will you be getting Henry?" She asked. Henry was Brad's five-year-old son, and Mary Ellen was dying to meet him.

"I'm not sure if she'll let me." He said sounding defeated. Mary Ellen didn't want to tell him how to handle his affairs, but she did tell him she was here if he needed her. He seemed genuinely grateful. Brad had been bullied from day one by his estranged wife and having Mary Ellen be so supportive was like a gift from heaven.

Steve had decided to go back to Nova Scotia to spend the summer with his father. Mary Ellen was heartbroken but had to let him go. If he had truly forgotten how his father had treated him, she had to let him find out for himself. Brad drove them to the airport and gave them a moment alone to say their goodbyes. When Mary Ellen returned to him, she completely fell apart.

"He's going to get hurt" she said. "Andrew hasn't changed and Steve's going to get hurt." Brad took her into his large embrace and tried to comfort her. By the time they got home she had regained her composure. The last thing she wanted was for the rest of the kids to worry, she would do that for all of them. Her relationship with Brad was growing stronger with each passing day. She still hadn't met Henry, but Brad assured her it would be soon.

As the summer days passed, Mary Ellen grew comfortable. Something she hadn't ever been before. She was still working at the bakery but only days. She was able to be home for dinner every night with her family. Brad was working at the factory and was able to secure days as well.

"Mary Ellen" he called when he came in the door after work Friday night.

"In here." She had been home from work for about a half an hour and was in the kitchen getting supper ready. She felt him come up behind her. He had a presence that she could sense. She turned and to her surprise there was a child with him. He was tall for a five-year-old and had the same blue eyes as his father and white, blonde hair.

"Henry, this is Mrs. Allen." Immediately Henry clung to his father's leg

"Hi Henry, are you hungry? She asked with a smile.

"Actually, Mary Ellen we're going to have supper at my mother's." He looked at her sheepishly.

"Oh, I thought. Well, it doesn't matter what I thought" she said. "Please tell her I said hello."

"Henry, why don't you go to the car. I'll be right there." Henry left his father's side reluctantly.

"Mary Ellen I'm sorry. Rebecca was livid when I told her I was bringing Henry here. I told her I would bring him to Mother's house, and she settled down."

"Brad when you are going to stand up to her. You live here and he's your son." Mary Ellen was seeing a chink in his armor, and she didn't like it.

"I will Mary Ellen soon, I promise." With that he kissed her and left. Clark came in the back door out of breath and smelling like little boys do.

"Where is Mr. Diggins going? I thought we were going to play catch?" He looked at Mary Ellen and she instantly hurt for him.

"Oh, Clark, something came up and he had to go. I'm sure he will make it up to you." Clark turned disappointed and sat at the table waiting for his supper.

"Go wash up, okay? Supper is almost ready." He left the table without a word.

Chapter 37

Summer turned to fall and the return of her eldest son. As she expected he was completely let down. His father had a girlfriend, whom his father worshiped. Steve took a back seat and was constantly berated in front of her two children. It wasn't long before Steve stood up to his father. Which of course, Andrew didn't stand for.

"Go home to your ungrateful bitch of a mother!" He yelled. Steve was on the next plane. Mary Ellen was so happy to have Steve home again where he belonged. Steve had dated a local girl a few times before he left for the summer with his father and picked up where he left off when he returned.

It was a Sunday that Mary Ellen would never forget. Steve walked in the door looking like he had the weight of the world on his shoulders. Just as Mary Ellen was about to ask him what was going on a young woman came into the kitchen behind Steve.

"Hello, you must be Rene." Mary Ellen didn't like surprise guests at dinner but this was the first girl her eldest son had brought home so she would let it slide. She was good at making meals stretch.

"Hello" was all Rene said. Steve then took over.

"Mom, we need to talk to you." Mary Ellen could feel the hairs on the back of her neck stand up. "Rene is pregnant and we're getting married." He wasn't asking permission; he was telling her. Mary Ellen realized her other children were sitting at the dinner table in total silence.

"Sara, get the little one's dinner." Mary Ellen could feel her blood pressure rising. Mary Ellen walked into the living room and motioned for Steve to follow. Rene took his hand and clung to him.

"What do you mean she's pregnant? How far along?" Mary Ellen was trying hard not to scream.

"Mom! It's mine and I'm going to marry her!" Steve was surprised that his mother would assume it was someone else's.

"Steve" Mary Ellen was trying to control her breathing. "You were in Nova Scotia; it can't be yours." She was eyeballing Rene now. "Rene, I'm not stupid. Weren't you seeing that boy from Essex while Steve was away?" Mary Ellen was seeing all of this clearly but knew she had to paint a picture for her son.

"We went out a couple of times but just as friends. It's Steve's." she said defiantly. There was no holding back now. Mary Ellen was shaking and yelling at her son not to be taken in by this Tramp. Steve would hear none of it.

"You can't talk to her like that. If you won't support us, I'm leaving!" Steve grabbed Rene by the hand and stormed out. He turned around only to tell her he would be back for his things when she was at work. Mary Ellen sat on the couch for what seemed an eternity.

Sara made sure the two little ones had their homework done and were ready for bed.

"Mom are you alright?" Sara asked in a whisper. Mary Ellen looked at this wonderful young lady and burst into tears. Mary Ellen's protests fell on deaf ears. Her eldest son was married and expecting a child. A child that Mary Ellen would love but one that she was sure wasn't her sons. Brad was becoming adept at splitting his time between Mary Ellen and her children and his ex-wife and his son.

Christmas was just days away and Mary Ellen and Brad swore it would be the best Christmas yet. They stayed up late after everyone was asleep and wrapped presents. Her kids would be overwhelmed this year. It was the first year that they would each get multiple presents. Brad insisted. She was grateful that even though he wasn't what she hoped he'd be with her children; he was good to them.

It was a cold miserable winter day and Mary Ellen was glad the weekend was finally here. She stepped of the bus and began the short walk to the house. Brad was taking Clark and Diane snowmobiling after supper with a group of guys and their kids, and they had been looking forward to it all week. When Mary Ellen stepped into utility room, she saw Clark sitting at the table alone.

"Hey there. Do you have all your stuff ready? Brad will be here soon, and you still need to have something to eat. Where's your sister?" Mary Ellen had been too busy to notice that Clark had been crying. "Did you hear me, Clark? You don't want to keep Brad waiting."

"He's not coming." Clark said.

"What? Who told you that?"

"He did." Just then Sara came into the kitchen.

"He called, mom." He said he was sorry, but he had to take Henry." They were looking at Mary Ellen with confusion. Mary Ellen was livid. She could put up with almost anything. As a matter of fact, she pretty much had. But no one was going to hurt her children not even Brad. Mary Ellen didn't hear from him until late Saturday, and it was clear to her that he had been drinking. The phone rang

"Mom it's for you!" Diane yelled from the kitchen.

"Hello" she said. Brad was trying to explain but Mary Ellen wouldn't listen. I told you no one would hurt my kids again. How could you?" Clark had been looking forward to going with you all week. And Diane told me that she never wants to go anywhere with you again." Brad tried again but Mary Ellen interrupted him. Look Brad, I think it would be best if you stayed at your mothers tonight." And she hung up.

Brad came to the house the next day, but Mary Ellen had made her mind up.

"Mary Ellen, can we talk?" He asked standing on the back porch looking through the screen door.

"Come in, you're letting all the heat out." She moved away from the door to give him room to enter.

"I'm sorry."

She looked at him in disbelief.

"Is that all you have to say?" There was an uncomfortable silence that she broke. "Look Brad I didn't leave one man to take care of another. My kids mean as much to me as your son means to you. I have been taking care of you since the factory closed. You have the nerve to put my children second after everything I've done for you." He hung his head in shame.

"Mary Ellen please, I'll do better."

"I think it would be best if you moved out. I'm tired Brad, and I can't allow anyone to treat me bad again." Her heart was breaking.

"I'm going to win you back; I love you, Mary Ellen." He turned and left. Mary Ellen tried to fill her days and nights with busy work. Brad called daily. At first Mary Ellen would tell him she was busy or tired, but he never gave up.

Meme called and invited Mary Ellen and the kids for dinner on Sunday and Mary Ellen was more than happy to accept. She had told her Meme what had happened with Brad and although she was proud of Mary Ellen, she was also sad because she really liked Brad.

"Hi Meme." Mary Ellen said as she and the kids filed into the living room.

"Bonjour" she responded. The kids always got a kick out listening to their great grandmother and mother talk to each other in French. Pepe had a big hug for each one of them. Mary Ellen grew to love the man who had taken her meme away from her.

"Hi Pepe." He wrapped is big arms around her and gave her a bear hug.

"Kids go sit in the living room and I'll call you when dinner's ready." She was always proud to take her kids anywhere because they were so well behaved.

"What can I do to help?" She asked.

"Set the table and tell me what's going on with Brad."

"Oh Meme, I just don't know what to do. I know I love him, but I can't let him treat the kids that way."

"Your right dear. I hope he smartens up though, I really do like him." She smiled. "Okay get the kids." Mary Ellen walked in the living room and just as she expected they had done just as they were told.

"Come on kids' time for some of the best cooking in the world!" They all came running. As everyone was finding their seat Meme yelled for her husband but there was no answer.

"Oh, she said he's going deaf." Mary Ellen looked at Diane and told her to go get Pepe. She could hear Diane telling Pepe to come for dinner, but he wasn't answering. Mary Ellen was helping Meme put the food on the table when Diane came into the kitchen.

"Mom he won't move and he's really red." Diane was a little dramatic, but Mary Ellen went to check on Pepe. By the time she got to him he was almost unconscious.

"Meme, call an ambulance!"

"What?" Meme stopped and began to yell to Pepe." Mary Ellen ran to the phone and called an ambulance. By the time they got to the hospital he was gone. Massive heart attack they said. When Mary Ellen returned to the house, she was practically holding her meme up. She tucked her into bed and went into the living room where her children were all sound asleep on the couch and floor. Sara woke up and looked at her mother with her big brown eyes.

"Is Pepe, okay?" She asked.

"No sweetheart he's not. Can you help me get the little ones into bed?" Sara shook her little brother awake and walked him to bed while Mary Ellen woke Diane.

The next morning with all the family gathering at her Meme's house Mary Ellen called a cab to take her children home. Her Meme stopped her in the living room and asked her to stay.

"Meme, I have to get the kids home and I'll be back."

"I need you. Can you stay, I mean move in?" She had tears running down her cheeks. Mary Ellen didn't know what to say. Her life was a mess and she needed to start again.

"I'll be back Meme, I promise." She bent down and kissed this fragile woman's cheek. Mary Ellen called her landlord and explained the situation she found herself in and to her surprise he was very understanding. She told him she could be out the following week and he said that would be fine. Now she had to let Brad know so he could gather his things. Brad was not about to give up on Mary Ellen. If she was going to move to her Meme's house, he would prove to her and her Meme he could change.

They would stay in the two-room apartment above her Meme's house. How on earth was she going to make this work. It had a small kitchen with a small dormer that led to a small bathroom. And a fair-sized living room that would double as a bedroom for her kids. With a fold out couch and a foam mattress pad she could make it work. She would sleep in the dormer off the kitchen. Her Meme gave her a cot that folded in half so she could store it away during the day. She told the kids that it was temporary, and they needed to be strong because their Meme needed them. Although there was a little complaining as Mary Ellen thought, her children came together to help her make it work.

Brad continued to peruse her. Now that Mary Ellen lived across the street from his aunt, he had his family helping him. Aunt Trina became a friend that Mary Ellen needed more than she knew. Kathy had married her long-time boyfriend and didn't have as much time to spend with Mary Ellen. Life was changing. Steve was now a father, and with no real example set for him he was doing his best. Steve was more like his father than Mary Ellen liked to admit. She had to let him go. The mistakes he would make would have to be his own. Claire was thriving in her new school and was able to come home on weekends. Mary Ellen would make the five-hour bus ride each way to act as a chaperone. If she did this Claire could ride for free. She would work late Thursday at the bakery so she could have Friday off. Early Friday morning she would meet the bus in the large parking lot of K Mart. When the bus returned it would be full of handicapped children. Some deaf, some blind. Waiting for them whenever he could, was Brad. She had to admit she was grateful. Finally, he wore through her defenses.

"Just dinner" he promised. And he was true to his word. He still wasn't working, and he was spending too much time with his brother Bernard which meant too much drinking but, on this night, he arrived on time, and she had to admit he looked good. He was so tall and those eyes, they always seemed like they were laughing about something only he knew.

"Hi" he said when she opened the door.

"Hi yourself." She said with a smile she couldn't hide. He took her out for Chinese food because he knew it was her favorite. They had a wonderful time. She was still unsure about where this might go but she knew she only wanted to be in his arms.

"Brad, Brad." She was shaking him awake. "You need to get up. I don't want the kids to see you here. Not yet." He rolled over and kissed her.

"Do we have time for this?" And he wrapped her up in his arms.

They continued this for another two weeks and tonight he was coming to visit with the kids and her. She didn't want to say anything to the kids. She wanted it to all work out with no expectations.

"I'll bring Chinese for us for later, okay?" He asked.

"Sure Brad. I'll feed the kids and I'll wait for you."

"I love you, Mary Ellen."

"I love you too."

Brad told his mother about his plans. How he would show Mary Ellen how much she meant to him. He had almost blown it once; he wasn't going to make that mistake again. This time he would marry her.

"That woman has been through enough Brad. I don't blame her for not putting up with you. It's time to grow up. Of course, you love Henry, but she must look out for her children too. And to tell you the truth I admire her. She reminds me of myself when I was her age. No one helped me raise you and your brother and let me tell you young man no one would have treated either of you as badly as you treated her boy." She was the one person in this world that Brad respected. And if she like Mary Ellen he knew she was the one.

"I'm going to go to Mary Ellen's tonight. I'm going to see the kids and when their asleep mom I'm going to ask her to marry me." He went to the cupboard where his mom kept the wine and reached in a grabbed a bottle of Cabernet.

"You don't mind do you mom?" He went to the phone and ordered Chinese takeout. It was eight o'clock he kissed his mother on the cheek and said, "Wish me luck." He was on his way.

"Brad!" She called after him. He turned and she said, "I'm proud of you." He gave her that smile and shut the door behind him.

Mary Ellen had taken a bath and put on a touch of perfume. She finished feeding the kids and they were watching the Partridge family and then the Brady Bunch. She loved the sound of their laughter. She sat at the kitchen table trying not to watch the clock. It was nine o'clock and there was no sign of him. She wondered if she should call his mother's house but then decided against it. One by one the kids came into the kitchen to say goodnight. Sara was allowed to stay up until ten on Friday, so she was the last to come into the kitchen.

"Good night mom. Is everything okay?" Sara was the one Mary Ellen relied on the most, but this was something she didn't want to worry her with.

"Sure honey. Have a good sleep." She kissed her daughter on the cheek and sent her on her way. Mary Ellen couldn't believe he stood her up. How could she be so stupid. He was probably with his brother getting drunk and she was sitting here like a fool. Well, this would be the last time. She pushed the table against the wall and opened the cot. Just like every night Mary Ellen said her prayers. But this night she really had a conversation with God.

"Please Lord, give me strength, the strength I'm going to need to say goodbye once and for all to this man I love. I've really tried Lord, but I just can't put my children through this kind of hurt again." With the rosary her Meme gave her firmly grasped between her fingers, she began to follow the ritual she had been taught as a child. One prayer after another until sleep came.

The sun was just starting to come up when the doorbell rang. Mary Ellen couldn't believe the nerve he had. She grabbed her robe and swung it over her shoulders. Slipped her feet into her slippers and headed down the stairs before he could ring the doorbell again. Please Lord, give me strength. She took a deep breath and opened the door.

Standing on the porch were Brad's Aunt Trina and his brother Bernard. Mary Ellen froze.

"Mary Ellen, can we come in?" His Aunt's voice was nothing more than a whisper.

"What's going on?" Panic was rising in her throat.

"Mary Ellen please." Aunt Trina reached for Mary Ellen. Mary Ellen turned toward her Meme's door instead of going upstairs to the cramped space.

"Mary Ellen, what's going on here." Her Meme was coming into the dining room wiping her hands on her apron. She was always up before sunrise.

"Sit down Mary Ellen we have some bad news." Bernard was at her side trying to sound strong. Mary Ellen still has a hard time remembering exactly what was said. Brad was on his way to see her when a drunk driver crossed into his lane. Brad died instantly.

Mary Ellen knew life would never be the same. She turned to her Meme, who looked at her with such loving eyes. Oh Meme, what am I going to do?

"Pray Mary Ellen. He knows your name. He will give you strength." She took Mary Ellen into her arms, and they wept.

Chapter 38

The next few days were the worst days of Mary Ellen's life. Funeral arrangements were made, and she had no input. Brads almost ex-wife took care of that. Mary Ellen and her children would be allowed to follow in one of the limousines but not after the Hearst, and not the second car which was for his mother and brother but the third car. Mary Ellen later found out the only reason she was allowed to be a part of the funeral was because Brad's mother insisted.

Because the divorce wasn't final Brad's wife would not only get everything including insurance, but she was able to exclude Mary Ellen from everything. Mary Ellen was heartbroken. She stayed close to her Meme because they now had loss in common. Something neither wanted for the other. Mary Ellen also stayed close to Aunt Trina and now Kathy was back in her life.

"Mary Ellen please come out with me; you can't sit in the house forever." Kathy was trying everything to shake Mary Ellen out of her grief.

"Thanks Kathy but I'm going to pick up an extra shift. I'm trying to save enough for a place of our own."

"Mary Ellen I'm not going to stop asking so you might as well give in."

"Thanks Kathy, I just can't." The pain was growing less with each passing day. Some days were harder than others, but they were getting fewer. She was torn between the feeling that he was on his way to her and that if he hadn't been he would be alive today. She didn't think she would ever reconcile the two emotions. Meme was getting stronger as well. Mary Ellen felt like she would be fine on her own.

"Meme, I found a house here in town. I'm going to go to the bank and try to buy it." She wanted to prepare her Meme for the possibility that she might be able to do this.

"I understand Mary Ellen. I guess it is time."

"We're going to be okay aren't we Meme?" They were two women trying to find their way. Mary Ellen was waiting in the outer office wishing she could disappear. What was she thinking? The bank manager was never going to approve a mortgage for her.

"Mrs. Allen?" He said extending his hand. "Please follow me." He led Mary Ellen into his office and closed the door behind them. "What can I do for you Mrs. Allen?"

"Well, I ah, I want to buy a house. I was hoping you could give me the money." Mary Ellen handed him a copy of the listing. It was a cute little two-bedroom house just waiting for a family to take care of it.

"Twenty-three thousand dollars is a lot of money. How much so you have for a down payment. And of course, there will be additional expenses. Closing costs, insurance and turning on all the utilities. Now where was I, oh yes how much money do you have?" He sat patiently waiting for Mary Ellen's response. Mary Ellen had saved five hundred dollars and her Meme gave her an additional five hundred. She threw her shoulders back and said,

"One thousand dollars." It was more money than she ever thought she would have. He sat quietly for a long time. Mary Ellen was starting to feel uncomfortable. The silence was broken when he cleared his throat.

"Mrs. Allen your application shows that you've been employed by the same company for several years. First in Nova Scotia and now here is that correct?"

"Yes sir." She answered,

"And your divorced?" He asked without looking at her.

"Yes sir."

"You have five children?"

"Yes, I do. Is there a problem?" She was beyond nervous.

"I have to say I am impressed that you have managed to save one thousand dollars Mrs. Allen. However, it really isn't enough to purchase a home. Regretfully our bank will have to decline your request." Mary Ellen didn't come here to take no for an answer.

"What can I do to change your mind? I promise to make my payments on time. We need to start over in a home of our own. I'm a hard worker and I swear I won't let you down." Something softened in him. He had to admit he had given more to people that deserved less. He sat quietly for another minute then looked her straight in the eye.

"Mrs. Allen we all deserve a second chance in this life. I think we can make this work."

Mary Ellen had unpacked the last box when there was a knock on the front door. Brad's mother was standing on the front porch with a casserole dish in her hand. Mary Ellen opened the door with a grateful smile.

"Come in please. It's so nice to see you." Brad's mother was a kind a gentle woman. She had been torn between Brad's ex-wife and Mary Ellen. If she rocked the boat too much, she was afraid she wouldn't be able to see her grandson. It was a fine line she walked. She loved Mary Ellen and wished more than anything that Brad would have lived because they would have had a beautiful life together.

"How are you dear? I hope I didn't come at a bad time." She asked.

"I'm getting stronger every day." Mrs. Diggins looked around and gave Mary Ellen an approving smile.

"I'm truly happy for you, Mary Ellen. It looks like you're going to be just fine dear." She sat at the kitchen table that Mary Ellen's Meme had given her and had a nice visit. "I needed to see for myself that you were okay Mary Ellen. I think I'll be a reminder of the past dear and you need to focus on the future. If you ever need me, please don't hesitate to call." She hugged Mary Ellen and then left.

Steve was still married with a beautiful baby girl; he was too young, but he was as bull headed as his father. Claire had graduated from school and was home full time now. It was a difficult transition for everyone. But they were family, and they would make it work. Sara was working at a local nursing home and helping Mary Ellen with everything. Cooking, cleaning, looking, after the two little ones, everything. There were days Mary Ellen wasn't sure she would have made it without her.

Life was quiet in this sleepy little town and Mary Ellen was happy for the first time in her life. Her children were finding their way she was working she had even made a deal with local hardware owner to by a washing machine on consignment. He was a kind man who saw how Mary Ellen was trying to give her children a better life, so he let her take the brand-new washing machine home as long as Mary Ellen promised to pay him five dollars a week. The kids were overjoyed now that they didn't have to spend their Saturdays at the laundry mat.

Aunt Trina still stopped in now and then and told Mary Ellen she was too young to be alone.

"I don't know why you won't get back out there. There's no reason for you to sit in this house night after night. Alone." She stated.

"I'm not alone, I have my kids."

"Well, that's all well and good but those kids can't keep you warm at night."

"Look Aunt Trina, would I like to have someone in my life? Yes, probably but where do I even begin. Who's going to want me?" Mary Ellen looked beaten.

"You're a beautiful young woman, and God has a plan for you. Don't give up dear. You're coming out Friday night and I won't take no for an answer."

"We'll see." Mary Ellen said,

"I'll pick you up at seven so be ready." With that she was on her way. Friday came a little too fast for Mary Ellen's liking. She was in the bathroom getting ready when Diane came in.

"Where ya going mom?"

"Aunt Trina wants to take me out for dinner. I shouldn't be late. Your sister knows how to get ahold of me if she has to Diane so promise me, you'll listen to her. Diane was fourteen now and Sara was having a harder time getting Diane to listen. Teenagers she thought. And that goes for your brother to."

She was finishing the final touches to her make up when the doorbell rang.

"I'll get it" Diane yelled as she ran from the bathroom to the front door. "Hi Aunt Trina, come in." Diane gave her a big hug and followed her into the kitchen.

"Hi there Diane, how's school?" She asked,

"Not bad I guess." Mary Ellen came out of the bathroom feeling like she was making a mistake.

"Hey there you look great." Aunt Trina could see how uncomfortable Mary Ellen was.

"I don't know if I really feel like going out." She was trying to find a way to get out of this, but Trina was not going to give in.

"We're just going to have dinner and a few drinks. Percy is waiting in the car. You'll have fun I promise. After some kisses and hugs and see ya laters, they were out the door.

"Well don't you look nice" Uncle Percy said with a big smile on his face. They were such a great couple Mary Ellen thought. That was the kind of love she had hoped to find but it just wasn't in the cards for her. She shook off the feeling of emptiness and said thanks.

They finished dinner and Mary Ellen had to admit it was kind of nice having adults to talk to. She didn't have to prove anything to these wonderful people. They simply accepted her for who she was. The bill came and Percy snatched it before Mary Ellen could see how much her portion was.

"Let me give you my share uncle Percy." She was trying to get money out of her purse.

"Your money is no good here" he said.

"Let's go to the club." Aunt Trina said.

"Oh, I think I should get home."

"Are you kidding we finally got you out of the house, you aren't going home yet." Aunt Trina giggled.

The club was hopping. Friday nights brought out all the lonely people looking for that special person to make their lives complete. Everyone was on their best behavior. Uncle Percy secured a table near the dance floor. Mary Ellen was glad for the distraction. Watching the couples dance was very entertaining. She fantasized about what it must have been like when her mother was young. When men knew how to dance, and women were happy to let them lead. Her thoughts were interrupted when a young fellow asked her to dance.

"Oh, thank you but no." she said

"Come on" he said taking her hand.

"No thank you" she said again.

"You're not going to make me look like a fool in front of my buddies now, are you?"

"Really thank you but I don't want to dance." Mary Ellen said it a little louder than she had intended to. Uncle Percy stood up and put his hand on the man's shoulder.

"Look I think the lady said no."

"Sit down old man. Nobody's talking to you." Out of nowhere a man appeared at Percy's side.

"Take your hands off the lady and go back to your friends. Now." he said. The fellow left. Percy turned around and began to laugh.

"Sean? Well, I'll be damned." The two men embraced. "Trina, look who's here." He shouted over the music that had started again.

"Oh, my goodness, come her and give me a hug!" After their embrace she turned to Mary Ellen and said. This is one of our dearest friends Sean. Mary Ellen extended her and thanked him for coming to her rescue.

"It looked like my old friend needed some back up" he laughed. Mary Ellen was immediately taken with his thick Scottish accent. And she suddenly felt very shy.

"Sean how long have you been back in town?" Percy asked

"Oh, about a week."

"And we're just seeing you now?" Trina sounded disappointed.

"I've been trying to settle back in and well you know." There was a moment of silence that Mary Ellen sensed had more meaning behind it.

"Sure, sure." Percy said. "So, what are your plans now? Are you going to stick around for a while?"

"I think I will. The house is kind of big but, well, I'll figure it out." he said.

"Sit, sit." Uncle Percy was pointing to the empty chair next to Mary Ellen.

"Sure, thanks." The conversation was fun and easy. Mary Ellen thought she could listen to him talk all night. Percy took Trina's hand and said I think they're playing our song. She smiled and the two of them left Mary Ellen and Sean alone at the table.

"Would you like to dance." He asked Mary Ellen.

"I think I would" He was a good dancer and had a nice smile. Mary Ellen could tell he was a little nervous and she was glad because she was too. He told her how he had lived in several different countries for his work. He asked her about her family.

"Well, she said, I have five children." They really are my world. The oldest is married."

"I can't believe you have a child old enough to be married." He smiled. She laughed and said,

"Well, I was a child bride."

Chapter 39

Things were easy between Sean and Mary Ellen. He was a little awkward and she liked that. He was a brilliant man and had made his living as an engineer. He understood loss to. His wife and son had been killed in a car accident just over a year ago. He had two daughters, one in nursing school and the other married to an ambassador to India. Mary Ellen felt inadequate, but he assured her she was perfect. Mary Ellen wasn't sure she could love again but slowly Sean was winning her over.

When Mary Ellen would leave work, she would find him sitting patiently on the bench so he could drive her home. Or when something needed to be fixed at her little house, he was ready with tools to take care of whatever the problem was. Mary Ellen was starting to relax into their relationship. His home was the opposite of hers. With French doors and hardwood floors. It was a sprawling estate on a beautifully wooded lot. She was overwhelmed with the serenity of this place.

"Mary Ellen stay with me." He said one night as they finished the dinner that she prepared for him at his house.

"Sean, I don't know. I'm not sure I can do this again." She said unable to look him in his sea green eyes. He gently lifted her chin and kissed her slowly.

"Let's try." He whispered. She took his hand and followed him into the bedroom where he showed her a gentleness that she had never experienced. This is a comfortable love she thought, and I am ready for it.

A few months passed and Sean explained that he thought it was time they got married. There was no big proposal, just that it was the logical next step. Mary Ellen only had Diane and Clark left at home and his daughter Rebecca was almost finished with her education and would be moving on soon. Mary Ellen had to agree that there was no reason they should wait any longer. The deal was done. Time to move on to the next step. She would sell her house and he would sell his. Now time to break it to the kids. Diane was beside herself. She just couldn't understand why she had to leave yet another school and what about her friends. How could they possibly do this to her? Clark was very unsure of Sean. He was only twelve and a half and he had already lost a father and a man he loved. He was being very standoffish with Sean and Mary Ellen couldn't blame him.

They found a farmhouse about fifteen miles outside of town. Sean told Mary Ellen it was time for her to quit work.

"Oh Sean, I couldn't possibly expect you to pay our way." she said.

"Look darling I think I can handle it. Besides you deserve to be taken care of." He smiled with his eyes, and she couldn't say no. Her old friend Kathy had married her long-time boyfriend and bought a beautiful piece of land with a new home on it only three miles from them. Mary Ellen was overjoyed. Sean and Kevin got along well enough, so they were always doing something together.

Mary Ellen began canning vegetables like her meme did when she was growing up and with her very own pantry, she was able to bake delicious treats for the kids to come home from school to. The wonderful smells would waft out of the kitchen and lull the kids into submission. Her days were filled with meal planning, working in her garden. Hanging laundry out to dry in the warm summer breezes. She had pickles curing in crocks in the cellar. She felt like she was living a fantasy.

She was a fast learner and becoming a stay-at-home mom was really growing on her. The kids were happier than she had ever seen them. They each had their own bedroom and always seemed to be outside discovering something or other. Mary Ellen tried to like Rebecca, but she was a very difficult young woman. Diane was three years younger, and they had absolutely nothing in common which made things very tense when she was home. To say was spoiled would be an understatement. After her mother died Sean really didn't know what to do with her. She had always been her mother's favorite and since Sean travelled so much, he left the child rearing to his wife. Unfortunately, his wife indulged her every whim. She was nineteen and on her third car.

"Daddy, I need this, and Daddy I need that." Sean simply said yes, and she would leave happy. Mary Ellen could see the jealousy building in her youngest daughter and really didn't know how to handle it. Her children were raided with all the love she could give them. However, money was never an option. Her children went without. Now Diane and Clark were forced to watch as their stepsister got anything she wanted while they were told no.

"Sean maybe you should say no." Mary Ellen tried to help him deal with his daughter, but her words fell on deaf ears. "You can't just give her everything she wants. You're not doing her any favors." But his guilt ran deeper than Mary Ellen knew. He had been driving the car the night his wife and son had been killed. He suffered from survivors' guilt.

"If it will keep her happy Mary Ellen, I'm fine with it." He would say. Rebecca had graduated and was spending more time at home. Things were more tense in the house, but Sean was good and showing them both how much he loved them. Diane and Clark were the only ones feeling left out.

Claire was going to marry a man she worked with at the local nursing home. He was older than she was, but he was kind and really loved Claire. Her daughter Sara was expecting her first child and Steven was the proud father of two girls. Life was wonderful.

"Sean, promise me our life will always be like this." She whispered one night as she laid in his arms."

"I promise darlin." Mary Ellen's mother was the only real thorn in their side. She was forever calling when she was drunk. Crying about some injustice from her past. Mary Ellen tried to reason with her. Tried to console her even tried to yell at her. But nothing worked. It was New Year's Eve and Sean, and Mary Ellen were getting ready to go to Uncle Percy and Aunt Trina's for dinner and drinks when the phone rang. Diane yelled to her mother

"Mom it's grandma, she wants to talk to you." Mary Ellen could feel the heat rising in her cheeks. Not tonight she thought. I can't deal with her right now. Mary Ellen was taking the rollers out of her hair when Sean said,

"I'll handle this." Mary Ellen had never seen him upset before and he was on his way downstairs to take the phone from Diane. Mary Ellen was on her feet trying to catch him.

"She's not coming to the phone." He said in a calm voice. "No, you cannot speak to her your drunk! Don't call here again like this, do you hear me." Mary Ellen stood next to him shocked. She had never stood up to her mother before and this man that she loved had taken care of years of hurt in an instant. He took her by the hand and led her back to the bedroom and told her to finish getting ready that he'd be waiting in the kitchen. She kissed him and hurriedly removed the last of the rollers.

When they got to Percy and Trina's all was forgotten. They had champagne and hors d'oeuvres, then a beautiful roast beef dinner with all the fixings. Followed by cream tarts and coffee. It was a wonderful night. Trina had prepared the guest room for them so they wouldn't have to drive home after a night of drinking. Mary Ellen was grateful. She called home and said good night to the kids.

They sat together enjoying a night cap after ringing in the new year, 1977 was going to be a great year she just knew it. They said their goodnight and made their way to their room. It was awkward making love in her friend's house, but they were quiet. Aside from the giggling anyway.

"I love you, Mary Ellen."

"I love you too. I had fun tonight. Did you?" She waited for an answer, but he was already asleep. Mary Ellen laid there for a long time thinking about how different her life was today. And how different love could be. With Andrew, she knew it wasn't love that brought them together it was necessity. With Brad it had been so passionate. They needed each other. Now with Sean it was comfortable. He was kind and she knew he would take care of her and even though Mary Ellen wasn't yet thirty-eight she was ready to let someone else take care of her.

She drifted off around two but was awake again at three. Sean had bumped his toe on his way out of the room.

"Sean? Are you okay?" She asked,

"I'm not sure." Mary Ellen sat up. She turned the light on next to the bed.

"What's the matter?"

"I don't really feel well. Must have been all the rich food, I've got some pretty bad heart burn." He was holding his chest as Mary Ellen slipped on her robe. Sit down here she said but he was already on his way to the kitchen.

"Sean" she said when Uncle Percy appeared in the hallway.

"Everything okay?" He asked

"Sean has heartburn. Do you have any soda?" She was following Sean into the kitchen. Trina was up now and heading toward the bathroom medicine cabinet.

"Here I have some Rolaid's." She said handing them to Sean.

"Thanks." He popped two into his mouth and began to chew. "I'm sorry you two, why don't you go back to bed." Just then Sean let out a moan and clutched his chest.

"Sean!" She yelled and ran to his side. Percy took his arm and sat him in the living room. "Trina, call an ambulance."

"What? What's happening?" Mary Ellen was frantic.

"He's having a heart attack." Mary Ellen froze. Aunt Trina was on the phone giving her address to the voice on the other end. Everything was happening in slow motion. She reached for his hand, and it was clammy. His skin was suddenly moist and sallow. He was gritting his teeth in pain and then it was done. His face relaxed and his had went limp in hers. The door flew open and men in white were at his side pushing her away. Trina took her to the other side of the room as the pushed on his chest and breathed into his mouth. This went on for what seemed an eternity. Then someone broke the silence by saying,

"Get him on the stretcher we have a pulse."

Uncle Percy ran to the bedroom and yelled get dressed we'll follow. Mary Ellen doesn't remember getting dressed or driving to the hospital. Her next memory is being led into an office at the hospital and a doctor saying I'm very sorry we did everything we could. Your husband died at 3:28 am.

Mary Ellen saw the room spin and fainted.

"Is she okay" Trina asked.

"I've given her a sedative. She'll sleep for a while then you can take her home."

When Mary Ellen woke, she was in an unfamiliar place. Trina was at her side.

"What happened?" But before Trina could answer it all came back like a rushing torrent. Mary Ellen began to sob. The drive to the farmhouse was like watching a movie. The scenery passed in a blur. Bare trees and snow-covered fields. Crows flying around trying to find something to eat. Telephone poles whipping by one after the other. Mary Ellen was so cold and yet numb all at the same time.

When they arrived at the farmhouse the kitchen light was on. Diane was an early bird and was already making breakfast. Aunt

Trina entered the house first followed by Mary Ellen and then Uncle Percy.

"Hi there" but Diane knew instantly something was wrong. Aunt Trina took care of all the phone calls and never left Mary Ellen's side. People began to arrive, and it was Trina who greeted them. The funeral arrangements were made, and visitation had come and gone.

Sean's two daughters were complete opposites. They barely spoke to one another and stayed on opposite sides of the funeral home. Mary Ellen's children had been through this before and understood they were second to Sean's girls. Mary Ellen was heartbroken not only for herself but for them. They sat quietly almost an afterthought amongst Sean's children and all their friends.

When they got back to the house Kathy took over for Trina who was exhausted.

"Mary Ellen please eat; you have to keep your strength up." Kathy pleaded

"I can't, I just can't eat Kathy. Have the kids eaten? Are they okay?" She asked

"They're worried about you. Please talk to them."

"What can I say. I don't understand why this happened. What am I supposed to say to them?"

"Mary Ellen, they know you can't answer why; they just need to make sure you're going to be alright. That your still their mom." Mary Ellen began to cry.

"Oh, Kathy I'm so tired. I'm tired of trying. I'm tired of being the strong one of fighting for every scrap. What am I going to do now?" But Mary Ellen didn't need Kathy to say anything. She knew what she had to do. She had to start over again. It's what she had done her whole life. Why should this time be any different she thought? She was weary. But the hard work was about to begin.

One week after Sean's funeral Kevin and Kathy called and asked if they could come over, they needed to talk to her about something. Mary Ellen tried to fix her hair and put on some lipstick but when she saw herself in the mirror she was overtaken with emotion. She had aged so much in this past week. She had dark circles under her eyes, and she was sure she had lost about ten pounds because her clothes were hanging on her. Snap out of it she told herself. You've been here before and you survived, you'll survive again. When Kathy rang the doorbell Mary Ellen jumped out of her skin. Why was she so on edge? She could do it. Walk to the door and answer it she told herself. It seemed like every step she took was like wading through quicksand. Her legs felt heavy and as hard as she was trying, she felt like she was going nowhere.

"Hi" she said as she opened the door to her dear friends. "Come in." Kathy and Kevin were familiar with Mary Ellen's house. They had spent many nights here, the four of them laughing and drinking, eating and telling stories. Kathy shook her head knowing it would never be the same.

"How ya feeling Mary Ellen?" Kathy asked already knowing the answer.

"A little foggy. I don't know why."

"Are you still taking those pills the doctor gave you?"

"Yes, do you think that's why?" She asked

"Well, he said to take them if you needed them so maybe you don't need them anymore." Kathy knew they were strong but didn't want to alarm Mary Ellen.

"Yes, I think I'll stop. I need to think clearly. Can I get you anything?" Mary Ellen really wasn't sure what she had in the house. But the kids were eating well so she assumed people had brought over food.

"No, we're fine Mary Ellen please come and sit down." Kevin was being extra gentle which set off alarm bells in Mary Ellen's head. Once seated Kevin told Mary Ellen that although Sean thought he had homeowner's insurance coverage in case of death, he didn't. Sean was not good at keeping up with his paperwork.

"He never finished filling out the forms" Kathy added.

"So, what are you saying?" Mary Ellen had that old familiar knot in her stomach.

"You and the kids can stay here for about four months but then you'll have to sell. I looked over all your financials like you asked me to Mary Ellen and after paying for Claire and Rebecca's wedding's and paying the mortgage for three more months. You'll have enough to pay first and last months' rent somewhere and support yourself for another two months." He informed her. Rebecca had announced at Christmas that she and her longtime boyfriend Kent were getting married in February. It would be a short engagement because she had taken a nursing job in Toronto.

"What about the insurance money?" She hated to ask, but she had to know.

"The beneficiaries are his two daughters. I'm so sorry Mary Ellen. He thought he had time. We all did." Kevin hated to have to be the one to tell her.

"His will leaves everything to his daughters. All the furniture and the car and the truck. They can't touch the joint bank account, but all the savings and investments are theirs. Mary Ellen began to laugh. Kevin and Kathy looked at each other perplexed.

"Are you alright?" Kathy asked. Mary Ellen sat back in her chair and said

"I lived without Wedgwood China before, and I guess I can live without it again. My mother taught me that. I understand now what she was talking about. Why did I ever think I belonged here?"

She got up from her chair thanked them and said she'd call them in the morning. Kathy and Kevin hated to leave her, but they knew she needed time to process everything. Mary Ellen spent another sleepless night. She was exhausted but no matter how hard she tried sleep wouldn't come. She had the pills the doctor gave her but when she took them, she found it hard to focus. She was even having a hard time remembering the funeral. She had been walking around in a fog. She hadn't paid attention to the needs of her kids or herself but that's about to change.

She sat at the kitchen table and came up with a plan. First, she would list the house, once she had a closing date, she would have an auctioneer come in to sell everything. His girls could have everything she would leave with what she came into this marriage with. How on earth was she going to tell her kids. She'd cross that bridge when she got to it.

The sun was coming up and she finally felt tired. She headed upstairs to Diane's room and crawled into bed next to her. And sleep came.

"Be quiet Clark, moms sleeping." Diane was so worried about her mother. She had never seen her like this. She was grateful she was sleeping. It was late afternoon when Mary Ellen made her way downstairs.

"Hi honey" she said as she hugged Diane.

"Where's your brother?"

"He's outside shoveling the driveway. We had more snow last night mom. Are you alright? Want a tea?" Diane was tripping over herself trying to make her mother comfortable.

"I'm fine sweetheart. A cup of tea would be great. Thanks." Mary Ellen sat at the kitchen table. She could see Clark shoveling the driveway through the window.

"Has he been out there long?" She asked,

"No not very long." Diane said. "He'll come in when he gets cold mom don't worry."

"I am worried about both of you. Come sit down."

"We're okay mom." Diane tried to reassure Mary Ellen.

"There's going to be a lot of changes and we're going to have to stick together. She looked out the window again and her heart broke. He was fourteen years old and had already lost so much.

"Mom?"

"Sorry honey what were you saying?"

"What changes mom?"

"I'm not sure just yet, but we'll figure it out together, okay?"

"Okay mom" Diane said, trying to sound upbeat. The door

opened and a cold blast of air rushed into the kitchen. Clark was shaking the snow off his arms while kicking his boots into the corner.

"Thanks Clark." She yelled

"Sure." He said with his head down. He started up the stairs when Mary Ellen stopped him.

"Can you come here please." Clark stopped and let out a heavy sigh.

"What?"

"Are you okay?" She wanted to know what he was feeling.

"Ya."

"Do you want to talk?" She asked.

"Na." He left her standing in the kitchen. Mary Ellen could only imagine the pain he was in. She had no idea how to help him, but she would have to try. They spent the next week trying to understand what Sean's death meant for them. Diane and Clark would have to change schools again. Mary Ellen would have to find a job. But first they would have to find a place to live. The kids would start their new schools in September. So, for now she would work on getting Sean's two daughters together to separate their fathers' belongings. Rebecca had been staying with her college roommate and told Mary Ellen she was available anytime. Her sister Martha was another story. Unlike Rebecca, Martha had her own way of doing things and decided it would be in her best interest to move into her father's house.

Martha and her husband Richard arrived two days later. Mary Ellen couldn't believe she had the nerve to move in but here they were. Martha and Rebecca began to separate everything.

"I want Daddy's beer stein collection" Martha barked.

"Well then, I get Mother's teacup collection. Rebecca responded. Mary Ellen couldn't believe that these two women only had each other left in this world and they were fighting over cups. Diane and Clark stayed clear of all the bickering. In the end Mary Ellen decided she would hire an auctioneer to sell the rest. The girls would then split the money.

Chapter 40

Diane had her driver's license now and Mary Ellen was grateful since she still hadn't gotten hers. They were just two weeks away from the auction. Martha and her husband had finally left, and Rebecca's wedding was over and done with. Claire had fallen in love with her boss. He was a chef and Claire had taken a job working in the kitchen. Although he was older than Claire, Mary Ellen thought he would be good match for Claire since it was obvious, he loved her back. They also had an upcoming wedding. Sara had married a young man that was new in town, and they were expecting their first child. Sara was glowing. Mary Ellen wasn't sure she was going to get through it without Sean but somehow, she did.

It was May, and Mary Ellen was feeling like herself again. She found an apartment in the city. It was a two bedroom, on the bus line. It was also only a couple blocks from Sara and her husband. Diane and she would share a bedroom so Clark could have some privacy. It was all they could afford for now. She managed to stretch their money enough to stay in the house until the end of June. Kevin had listed it and it sold within a week. He told her she wouldn't have any trouble selling it and he had been right. She would have enough money to buy new living room furniture, maybe even new bedroom furniture. Time was going by fast and slow, all at once. She was staying busy, so her days were flying by, but her nights were long and lonely. She finally went back to her own bed. She realized she wasn't doing herself or Diane any favors by sleeping with her. The kids all rallied around her, and her new grandchildren were wonderful, but Mary Ellen was now afraid. Of what she wasn't sure. She hated staying alone. She had never been afraid before but now she was afraid of tomorrow and what that might hold.

"Diane come on; I need to get to the grocery store." She was calling up the stairs when the phone rang.

"Hello" she said.

"Hi mom, what can I do for you?" Mary Ellen's mother had been on her best behavior since Sean died. Helpful even, but today was different. Mary Ellen could hear the familiar sound of booze in her voice.

"Mother have you been drinking? Why she thought she would get a straight answer she'd never know. "Mother I don't have time for this right now. We'll talk later." She hung up the phone and found a new resolve. She was done, finished. No more grieving, no more letting her mother walk all over her. She would start fresh, and no one was going to get in her way.

"Diane let's go!"

"Mom, can I get Fruit Loops?" Clark had decided to come along, and Mary Ellen was already regretting saying yes.

"Clark you already have Cheerio's in the cart."

"What if I put it back?" He asked,

"Okay but hurry up we're almost done." Her patience was waning. "Come on Diane lets go to the check out." Clark managed to catch up with his box of cereal. He was growing so fast Mary Ellen was having a hard time keeping food in the house. They were walking out of the grocery store when Mary Ellen heard someone calling her name. She turned and to her surprise, Ken, her old neighbor was standing with a young woman at his side.

"Ken? Oh, my goodness, how long has it been? And who is this? No let me guess, is this Sandra?"

"Hi" the young woman said with a smile on her face.

"This is Diane and Clark. How are you?" She couldn't believe it; he hadn't changed a bit.

"Pretty good, now. When did you come back to Windsor? I thought you and Andrew were in Nova Scotia."

"Oh, I've been back for a few years. I'm getting ready to move back to Windsor in a couple weeks. How's Pearl?" The kids were starting to fidget.

"Hey, do you want to get a drink or something sometime? We could catch up." He looked a little nervous.

"Oh, I don't think I can?" She really wanted to catch up but now probably wasn't a good time.

"Come on, it'll be fun." he said. Diane poked Mary Ellen,

"Go mom you need to have some fun."

"Okay" she reached into her purse and pulled out a piece of paper and a pencil. She scribbled her phone number and handed it to him.

"Tell Pearl I said hi." He took the paper and smiled. Diane was a good driver, but Mary Ellen was still a little nervous, so she occupied her time remembering the past. She tried to remember what Ken and Pearl's other kids' names were. She wondered if they had more children like she did. Diane was only a year old when they moved to Halifax. She wondered if they still lived in the same house. She hadn't thought about that part of her life in a long time.

Diane pulled into the driveway and Mary Ellen was pulled back to the present. The phone was ringing as Mary Ellen walked into the kitchen. I'll get it yelled Diane speeding past Mary Ellen.

"Hello, oh hi, sure just a minute please."

"Mom it's for you." She handed the phone to her mother with a concerned look.

"Hello"

"Hi" he said, "This is Ken."

"Hi again." she said

"So, when would be a good time to get that drink?"

"Well, I really hadn't had a chance to think about it, I just got home." She laughed

"I can pick you up tomorrow at say seven?"

"Ken I really have a lot of things going on here. Maybe another time."

"What are you going to do at seven at night?" He had a point she thought. After a bit of a pause, she reluctantly said sure why not? She gave him her address and said goodbye. She didn't know why she was so nervous. She hadn't seen them in a long time, but they had all been friends. She would try not to share too much. She would just have a couple drinks a few laughs about how young they all were.

"Okay, if you need anything call Kathy okay. I shouldn't be late. Love you both." Just then he pulled into the driveway. She couldn't see in the car but rather than have them come into the house she went out to meet them. She opened the back door but when she went to get in, she realized Ken was in the front seat alone.

"Oh hi, where's Pearl?" She slid into the front seat.

"Well, I was going to tell you yesterday but, well, we're getting a divorce." He paused waiting for a response.

"What about you. Did you finally leave Andrew?" It just occurred to her that they never talked about their spouses.

"How did you know?"

"I didn't really, but I figured you would. You were always too good for him."

Mary Ellen laughed.

"Well, aren't we a fine pair."

"You still up for a drink?"

"Sure, why not." They sat in a booth in a dark little bar and told each other how their marriages came to an end. Pearl had cheated on Ken. And Andrew had cheated on Mary Ellen. They talked about their kids and what had become of all the neighbors. Mary Ellen was shocked to hear he still lived in the same house. She was surprised how easy he was to talk to. He was different from anyone she had ever met. He was rough around the edges. A real tough guy. His eyes where dark brown and he was starting to go bald. It suited him. He drank whiskey followed by beer. He made her laugh.

"Well Ken I really should be getting home. Do you mind?"

"No, no problem. I'll be right back." He went to pay the bill and came back to the table with an extended hand. She took it.

When they pulled in the driveway. They sat in silence in the car for a minute. Then Mary Ellen spoke.

"I was married to a man named Sean and he died. We were only married for two and a half years. And before him I was in love with another man, and he was killed in a car accident." There was silence again. This time Ken spoke.

"Well, I don't plan on dying anytime soon so would you like to go out for dinner this weekend?"

"Okay." And they both laughed. Mary Ellen got out of the car and bent back in and said, "Thanks Ken I had a nice time."

"See ya Saturday." He said and she closed the door. When she was securely in the house, he backed out of the driveway.

Chapter 41

The auction had taken place, and everything was gone. All the beautiful furniture, the China she had served so many dinners on for their friends. No more crystal or silver. The girls had taken what they wanted and now the money would be divided between them. Mary Ellen was anxious to close this chapter of her life. Diane and Clark had gone ahead with Sara and Steve. Claire and her husband followed in another car. Ken waited outside as Mary Ellen took one last look at the house, she called home for the last three years. She had been her happiest here. For the first time in her life, she had been cared for, completely. But in the end, she had nothing.

She slowly closed the door and walked toward Ken. I lived without Wedgwood China before she said to herself.

"Ready?" He asked,

"Ready as I'll ever be." She said as she slid into the seat next to him and he took her hand in his.

"Come on beautiful let's go."

Mary Ellen and her two remaining children, Diane and Clark, were settling into their new life. Diane was in love with a young man from a good catholic family and Mary Ellen hoped her daughter would fit in; she had been through so much. Diane was enrolled in hairdressing school and was pretty good at it. Clark was still in high school and was a handsome young man. Mary Ellen prayed for her children. Prayed that they would find their way.

Mary Ellen was spending all her free time with Ken. He has become an engineer with a crazy work schedule. But they made it work. Ken still had two children at home but like Diane and Clark they were very independent.

Mary Ellen was forty years old; she was a grandmother three times over and tired. There was something in her though that wouldn't let her give up. She was able to get a job at a variety store, so she had a little income. Enough to pay rent and get groceries. But that was it. Unlike Steve and Sara, Diane and Clark didn't really understand how tight things were. Ken did what he could without overstepping but in all honesty, she wished he would. He was a good man but a hard man. He too, survived a tough upbringing. One that he only shared with Mary Ellen after a few drinks.

"Look" he'd say, "I'm not looking for sympathy, it's just the way it was." They had that in common. It was a bond that they could build a life on. Diane was in a hurry to prove herself. So, after hairdressing school she decided to change direction and took a great paying job with one of the big auto makers. At nineteen she had secured an apartment and off she went.

Ken was never a father figure to Clark. He was busy with his own kids and Clark really showed no interest in him. Mary Ellen was aware of how many times Clark had been let down by the men in her life and she had decided she was not going to push them together. Times were getting harder and harder for Mary Ellen. She was finding it more and more difficult to make ends meet. She had never asked anyone for anything, and she certainly wasn't going to ask Ken. She made a phone call to her youngest daughter.

"Hi honey"

"Hi Mom, how ya doin?" Mary Ellen couldn't believe she was going to have to ask her own child for money, but she had nowhere else to turn.

"Well to tell you the truth not very well. I was wondering if I could borrow some money. I hate to ask but I don't know what else to do."

"Oh, Mom of course! Anything you need." Mary Ellen was grateful but at the same time a little disappointed that her daughter was doing so well and never thought that her mother was going without. I'm so tired she thought. Tired of just making ends meet. While she was always exhausted, Ken was always ready for a party. Drinking was becoming second nature for Mary Ellen. Although Bea was an alcoholic, Mary Ellen knew she would never be anything like her mother. Ken took Mary Ellen to all his local haunts. Fun followed him, and Mary Ellen loved being a part of it. When she was with Ken, he made her feel like she didn't have a care in the world. But she did. Clark was her only real responsibility and she was failing him. She didn't seem to have the drive to finish raising him and the more she was with Ken the less she cared.

"Hey, do you want to go up north fishing?" Ken was excited, but he never wanted to let her know how much. He really wanted her to go. He had a tough exterior that he had to uphold after all.

"Sure. When?" she smiled. Ken reached for her and pulled her close. He kissed her long and hard.

"What was that for?" she giggled.

"How fast can you get ready?" This is how their life together was. No responsibility, no worries or arguing. Just fun and adventures.

Mary Ellen knew that she loved this man. What she didn't know was if he loved her back. He said the words and he was very attentive. When they made love, it was all she ever wanted it to be. But there was something missing. Ken was humiliated when his marriage to Pearl ended. She convinced him she needed a break. To find herself. Ken rented an apartment for her and furnished it. He was sure she would be back. Instead, she had the perfect place to entertain her boyfriend. And Ken paid for it. It was only after a friend convinced him to sit outside the apartment one night that Ken finally believed him. No woman would make a fool of him again.

Mary Ellen got a new job working as a chef, preparing meals for an order of priests at an all-boys school. She was discovering a whole new side to herself. She ran the kitchen. Trying new recipes, learning food allergies. Caring for a bunch of men. She was discovering her passion. She was good at it. She did find it harder and harder to keep up with Ken and his lifestyle and Clark and his needs. It seemed her back was hurting all the time.

She and Ken had been seeing each other for a couple years now and she was wondering where it was going. Clark had moved in with Bea. Mary Ellen told herself it's what he wanted but, she the truth was, she wanted to move in with Ken.

"Clark are you sure about this?" She loved her youngest son so much but was ready to start her own life. Clark knew he was in her way, so he moved. Ken's kids had also moved out so there was no reason for Mary Ellen not to just stay at Ken's.

Chapter 42

Mary Ellen woke up early with a raging headache. This was really nothing new but this morning there was an unusual pain over her eye. Ken had left for work early because he was on the day shift this week. Mary Ellen made her way to the bathroom mirror. Her eye was a little swollen, and there was a small but distinct sore along her hair line. When she touched it, she let out a small yelp. Oh my, she thought what on earth. Mary Ellen headed to the kitchen to start the kettle for her morning tea. She tried to settle in with the morning paper but the discomfort she was feeling prevented her from relaxing.

Call Dr. Mando, she thought. She looked at the kitchen clock and realized they wouldn't be opened for a couple hours. She went back into the bathroom for an over-the-counter pain pill and decided to take two.

"Good morning this Is Mary Ellen Casey. I was wondering if I could come in to see the Dr. this morning?" Mary Ellen was wincing in pain now and was having a hard time staying patient when she was put on hold. "Yes, I'm still here. Yes, I can come right now." Mary Ellen hung up the phone and called a taxi. She hated to spend the money, but it would be the fastest. way to get there.

"Mary Ellen I'm afraid you have shingles." Dr. Mando said matter of factly.

"Shingles on my face?" Mary Ellen couldn't hide her disbelief.

"Yes, although we usually see shingles on the trunk, it is not unheard of to see it occasionally on the head.

"It's terribly painful." she said

"I'll prescribe something for the pain. Unfortunately, you will just have to wait it out." He was in a hurry, like every other day. And a little annoyed that his nurse managed to fit Mary Ellen in on his golf day.

"Can you write me a note for work? She asked.

"You can work. It's on your face not your body." Mary Ellen couldn't believe her ears. Without a note she wouldn't be able to miss work. She stopped on her way out and asked the receptionist to call her a taxi.

When Diane pulled into the driveway to pick her mother up for work, Mary Ellen was already coming out the front door. Her daughter was good enough to take her to work four days a week and if Ken was on nights, she would pick her up. When Mary Ellen slid into the front seat, she could see the shock on Diane's face.

"Mom! What happened to your face?"

"The Dr. says I have shingles."

"But your face is swollen?" May Ellen touched her cheek but didn't dare touch her eyebrow.

"Well, I have to work, so let's go or I'll be late." She let out a long sigh and Diane put the care in reverse.

Father Duncan was very sympathetic but also wanted his dinner.

"Mary Ellen dear, if you will just get our supper tonight, I will get someone to cover your shift until you feel better."

The next few days were a bit of a blur. Days that were filled with pain. When Mary Ellen stepped back into the doctor's office, he was visibly alarmed.

"I think you need to stop working." Had Mary Ellen heard him correctly? "I'm concerned about your eye. We don't want the shingles to reach your eye." The pain was so intense Mary Ellen could feel the tears beginning to swell in her eyes. As the tear made its way slowly over her lower lid and slid down her cheek Mary Ellen let out a cry that stopped the Dr. In his tracks. He quickly wrote a prescription and hurriedly passed it to Mary Ellen.

"Take this downstairs to the pharmacy and tell them I said to rush it. You need to apply this directly to the open sores as needed for pain. I want to see you back here in a week." Mary Ellen's hand was trembling hand.

Later that night, as she sat in the long shadows of the decreasing sunlight, she wondered what was to become of her. Life was passing her by. Ken had his life and she supposed she had hers. The problem was she realized she was living his, for him. Caring for him, cleaning for him, cooking for him. What was in it for her?

It was now dark in the family room where she had settled in for the duration. When she stood to make her way to the light switch the air that her movement generated wafted against the open sores on her forehead, and it took her breath away. She could feel the tears begin to swell in her eyes, but she was unable to stop them. Just then Ken appeared in the doorway. Mary Ellen collapsed into his arms. The pain was unbearable.

"Sit down beautiful." Ken was being as gentle as he knew how to be. His heart was breaking to see her in so much pain. Ken had told a guy he worked with about Mary Ellen having shingles and this guy was all too happy to tell him that shingles were brought on by stress. Had he caused this in her? He wondered. If so, he would make it right. He got Mary Ellen to the chair and sat at her feet.

"What can I do Mary Ellen?" He asked. But all he heard were whimpers. "Marry me." he said.

Had she heard him correctly? She would wait, if he said it again, she would know. If not, she was hallucinating.

"Mary Ellen, marry me."

"Okay" And it was done. She had been waiting and now it was done. No dinner, or flowers, not even a ring. And still, it was perfect.

Chapter 43

Time seemed to fly by now that her shingles had cleared up. She and Ken would be married by the end of the day. Kathy would stand with her, and Kevin would stand with Ken. They had all become close and it just made sense that the four of them would be the only ones to celebrate this event. For now, anyway. They decided they would tell the kids in a couple of days. Today would be just for them.

Mary Ellen was completely relaxed when they arrived at the minister's house. It was his wife who answered the door and showed the four of them into a makeshift chapel/living room. Mary Ellen had bought a new dress and had her hair done and Ken was in a suit. Vows were exchanged, rings were placed on the appropriate fingers, and it was done. Ken looked at her like she was a gift that he had just realized he always wanted. She was overjoyed. The four of them laughed and hugged and paid the minister. Out they went, husband and wife. That's when she realized it was Friday the thirteenth. And she thought, of course it is. Not one of the children were happy to be left out. They were, however, happy they were married.

Life was going to be everything she had dreamed. Mary Ellen discovered she had a green thumb. And with a little coxing, Ken dug gardens for her. She would just finish with one and she would already have her next one staked out. Ken didn't seem to mind. He seemed proud of her. Work was another thing.

She was quickly losing her passion for taking care of the priests she once revered. They were like children, always wanting her attention. This one needed this and that one couldn't eat this. She now found herself pealing tomatoes for one of them.

One evening while standing at the sink filling one of the huge pots for potatoes she felt a sharp piercing pain shoot up the center of her back. Unable to move, she yelled for Father Cooper. Within seconds he was at her side.

"Just leave everything to me, Mary Ellen. Now let's get you home."

Ken was at home and met them at the door.

"What's going on Padre'?" She hated it when he called Father Cooper that, but he seemed to take it as an endearing term. What did she know?

"Well, it looks like our girl has hurt her back. She won't go to the hospital so maybe you could get her to the Doctor tomorrow." Father Cooper was almost paternal.

"Will do Padre', thanks." Ken had been home for a couple hours, but it was clear he had been drinking. There was a burning pain in her back, and she was having a hard time getting comfortable.

"Do you want me to rub your back? Ken was trying, but she just wanted to go lay down.

"Thanks, but I'll be alright." She lied.

After some tests the doctor told Mary Ellen she had osteoarthritis. He also told her that there was evidence of bulging disc. He asked if she had ever been in an accident. Yes, she had, memories of being thrown from the snow mobile Brad was driving years earlier came rushing back.

"I'm suggesting you stop working. I'll fill out papers for disability and you can apply for that. Of course, there are no guarantees, but you clearly can't continue to do manual labor."

Although Mary Ellen was relieved, she was still nervous. How would she tell Ken? He would think she was taking advantage of him. She had always worked. She was proud of how she always took care of herself. She would be totally reliant on him. Ken wasn't the type of man to show sympathy, in fact Mary Ellen knew he wouldn't. He instead, teased her.

"So, I guess you think you'll get to lay around and become a lady of leisure?" He said with a wry smile. "Well, we'll see about that." There was no more to be said. Ken had told her in his own way that he would take care of her.

Chapter 44

Life was going along just fine. Bea, again, was always on her best behavior when Ken was around which made life easier for everyone. Steven was settled in Calgary and was now a father and a widower. He had remarried a wonderful woman who suffered from severe arthritis. Eventually it took her life. Steven was starting over for the third time in his life, raising his young son.

Claire had a tougher road at the moment. Her husband was suffering from lung cancer. He was also a diabetic which complicated things further. Sara was the proud mother of two beautiful children and on her second marriage. Mary Ellen was extremely proud of her hard-working daughter. Starting over hadn't been easy for Sara but she was full of determination. Sara's second husband was a good man and loved her very much. Mary Ellen couldn't ask for much more. Diane had taken a different path. Much to Mary Ellen's disappointment Diane was not lucky in love until a little later than expected. She fell in love with a younger man from the United States and promptly married and move to the South. Unfortunately, children were not in the cards for Diane which was a cross only she could bear.

Mary Ellen's youngest son, Clark had married the sweetest girl. They had two children together and although they endured some rough waters over the years, somehow managed to find their way.

Things started to go sideways one night, when the phone rang and Ken almost knocked Mary Ellen over to answer it. The conversation was short and to the point. He quickly hung up and headed outside. Mary Ellen was left to sit and wonder what just happened. When Ken came back in Mary Ellen was seated at the kitchen table. She knew better than to jump on Ken, so she waited until he had a beer in hand.

"Who was on the phone Ken?"

"What?" His question seemed odd.

"The phone, who was on the phone? You were awfully short." She tried not to sound too curious.

"It was just one of the guys from the club." His answer seemed satisfactory but somehow, she didn't believe him.

Mary Ellen decided to stop drinking. Partly for her own health but mostly because she found it impossible to keep up with Ken. He could drink from morning till night. Get up and work the next morning without missing a beat. Mary Ellen, on the other hand, was almost drunk after a few beers. She realized it wasn't fun anymore. She tried to go to the club and Ken's favorite bars with him when she first stopped but she didn't like to be the only sober one. It was like she was always left out of some hilarious joke. Mary Ellen would sit at home for hours alone waiting for Ken to come home. He always did.

A week went by, and Mary Ellen found herself sitting in the kitchen staring at her dinner and his empty chair. What was she going to do? Live like this forever? She had made up her mind to say something to him in the morning. No sense in talking to him when he was drinking.

Just then the phone rang. It's probably him, she thought. Ken would call her from the bar to see if she wanted him to bring her home anything. She occasionally did, but not tonight.

"Hello." There was silence on the other end. "Hello." She said again with a little more vigor.

"He's mine. He wants me. Why don't you just let him go!" Mary Ellen stood in the kitchen, and she felt like the floor had fallen out from under her feet.

"Who is this!" She demanded. It was a familiar voice, but she couldn't match a face to it.

"Did you hear me! Who is this?" This time she heard a distinct click and a dial tone. Mary Ellen sat down and began to shake. Was he cheating on her? Why? She did everything for him. Then it came to her, the voice. It belonged to one of the women that hung out at the bar. Mary Ellen had talked to her a few times when she first stopped drinking. What a fool, she thought. How could I be so stupid. Mary Ellen thought she was a nice enough person, but Ken told her to stay away from her.

"She's no good Mary Ellen. She's nothing but trouble." Mary Ellen took him at his word.

When Ken walked in the door all hell broke loose. There would be no waiting. Not this time. Ken started out denying anything was going on. The angrier Mary Ellen got, the calmer his denials became. Mary Ellen felt anger and frustration like she had never felt before. She was hanging on to the kitchen counter with her back to him when she reached for the canister filled with flour. Before she knew what was happening, she hurled it across the kitchen. The two of them stood motionless as the white fog of flour blanketed everything. Mary Ellen slowly moved to the phone hanging in its perch on the kitchen wall. She lifted the receiver and dialed Sara's number.

"Come and get me now!" Sara lived only blocks away and was there in five minutes. Mary Ellen was covered in flour when she walked out the door and into Sara's car.

"Mom?"

"Not now, please." They drove to Sara's in silence. Luckily Mary Ellen's grandchildren were already in bed. After Mary Ellen showered and put on one of Sara's house coats, she joined her daughter at the table. Mike, Sara's husband had already excused himself, so they were free to talk.

Mary Ellen, regrettably, had always shared too much with her children but Sara was her confident. Years later she would realize her mistake in treating her daughter as a friend but right now was not that time.

"What am I going to do?" It really wasn't a question she expected an answer to, but true to form her wise daughter had one.

"Nothing, absolutely nothing. You'll stay here until he comes to you. And he will." Sara said with confidence. Three days had passed and there was still no word from Ken. He was more stubborn than she had anticipated. Sara and Mike were at work and the kids were at school, Mary Ellen summoned up all her nerve and picked up the phone. After four long rings she heard his familiar voice.

"Hello."

"Hi" she whispered.

"Well, I didn't think I'd hear from you anytime soon. What can I do for you?" Was he serious? After everything he did, this was how he greeted her.

"We need to talk."

"I said everything I need to say." He was determined not to give her an inch.

"Well, I need to talk. Will you give me that?" She asked.

"Sure, I'll come and get you."

"How do you know where I am?" She sounded puzzled.

"I'll be there in a few minutes." And he hung up.

Mary Ellen slid into the front seat of their new full-sized SUV. She was so proud to sit in the passenger seat. He had paid cash for this vehicle and told her she deserved to ride in comfort.

"Hi," she said not really making eye contact with him.

"Hi yourself." They drove in silence the short distance back home. Mary Ellen stepped onto the driveway and walked slowly up the familiar steps of the front porch.

The smell of the peony bushes she planted to act as a hedge around the elevated porch, enveloped her as she opened the front door. What she saw next stopped her dead in her tracks. The flour she had hurled across the kitchen days earlier was still blanketing everything. She stood in total disbelief and silence.

"You didn't expect me to clean this mess up, did you?" He said, as if she had asked him why he hadn't. Mary Ellen turned and stepped back onto the front porch. She took her familiar seat and waited for Ken to join her. He did.

"Ken, do you not feel bad at all about what you did?" She didn't want to sound like a scorned woman but after all that's what she was.

"I would if I had done anything. But like I tried to tell you I didn't. I don't know what you think I did but I can promise you if I did do something I sure in the hell wouldn't get caught. I think you know that." His eyes were almost black. That always alerted Mary Ellen to the fact that he was really starting to get angry.

"She called and told me. She said I was in the way." Mary Ellen was fighting tears that were winning.

"She, who?" There was a level of impatience in his voice that made her even more insecure.

"Jackie, from the bar." She spat the words. Ken began to laugh.

"And you believed her? I told you to stay away from her. She a nut case. Come with me." He took Mary Ellen by the hand and led her through the flour covered house. He picked up the phone and call Nelson at the bar.

"Hey, hi Nelson, this is Ken, is there any chance I can talk to Jackie? Thanks." Ken held the phone between himself and Mary Ellen so she could hear everything that was said.

"Hello this is Jackie." Mary Ellen could feel her blood run cold.

"Jackie this is Ken."

"Oh, hi Ken. What can I do for you?" Mary Ellen kept her eyes locked on her husband.

"You can tell me what the fuck you think you're doing calling my wife."

"What are you talking about?" She was a terrible liar.

"Don't screw around Jackie, I want an answer." Mary Ellen was almost afraid for this woman.

"Awe Ken, I was just screwing around. I just wanted to shake her up a bit." Ken was livid.

"If you ever call my wife again, I'll fuckin kill you." Mary Ellen had known about this side of her husband but had never seen it. She was already sorry she had ever questioned him. Ken hung the phone up. He looked at her without missing a beat said I need to get ready for work. You might want to clean up this mess, after all you made it.

Chapter 45

Christmas was always eventful in their house. Blending the two families had its challenges. They managed to keep their children in two separate camps. His kids were tough and hers were soft. Ken and Mary Ellen would go to see his kids on Christmas eve and hers on Christmas day. The problem was her kids needed to be with in-laws or they wanted to be home with their own kids Christmas day, so jealousy was sneaking in.

"Why can't we have Christmas eve this year. And you can spend Christmas day with Ken's family this year." Were the questions she would have to deal with. This year would be different.

"Ken, how about we do Christmas dinner here this year?" If the kids want to come, they can.

"Why don't we have Christmas the week before then everyone will be happy?" He suggested. The word went out. Christmas was going to be held the Sunday before, and everyone was welcome. The first few years were okay. Nice even. Presents were exchanged and food was prepared and then devoured. Everyone seemed to enjoy themselves. Before Mary Ellen knew it, word had spread to their friends and then their kids' friends and then people who were alone for the holidays. Mary Ellen and Ken would get up at the crack of dawn preparing food for over sixty people. As the day progressed their little war time home would swell with people. Family, friends and strangers. It was a battle all day to keep people out of her kitchen. Everyone wanted to help. Especially the girls. By the time dinner was put out Mary Ellen was exhausted. The last thing she wanted to do was eat. She would find a spot in the dining room and watch everyone find their way through the never-ending line, jostling for the best piece of turkey or ham. Loading their plates with all the fixings and balancing dinner rolls and silverware.

How she enjoyed feeding people. One beer would turn to two, then three. Before Mary Ellen knew it the night would be done. People would begin to make their way out the front door. Thank you and hugs. Call you tomorrow and see ya laters. Mary Ellen would help the girls find the right containers to store any leftovers. Dishes would be washed and dried. And most would be put away in the wrong place. Just one more thing she would take care of in the morning.

It wasn't until Mary Ellen realized Christmas was no longer for her family but for strangers that she decided to stop Christmas all together. Mary Ellen realized her own children were only showing up for a couple hours or not at all. Diane had voiced her displeasure. She had wanted Christmas with her family instead it had turned into a Christmas with total strangers, a house full of cigarette smoke and beer. It did hurt Mary Ellen, but she had to admit there was truth in it. It worked for several years but like everything this too would come to an end.

Mary Ellen decided right then and there that she hated Christmas. It was impossible to please everyone. When she was young Christmas was always such a disappointment. No father, an absent mother. The resentment she felt from her aunts and uncles having to share their presents with her. She had tried over the years to make it like she had dreamed it should be, but there was always something, divorce, a lack of money. The look of disappointment on her children's faces when they realized the gift, they wanted wasn't under the tree. Or worse yet how they tried to not look disappointed. It would be a burden to her for the rest of her life.

Chapter 46

Mary Ellen tried to keep up with Ken's friends and their drinking for years. They had had a lot of good times. Fishing and camping. Traveling to Florida or just plain hanging out. But it was clear that when Mary Ellen quit drinking these so-called friends quit her.

"Why don't you just have a couple beers?" Ken would ask.

"Because a couple leads to a few and then I'm drunk." Why couldn't he just quit with her.

"Angela and Frank only tolerate me, so you won't stop going over to they're house. Can't you just stay home?" She knew the answer before she let the words leave her lips.

"Listen, I don't tell you what you can and can't do so don't start telling me." He leaned over and kissed her on the lips like only he could and headed out the door. It would be another lonely evening by herself. Her kids were all living their lives. She was proud that everything had worked out for each of them. They would all have their own trials. She was sure of that, but at least she had raised five kind people. Too kind, according to Ken. He always complained that she had made her kids too soft. Funny though, when it came down to it, he really loved her kids. And for that she was very thankful. He had a special bond with each of them. He refused to lend money to any of the kids, after all there were ten of them. And he only gave advice when they asked but they all looked to him like a father. There was no bull with Ken and the kids all knew they could count on him. That was unusual to her kids. They're father had proven time and time again he was unavailable.

Lost in her thoughts, Mary Ellen made a cup of tea and sat in the sun porch Ken had built for her. She remembered the time Sara went to visit her father in Calgary. Mary Ellen didn't really want her to go but Andrew had paid for the airline ticket and genuinely sounded excited to see Sara. Mary Ellen and Brad took Sara to the airport and Mary Ellen did everything to help Sara squelch her fears. But when Sara walked through the door that led to the airplane Mary Ellen wanted to run after her. Brad's strong arm held her back and they simply waved when Sara turned around to look at them one more time. As Mary Ellen sat in waning sun drinking her now cold tea, she remembered the phone call she got from Sara like it was yesterday.

"Mom, I want to come home." Sara's voice was strong but there was an urgency only a mother could hear.

"Sara you still have three days." Mary Ellen wanted to sound interested but not concerned, even though she was very concerned. Sara was her rock, also a very independent, strong-willed child. If she wanted to come home, there had to be a reason.

"Sara put your father on the phone." Andrew had been married for some time now and his new wife seemed nice enough. So, Mary Ellen needed to know what was going on.

"Hello, Mary Ellen." There it was that voice that could make her angry just by hearing it.

"Hello. What's going on Andrew? Sara had been so excited to see you?"

"Well, she sure has grown up, hasn't she?" He sputtered.

"She's almost eighteen." What did he think she was going to stay his little girl forever?

"I think she would be happier if she left a few days early." Andrew sounded like he was looking for her permission. So typical Mary Ellen thought, rather than deal with his daughter he would just send her home.

"Can you put Sara back on the phone please?" There was no goodbye, just Sara's voice.

"Mom?"

"Look Sara, you wanted to go, don't you think you should stay for the rest of the week?" No, was the only response Sara gave.

"Okay, tell your father to let me know when he has the arrangements made and I'll pick you up. Sara, I love you." With that there was an audible exhale.

"Thanks Mom." Mary Ellen remembered how Sara looked when they met her at the airport. Her strong daughter looked like a lost child. Sara had always had a special bond with her father. Andrew wasn't afraid to show favorites and Sara was his. Seeing her father alone after all these years had been a real eye opener for Sara. When he realized she had a mind of her own and couldn't be treated like a child he dismissed her. If he couldn't control her, he really had no use for her. Which broke Sara's heart. Which in turn broke Mary Ellen's.

Why did these memories come rushing in when she was alone? Were they a reminder of what she once had and what she had survived? Maybe. She thought how far she had come and although her life wasn't perfect it was so much better than it had ever been. Ken was a good man and a good provider and even with his faults she loved him, and she had no doubt how much he loved her.

The sun had now set, and she found herself sitting in the darkened sunroom. As tough as Mary Ellen would like to have everyone think she was, she was really afraid. Ghosts of the past. Sounds that she couldn't quite discern. She quickly stood up and began turning on lights.

As she made her way into the kitchen, she heard the door opening.

"Ken?" she regretted saying as soon as she said it. What if it wasn't him.

"Yep, it's me." He answered.

"Well, I'm not going to lie, I'm glad your home early." She smiled and kissed him as he wrapped his arms around her. He held her for a moment longer than usual and although it felt wonderful, it set off alarm bells.

"Ken, is everything alright?" Mary Ellen hadn't slept much at all. Ken's confession rang in her ears. How could he have kept this to himself for so long.

"Well, I don't want you to worry. I just thought everything would be okay." He could hardly make eye contact with her.

"What is it, Ken? What's going on?" Mary Ellen felt as if she needed to sit down but didn't know why.

"There's blood in the toilet when I go to the bathroom. There has been for a while now. I thought it would go away. I'm tired. I'm tired all the time. I think I need to call the doctor tomorrow." He seemed genuinely afraid. This was the first time in all the years they had been together he seemed shaken.

"I'll call first thing in the morning." Mary Ellen walked to her husband and wrapped him in her arms. They stood for a long moment but when they broke their embrace he was back. The strength he had always shown her had returned as if it had been on a restful retreat. He took her by the hand and led her to the bedroom. He gently laid her on the bed, told her how much he loved her, then he began to show her.

The next few weeks were a blur. Doctor appointments, tests, medicine. And of course, all the phone calls. Ken insisted that each of the kids be told. Colon cancer. Could she ever get used to saying it? She told each of the kids and they each had the same reaction. Total disbelief.

When she called Diane there was an hour time difference. It was dinner time there, so she knew Diane would be home from work and probably in the kitchen. She was right. Diane answered after the first ring. After giving her daughter all the facts, she told her surgery was scheduled to see the extent of the spread. Diane said she would book a flight first thing in the morning. She would absolutely be there for the surgery. Ken had made it clear he didn't want any of the kids at the hospital for this. His kids listened hers didn't.

"What's he going to do?" Sara said. "Yell at us? Well, let him. You're not going to be alone." And that was that.

One by one they arrived at the hospital. It seemed like they had just wheeled him into the operating room when out stepped the surgeon.

"Mrs. Ingram?" Mary Ellen stood, and he walked directly to her. "Can you come with me?" He asked. Mary Ellen looked at all her concerned children and said,

"Can they come to?" The doctor smiled.

"Yes, right this way please." He led the family into a conference room with a large white board on the wall. He walked over to it and began to sketch. First a colon and then a liver. He then added circles inside the liver.

"This is Kens liver as I saw it. If there was one side of the liver untouched Ken would have a chance. Unfortunately, his liver in completely impacted so there really isn't anything we can do. I removed part of Ken's colon and that should prolong his life by a couple months." The silence in the room was deafening. Diane was the first to speak.

"There's nothing you can do?"

"Mr. Ingram will see an Oncologist and they will decide on a plan that works for everyone." Clark was holding his mother's arm, as if to steady her. Then Mary Ellen asked the question everyone was afraid to ask.

"How long do you think he will live?" As the words came out of Mary Ellen's mouth, she immediately wanted to take them back.

"It's hard to say, but I would think six months with the extent of the spread." He lowered his head as if something had fallen onto his well-worn shoes. "The nurse will come and get you as soon as he is in a room." He then walked over to Mary Ellen and took her hand and said.

"He's one hell of a guy, don't count him out just yet." On that they could agree.

Chapter 47

Ken did not disappoint. He never complained. He quickly made friends with every doctor and all their staff. He never met a stranger, Mary Ellen thought. When his chemo started, he insisted on going alone. His children felt excluded, but Mary Ellen wasn't surprised. He had acted like this was just something he had to get through. He immediately took charge.

"Mary Ellen, come sit down. There are some things we need to discuss." He was so matter of fact. Mary Ellen took her familiar seat across from him at their well-worn kitchen table. She was sure there were indents in the table where he set his elbows as he read the newspaper from front to back. Always ready to have a great discussion about this and that. Once she was comfortably settled, he began.

"There are some things we need to take care of."

"Sure Ken, anything." She couldn't imagine her life without this man. He really was her rock. She would do anything he wanted.

"I want you to come to the bank with me. We need to take care of some business. I want to leave my kids, my retirement savings." Then we need to go to the funeral home and take care of the arrangements.

I don't want you to worry about any of that." He smiled as if he had just given her a gift. Mary Ellen was still stuck on the, his retirement savings and his kid's part. As if he read her mind, he said,

"Now don't worry the money we put in your name will be yours. And of course, you can live in the house for as long as you want. If you do decide to sell it and move, the money goes to my kids." Mary Ellen swallowed hard. As if she had a great pill stuck in her throat. What was happening? This was her home. This was her kitchen. The family room where she sat and watched Western movies one after the other. The sunroom he built for her, where she sat waiting for the finches to come in the morning to the feeder, she had hung over the flowers she had planted. On and on. She had called this house home for longer than any of his children had lived in it. Was he serious?

That's when it hit her. Yes, she had been his wife for more than twenty-five years, and her children looked to him as a father. After everything they had been through together, she still wasn't family. There was a hardening that happened in Mary Ellen's heart in that moment. A hurt so deep it would never be reached.

"When would you like to go?" Showing him nothing but love. Real love. If this was how it was going to be, so be it.

When they left the bank, Mary Ellen felt a great relief. Everything had been taken care of. Nothing for her to worry about. She understood him better than he would every understand her. On to the funeral home. Mary Ellen felt like she was in an alternate universe. Was any of this bothering him? She thought.

They sat across from a man, young enough to be her grandson. He had only been working at the funeral home for a couple of months.

"Well, I think I have everything I need here. If you would both come with me, I'll show you the casket room. This was too much for Mary Ellen. I think I'll just wait here. Ken let out a chuckle and bent down and kissed her.

"No problem, I'll get you a nice one." He smiled and left her sitting in the office. Mary Ellen sat in total silence. She just about came out of her skin when she heard the basement door open and Ken and the young man came through it arm in arm laughing, as if they had been to a comedy club.

"Okay beautiful, all set." He reached down and took her by the hand.

"Listen Ken, you have my number. If there's anything I can do for you just let me know." Ken walked up to him and gave him a hug, then a stern slap on the back.

"Just make sure you take care of my wife when she calls."

"You got it Ken." The young man had a tear in his eye.

Chapter 48

Ken had been placed in a new trial for terminal cancer patients. Mary Ellen knew there wasn't really any hope, but six months had turned into almost three years. Ken had taken his last chemo treatment.

There was nothing more they could do. His oldest daughter had driven him. Mary Ellen went along for the ride. When Ken was leaving the building, the nurses who had cared for him, and even the oncologist came out to shake his hand. They all told him what a pleasure he had been to work with. They knew they would never see him again and so did he. Ken was weak but refused a wheelchair. "I'm good Doc." he said. Mary Ellen marveled at his strength, as did everyone. Mary Ellen set the phone back in its cradle and shared the good news with Ken.

"Diane and her husband were moving to Michigan. They would be here in just a few weeks.

Mary Ellen was exhausted. Between Ken's girls and her Sara, she pretty much had someone helping all day and night. She was so thankful.

Ken had lost so much weight. None of his friends tried to see him anymore. In the beginning they came non-stop. But as Ken got sicker, he told her to tell them no visitors. Mary Ellen felt like the bad guy and his friends looked at her like she was keeping him from them, but really it was because he didn't want to be seen like this.

When Diane arrived that freed Mary Ellen up to get out of the house. Sara would pick her up for an hour or so and Diane would sit with Ken. Claire wanted to help but she was nervous to be alone with Ken incase she didn't hear him. Mary Ellen assured her that when Ken passed, she would need Claire more than ever. That helped Claire navigate her own feelings of being left out.

It was around 5:30 on a Saturday morning when Ken took his last breath. Mary Ellen got out of bed and made her way to the family room.

A couple of weeks earlier a hospital bed arrived, and Ken was finally secure. He had fallen more than once when he got out of their bed trying to make his way to the bathroom. The Doctor finally convinced him it was for Mary Ellen's sake that he needed to use it. He stopped fighting about it and did it for her. Mary Ellen watched as the life drained slowly from her husband. Fear and panic would keep her up at night. Was she selfish to want this to go on? But if it didn't, she would be alone. Even in his present condition, his presence was larger than life.

Mary Ellen entered the family room to find her daughter sitting on the couch. Diane looked terrible. Oddly Mary Ellen had finally slept for more than a few hours. She would make Diane a good breakfast and then tell her to lay down. She leaned down to kiss her beloved Ken. Good morning darling. Somehow Ken responded. It was a groan, but his eyes met hers.

"He had a tough night mom." Mary Ellen smiled at Diane and asked her if she'd like a tea.

"Sure mom, that would be great." Mary Ellen was in her favorite place. The kitchen. She remembered how Ken would sneak up behind her and pinch her bottom, scaring her half to death. Then he'd wrap his arms around her, so she had to stop doing whatever it was she was doing. Oh, how she wished he could come in the kitchen now.

"Mom?" Mary Ellen turned and knew instantly by the look on Diane's face.

"I was just with him." And then it hit her. Mary Ellen had never felt such emptiness. Diane wrapped her arms around Mary Ellen for a moment, and then Mary Ellen went to Ken.

Diane called Ken's kids first. One by one, she told them how their father went peacefully mom kissed him good morning.

The sun was finally coming up and the kids were arriving. Each took time with their father. Mary Ellen joined them as they stood around his bed. Diane had done such a good job straightening the blankets and fixing his hair. Mary Ellen looked at all these adults standing around her husband's bed and saw the pain and loss on each of their faces.

"Let's pray" she said. No one was more surprised than she was that she had said it, but there it was. She began the Lord's prayer. They joined in. It was Diane who spoke next. She thanked God for Ken. For his life and all he had given to each of them. When she was done there was a peace that fell on the room. Mary Ellen literally crawled into bed and laid next to her husband and cried

Chapter 49

If anyone ever doubted Mary Ellen's character, they didn't any longer. Mary Ellen followed Ken's wishes to the letter. Really, she didn't have to. Everything was in her name. But over the next couple of months as retirement certificates came due Mary Ellen would call each of his children as he instructed, and they would go to the bank, and she would sign them over. One by one until all five were taken care of. Ken had gifted each of his kids a sum of money the Christmas before he passed so that was that.

Mary Ellen stayed in the house for three years. She remodeled the kitchen with the help of her kids. She had always wanted a new kitchen but now that she had it, she felt like she lost Ken all over again. Mary Ellen was always afraid to be alone in the house now that Ken was gone. And she couldn't continue to ask her kids to stay with her. Mary Ellen knew it was time to move on. It didn't take long to sell the house. The house she had lived in for thirty years. How was she going to do this? She could feel the hurt her children felt. She could see how disappointed they were in not only Ken but also her. Why didn't she fight him on this? On any of it? She was sorry she hadn't. now it was too late. She could keep the money from the house. It was in her name. How would she live with herself? And there it was. I lived without Wedgewood China before, and I can live without it again.

The house was sold and the money split. Done. Mary Ellen was starting over at the age of seventy-two. A nice three-bedroom apartment. She decorated it the way she wanted. She ate when she wanted, and she made a new friend. Karla. A divorced woman in her sixties who liked to travel and shop. Just what the doctor ordered. Mary Ellen was living her life without any restrictions for the first time in her life. She came and went as she pleased. Bought what she wanted without looking for approval from anyone. She even travelled. She was going on a Mediterranean cruise with her new friend. She had the time of her life. Sightseeing during the day, then dressing up for a late dinner then a trip down to the casino. Life was good. Mary Ellen felt like she had just started to live. She missed Ken but now instead of sitting around thinking about him and nothing else she was enjoying her life.

All good things must come to an end. Mary Ellen had heard that saying one time to many in her life. This time it was a devastating blow that affected her daughter more than herself. Sara's only daughter had been diagnosed with cervical cancer. She was a young woman with a child of her own. Life is so cruel she thought. Why her? Why not me? It was over almost as fast as it had begun. Her precious Sara was now raising her granddaughter.

It wasn't long after that that she received word that her sweet Steven had passed away with a heart attack. Mary Ellen felt that hand reaching for her again pulling her down. Deeper and deeper. How could she recover. Her first born. The pain was too much.

Mary Ellen sat in her living room after returning from the west coast where she buried her son. The sadness was so heavy she felt it in her eyes. She thought she was going mad. The vision in her right eye was disappearing. Like a curtain was being closed. What the hell she thought. Her heart started racing and her breathing was uncontrollable. And as quickly as it happened it was gone. Her vision was restored, and her heart rate started to normalize. Stress she thought. This too shall pass.

Unfortunately, it didn't pass. After three more episodes Mary Ellen decided it was time to tell someone. Karla immediately advised her friend to contact her doctor. Mary Ellen thought that was sound advice, so she did.

"Mary Ellen the symptoms your describing is leading me to the conclusion that you're suffering from mini strokes. I want to run a couple tests and put you on a blood thinner." Mary Ellen sat in total disbelief. How? Why? She unfortunately already knew the answer. Although Mary Ellen had quit smoking it was too late. The damage had been done. She had heard the warnings, but it was like they were talking about someone else. It wouldn't happen to her. Would it? Sure enough, the results were in. Mini strokes.

"You are at increased risk for a real stroke, Mary Ellen. You need to take better care of yourself, and I want you to keep a check on your blood pressure. Stay on the blood thinner and I'll see you back here in six months." That's it? Mary Ellen was screaming inside but, on the outside, she heard herself saying okay, thank you.

Mary Ellen called Sara and before she knew it, she had given up her apartment and moved in with her already overburdened daughter. It didn't take long before the difficulties surfaces. She knew better than to move in with one of her kids. But she did it anyway. There was such a rift building between her darling Sara and her that she didn't even recognize herself anymore. Arguing was a daily occurrence. In hindsight, Mary Ellen could see that she was so unhappy that she took it out on Sara. Sara was still reeling from the loss of her own daughter and trying to hold it together for her grand-daughter and now her mother. What was Mary Ellen doing, adding to Sara's stress?

It had been a year and it was time for her to take charge of her own life. Her so-called friend, Karla had decided Mary Ellen lived to far or something because she stopped calling and never came out to see her. Mary Ellen couldn't complain however, since she never did get her driver's license. Mary Ellen found a wonderful little place right down road from Claire. Perfect she thought. Close but not together. Sara was hurt but if she was being honest Mary Ellen knew she was probably glad to see her go.

Mary Ellen loved her little place. Starting over was a way of life for Mary Ellen. I can do this she thought. And she did. She made a nice life for herself. Diane came to visit once a week. Clark was just around the corner and would bring her great-grandchildren to visit and Claire would stop in daily. Sara worked, but always made a point of stopping in or taking her to a Bingo. What more could she ask for?

Chapter 50

The day started like any other day. She got out of bed, thankful to still be alive. Not that she felt good because she didn't. Yesterday was just another day too, filled with abdominal pain, neck pain and heart palpitations. No one seemed to care, not really. Another trip to the doctor, this time she took her youngest daughter with her. Complaints about the pain in her abdomen were answered with a response she never expected.

"Well Mary Ellen, we have a bit of a problem." The doctor's concern sent up all kinds of red flags in her already overloaded pain filled mind.

"What kind of problem?" Diane couldn't help but interrupt. Mary Ellen immediately shot Diane a disapproving look.

"Your kidneys are not functioning where we need them. An acceptable level for your age is 115. Your kidneys creatinine level is 190. Are you drinking enough water?"

"Yes, I have a glass of water that I refill all day." She answered,

"How many times do you refill it?" Although frustration was building with these asinine questions Mary Ellen managed not to tell the doctor something she might regret later.

"Look I drink about four bottles a day." Diane didn't really believe her since she had spent the day with her mother and had only seen her drink decaf coffee. She knew better than to contradict her mother in front of the doctor.

"Ok Mary Ellen, I want you to stop your blood pressure medicine for a few days and then go for blood work again. You have to continue your A-Fib med because we don't want you having a stroke." To which Mary Ellen immediately agreed.

Having a stroke was at the top of the list of Mary Ellen's fears. Having suffered mini strokes in the past made Mary Ellen realized she was not going to languish in a bed somewhere unable to speak or walk or wipe her own ass. Oh no way!

When she got home from the doctor, she began to drink water, she had made up her mind she would get these damn kidneys back in line so they could then do a CT scan of her abdomen since she was just about at the end of her rope as far as that pain was concerned.

Today was a new day. She sat at her little table quietly drinking her decaf coffee. As the pain increased, she began the ritual of rubbing her belly. She would wait to have a bowel movement. At last, the urge hit her. And it was all she could do to make it to the bathroom.

She had been on antibiotics for a week and the doctor re-upped them for another week. She would have to endure the awful taste they left in her mouth a little longer if it meant ridding herself of this horrendous pain. Finally, the pain was finally dissipating, now she could get on with her day. Claire lived only a few doors down the street. She knew she would see her later and she looked forward to the visit. It would break up her day. Besides she always had interesting stories about the comings and goings of her neighbor. Mary Ellen washed her face put on her hearing aids, read the paper and then put it back in the paper box sitting outside her front door so the neighbor could enjoy it. She knew she was a dying breed. Her grandchildren told her she could get the paper online. If only she knew what that meant. After doing the dishes she decided to strip her bed. It was going to be a beautiful day so a little fresh air would do her good. The laundry room was outside and a couple of doors away. She loved her little place, but she could also go stir crazy in the two rooms she called home. She had decorated it in light colors but even that couldn't hide how small it was. What she loved the most was that she had a front door as well as a back door. She had her own shed and a shared clothesline.

Mary Ellen had a little patio with a screened gazebo for relaxing in on nice days. Life was pretty good. The days of longing for her beloved Ken were behind her. Now she looked at each day as it came. Just putting in time. It was hard to believe forty years had passed. It seemed like yesterday to her. Time has a funny way of doing that, sneaking up on you. They're relationship had been moving along nicely and they seemed content living together. Mary Ellen had been working as a cook for the Priest's as their resident chef when a minor skin irritation on her forehead turned into a painful rash. Quickly diagnosed with shingles she was beside herself in pain. There was the fear that the shingles would reach her eye. Ken worked, then came straight home to be at her side. This was a side of Ken she didn't realize existed. Mary Ellen had a particularly difficult day. The pain had been intense all day and if she dare cry, the tears that fell on her cheeks were excruciating. Ken came home from work and took his position at her side. Something had changed in him, and she could see that this was having an unusual effect on him. Without warning he said, "Marry me." It was, in typical Ken fashion, more of a statement than a question. She simply said yes.

When she looked at pictures of him, she saw a handsome young man full of life. Or a graying man wise beyond his years. She missed his sense of humor and the way he devoured the newspaper in the morning. It was hard to believe that a chance meeting in a grocery store all those years ago would have turned out so amazing. They were inseparable after they left the home she had shared with Sean. They didn't marry for a few years but when they did, they were sure they would always be together. They would sit at the kitchen table, he with his coffee and she with her tea, and discuss the news of the day.

Here in her little flat she had only her own thoughts and opinions. She had no one to share her views with. She let her thoughts journey back to those days only a little at a time now. Remembering was sometimes a little too painful.

He has been gone fourteen years now. Fourteen years and a week to be exact. For her he had been the perfect husband. Maybe not always the perfect man but then again, she was far from perfect herself. He loved her though even with all her baggage. She stopped the memories before she let the morning slip away.

She finished the dishes and headed to the bedroom. Stripping the bed was easy, it was remaking it that was a challenge these days. Oh, how she hated getting old. As the thought came to her, she could hear him saying "it sure beats the alternative" but she wasn't sure anymore.

It took her by surprise when the numbness started but then as if a bolt of lightning struck, she knew. Stroke. Mary Ellen could feel confusion setting in and a heaviness like nothing she had ever experienced.

"Oh, dear God Please!" The thoughts were correct, but she couldn't understand her own words. She managed to get to the phone that was sitting waiting for her on the cradle next to the love seat. She fell into it no longer able to feel her right leg. The pain was intense. She pushed the button that automatically dialed Claire.

"Help me, please." Again, the words made no sense. Please God let her understand, she begged. Claire answered the phone and instantly knew something was terribly wrong.

"I'm on my way mum." Throwing clothes on she ran out the door. When she entered Mary Ellen's place shock washed over her. She began to shake.

"I'm here mom." She grabbed the phone and dialed 911. But nothing happened. What was wrong? She thought. Being hard of hearing was something she had dealt with all her life but at a time like this she almost lost it. She ran out the door turning on the grass still wet with morning dew and rushed to the neighbors. She pounded on the door as hard as she could, so there would be no mistaking the sound for anything but what it was, a frantic woman.

When the door opened, she thrust the phone in Cora's face. Without hesitation Mary Ellen's neighbor and friend dialed 911.

"Mum had a stroke call 911." Without looking back, she ran back to her mother's home.

"The ambulance is on its way mum, I'm here, I'm here." All the while fighting back tears. Mary Ellen was slumped over on the loveseat. Claire was so impressed with her mother's strength. How was she able to hold herself up she thought?

The ambulance took five agonizing minutes. When they began to ask Claire questions, she dialed Diane's cell phone and handed it to the paramedic. The paramedics questions were mainly about what medication Mary Ellen was taking. Satisfied they had what they needed they transported Mary Ellen to the hospital.

Mary Ellen was on the best blood thinner available, so what happened would be a mystery. Yes, she had A-Fib but the medication she took was to control that and so far, it had. This was the one in a million you hear about. People were poking her and asking the same questions over and over.

"Shit, shit, shit!" What could she have done different she wondered? Fear and panic set in when she realized she couldn't move her arm or leg and although she knew what she wanted to say, the words weren't coming out. Sleep she thought, when I wake up it will be over.

When Mary Ellen opened her eyes, her kids were with her. Staring at her in disbelief. The look of pity on their faces was hard to mistake.

"Rest mom, it's okay we've got this."

"Got what? Me?" But when Mary Ellen again tried to tell them what happened a mass of garbled words spilled from her mouth. Tears began to fill her eyes.

"Please mom, it's okay.

Take your time, go slow." Sarah was directing her. Did they think she was stupid? She knew to go slow; she was going slow!

Mary Ellen closed her eyes and tried to not feel claustrophobic. She slowed her breath and began to think of better times. Times with Ken. Fishing. Oh, how they loved to go fishing. Ken had a wonderful fishing boat that he masterfully handled. He always knew where the fish were biting. They would set off early in the morning and as the sun would rise the fog would lift off the water. She could feel the moist air on her cheeks.

"Mary Ellen? Can you hear me? This is Dr. So, and So. How do you feel?" He asked in a voice just a little too loud. Geese, do they think I'm deaf?

"I feel terrible. My head is pounding, and I can't move." But again, the sounds coming out of Mary Ellen's mouth had no resemblance to the spoken word. Frustration led to anguish and then sleep again.

This time she and Ken were on the road traveling south through the States. Florida, she couldn't wait to get out of the cold. She had a hard time believing they were living such a wonderful life. Kens beginnings like hers were less than desirable. An absent father and an alcoholic mother. Ken ran away from home at a very early age. Only to return to a mother who barely noticed him gone. He would steal chickens for his mother to cook and anything else he could get his hands on. He was always looking out for his little sister, and she adored him.

Ken was a tough guy but had nothing but love for Mary Ellen. It was a miracle they found each other after all those years. There was something mysterious about Ken when they had been neighbors all those years ago, but now knowing him the way she did it was a kind of kinship. Each living a life of secrets and shame. But not with each other. No secrets and no shame. Simply a deep understanding.

When Mary Ellen woke this time, she was on a gurney moving through the halls of the hospital. The lights were flashing overhead and there was noise coming from everywhere.

"Mary Ellen I'm nurse so and so. We're in your room now and we're going to lift you into your bed, okay?" With a great hoist and a quick movement Mary Ellen was laying like dead fish on the bed. As she flopped around, they got her into a position that was comfortable or so they thought. Off came her night gown, on went a johnnie shirt and diaper. Sheets were piled on her and blood pressure was being taken. Mary Ellen wanted to scream.

"Mary Ellen I'm Dr. So, and So. Well, it seems you suffered a significant stroke. It's early so we will keep an eye on you and see how you do Okay?"

"See how I do. Are you kidding me? I had a stoke now fix me!!" Shit, can't you understand me, she thought. Dreams were Mary Ellen's happy place. She dreamt of being in her house again with Ken. Working in her garden. A garden, by the way that was the envy of everyone who visited. Sometimes she was young again and helping her Meme in the kitchen. In her dreams she was young and strong. Thoughts came quickly and her movements were fast and precise. This is where she wanted to stay.

When she was awake, she was in pain. Someone was always poking her or testing this or that. Couldn't they just leave her alone. Each one of her surviving kids were here. Sometimes together sometimes alone. They were like her guardian angels, never leaving her side.

Oh, how she wished they would stay home. She knew better though, after all she raised them. They would stick together and protect her with their last breath. Don't get upset she thought. They can't understand me anyway. Diane explained how Mary Ellen had just been at her doctor the day before complaining of abdominal pain.

"Her doctor wanted a CT scan" Diane was trying to explain that her mother was still in pain.

"Just because she had a stoke doesn't mean all the other issues would just magically disappear. The neurologist agreed but explained until Mary Ellen could swallow, they couldn't use contrast.

"We'll send her for an ex-ray.

As soon as I can swallow contrast, they will do a CT of my abdomen to see if they can find out what's going on. Ha this has been the same for years and they haven't done anything yet. Now I had a stroke and they're going to fix my abdomen. I'll believe it when I see it.

"Diane, how many days have I been in here?" There it is that look again. She should know me well enough to know what I want.

"Hey momma, how ya doin? I brought the newspaper. Can I read it to you?" Diane asked.

"What day is it? Just tell me what day it is." Mary Ellen was getting agitated, so Diane assumed she didn't want the paper read to her. Mary Ellen tried to smile so Diane wouldn't feel bad.

"It's okay mom, no worries. Oh, by the way it's Wednesday. You've been here five days now and you're doing great.

"What, five days! Are you kidding me? Oh my God! No, no this can't be happening. Lord why?" Mary Ellen closed her eyes and tried to slow her breathing. Don't cry, don't cry. She fell fast asleep again.

Mary Ellen found herself sitting in the kitchen she shared with Ken for almost thirty years enjoying a cup of tea. "Hey beautiful" Ken smiled at her like only he could. Mary Ellen smiled back and stood up.

"Are you ready to go to work?" She asked.

"Yep, no rest for the wicked." Mary Ellen hated it when he worked nights, she was always afraid when he had to work all night. "I'll see you in the morning. You, okay? "He could see the fear in her eyes.

"Oh sure" she said not very convincingly.

"Okay, lock up behind me." And out the door he went. She stood in the front window watching him drive away.

"Come on Cody let's go watch tv." The big black lab never left her side. She wasn't sure exactly what it was she was afraid of but having Cody with her always made her feel better.

When Mary Ellen woke up, she had new surroundings. They had moved her while she slept. She had been in a large room with only one other patient and now she was in a room with three other women. One was of Italian descent and spoke with a thick Italian accent. That was Maria, in the bed next to her was Joan. She knew her name because she heard Diane praying with her. She said her name clearly to God when asking for His mercy. Well, it worked because the next day the Lord took her home. Across the room was Miss Alice, a ninety-three-year-old sweetheart. Her daughters said she wasn't always that sweet but since her stroke she had a new personality and they loved it. All of them had the ability to speak. Only one of them had lost the use of her arm. I guess that makes me the worst of the bunch. I can't talk or move.

They threatened to put a feeding tube in if I didn't start swallowing. Damn it, no one is going to put a feeding tube in me. I'll show them. Mary Ellen began to swallow as if her life depended on it. Soft food to follow. The speech pathologist evaluated my ability to swallow, and I'll be damned I did it. I passed the test and before you knew it, they were pushing some lasagna in front of me. Much to my surprise it's not bad. Not as good as mine but better than that frozen stuff everybody raves about. They really don't have a clue. I was able to feed myself; one handed no less. The kids will be happy because they were afraid, I was going to starve to death. I was happy for a chance to get a few pounds off. I thought I did pretty good until Sara took the towel away that was draped across my chest, and I realized half the lasagna was laying on the towel.

Sleep came easy after dinner. Nighttime however was a different thing. Mary Ellen laid awake for what seemed hours, beeps and buzzers were going off all night. Instead, she let her mind wander back to better times.

She was on a boat with Ken, and they were racing across Lake St. Clair. The air was warm, and the sun was shining on her making her skin turn a beautiful golden brown. The water sparkled like a million diamonds dancing like fairies on the water. When Ken sped up the splashing waves hitting the boat sent a cooling mist up to freshen Mary Ellen's skin. It was hard for Mary Ellen to believe this was her life now. After all the heart ache and disappointment, she would end up marrying Ken. The neighbor that wouldn't get involved in her fight over Claire falling in the trench. Mary Ellen had always been intrigued by him but was also a little afraid of him. Now here she was all these years later and he loved her.

"Do you want to go to the island? We can throw the blanket down and have a picnic." Ken wasn't the picnic kind of guy, but he knew she had worked hard packing up a lunch for them, so he didn't want to disappoint her. Besides he was hungry and could use a beer.

"Sure, I'm ready when you are." The memories were washing over her in waves. The blanket almost floating in the air as he threw it down onto a soft patch. Like watching everything happen in slow motion. Ken laid down on his side propping himself up on one elbow. He lit a cigarette and settled in. Mary Ellen busied herself getting their lunch out of the little cooler she so carefully packed earlier in the day. After they had their fill, they laid side by side on the blanket and stared at the blue sky. Guessing what each cloud resembled. Soon Ken was sleeping.

Mary Ellen wanted to hang on to this memory. He was so handsome and when he slept all the lines on his face disappeared. He woke fresh and ready to go. Mary Ellen had already packed away all the trash, so she was ready for their return home."

Mary Ellen, I'm your night nurse, I'm just going to check your vitals, okay?" Was she kidding no it wasn't, okay? She had finally dosed off and this nurse had the nerve to wake her up. But Mary Ellen's protests were misunderstood for compliance.

"Okay Mary Ellen, everything looks good now go back to sleep." Oh, if only she could understand me, she thought. Maybe it's better that she can't. It was hard for her to fall back to sleep this time. The sounds at night were different from the day. Sounds of snoring and nurses prattling on about who knows what. Words that were just sounds off in the distance. The next thing Mary Ellen knew it was morning. She must have fallen asleep at some point but now the activity on the floor had quickened. Lights were turned on and people were rushing here and there. Oh, how she wished she could communicate with someone, anyone. Maybe I'll try again she thought.

"Hello, hello." Shit, just noise! Was she ever going to be able to talk again? She knew the words she wanted to say but they wouldn't come out.

Dear God, why is this happening to me? Have I done something? Haven't I tried to be a good person? The tears started but she was careful not to make any sounds. Think about Ken, she told herself. She let her mind wander to better days.

The doorbell was ringing, and Mary Ellen was making her way to the front door.

"Well, hi there, come on in." Her Aunt Louise had taken a bus and walked the block from the stop to come to see her. They embraced and Mary Ellen felt like she had a friend and a big sister all rolled into one Aunt. They had become close over the past few years, and she was grateful to have her in her life.

"Ken just left for work; he'll be sorry he missed you." She led Aunt Louise to the kitchen and put a bottle of beer and a cold glass in front of her. They could sit for hours chattering on about absolutely nothing, smoking cigarette after cigarette. Mary Ellen tried desperately to remember what she looked like, but that memory was fading away. She found herself bent over her peony's dead heading. The smell of them filled the air. If it wasn't for the ants, they attracted she thought they might be her favorite flower. Her dahlias were beautiful this year as well. Must have been all the rain and pigeon shit. Ken raced homing pigeons for as long as Mary Ellen could remember. There was good money to be had if you knew what you were doing. And Ken knew exactly what he was doing. No one was allowed in his coup, not even Mary Ellen. They would sit in the back yard or the sunroom on race days waiting for the pigeons to return home after a grueling two-hundred-mile race. She was fascinated with how they found their way home.

Ken knew what time the birds would begin to arrive. He would start looking to the sky in the direction they were expected and sure enough without fail they would come into view.

"Mary Ellen they're coming." He would watch as they would land and enter the coup. He would rush in grab ahold of them and place the band on their leg into a clock that was designed to mark the exact time of their arrival. Once they were all timed Ken would head to the club, clock in hand. All the clocks from all the pigeons would be read and the winner announced. Ken would collect his money having bet on himself buy a beer or two and head home. Mary Ellen usually had dinner waiting. They would have a few laughs and call it a night. Curling up next to him was like wrapping herself in a warm familiar blanket. She would fall fast asleep.

Memories were just that, memories. Oh, how she wanted to live in the past. She wanted to know what was happening to her, but she was unable to ask. She was relying on bits of information she overheard from whispered conversations. The problem was she didn't know if they were talking about her or someone else.

Each one of her children would come in and share what they knew to the best of their ability, but damnit she needed to know the facts. How long would she be here? When was her speech coming back? She presumed her leg and arm were caput. That must have been what they were talking about when she heard catastrophic.

"Mary Ellen, how are you today?" The nurse wanted to know but since she couldn't answer what was the point?

"What day is it?" "Hello, can anyone hear me? What day is it?"

"Hi mom, how did you sleep?" Clark was a man and yet she looked at him like her baby. Her oldest son Steve was gone, had a heart attack ten years ago. Where did the time go?

Mary Ellen worried about Clark constantly. He was always tired and although she knew how hard it was to quit smoking, since she herself had quit, he wouldn't even try. What if he had a heart attack like Steve, how would she stand losing her baby boy? With a coffee in his hand Clark sat next to her. He took her hand in his and told her about his day. Talked about his grandchildren with such affection it warmed her heart. Did he know how much she loved him? Had she told him enough. She tried now but babble spewed forth. Clark smiled and I know mom, I know. But did he?

Mary Ellen closed her eyes and let her thoughts drift back to the time she worked with the priests. A time when she was happy and full of creativity in the kitchen. She started in housekeeping but quickly moved into the kitchen. Before she knew it she was their most prized chef. She wished she could remember the recipes. She cooked for twenty priests daily. Everyone had special requests and she was always accommodating. One priest loved tomatoes but couldn't eat the skin, one only liked green tea while another couldn't stomach it. Mary Ellen knew everyone by what they ate. She was like a mother hen. She took a lot of grief from her grown children though because she didn't want to cook family dinners anymore. It was like anything she supposed, if you did it for a living you didn't much feel like doing it at home. Her youngest daughter had been a hairdresser for a short time, she would complain when people wanted her to cut their hair after work. Like that, she thought, it's just like that. She was almost fifty when she had worked for the priests. All the kids were happy and independent. She finally felt free to live her own life, not that you're ever free of your children but for the first time in her life she didn't feel the fear of paying bills or how she was going to put food on the table for five growing mouths. Ken had showed her a new way of living. She was loved and protected.

Mary Ellen was brought back to the present by the incessant chanting of her roommate. Repeatedly she would yell "somebody help me please!" Finally, one of the visitors would take pity on her and after trying to help her they would give up and the chanting would begin all over again. Mary Ellen looked around the drab room. Why wouldn't they paint these rooms a bright color she thought. That would probably cheer everyone up. She was trying to figure out how long she had been in the hospital. One week? Two? She would have to ask someone she thought. Somehow.

The nurses were coming and going and one of her children were always on hand to make sure their mother was being properly cared for. She really did appreciate each one of them, but she wished they would go home. Just then her youngest daughter leaned over and said,

"Hi momma, well you've been here two weeks today. I think it's time to get moving. I want you to try to talk mom. I don't care if it sounds like a bunch of mumbo jumbo, just try. Time to retrain your brain."

"Wait did you say two weeks?"

"That's it, mom just try."

"Shit! Shit!" I bet she didn't understand that! How could two weeks have passed. Mary Ellen could feel herself starting to panic. She felt trapped in a body that wasn't hers. She closed her eyes and tried to slow down her breathing. Relax, she thought. Just focus on getting out of here.

When the physical therapist showed up the next morning Mary Ellen made her mind up that she was going to try her hardest. This nice young girl smiled and told Mary Ellen what they were going to do.

"Now we're going to move your fingers, okay good. Next your arm, now your shoulder. And so on and so on."

Was this it? How was she going to get out of here if that's all they were doing? She would have to tell the Doctor, if she ever got to talk to her. The morning came and went, and Mary Ellen drifted in and out of sleep. Every time she opened her eyes one of her children was sitting at the foot of her bed. Different child, different day.

Mary Ellen let her mind wander to a time when Ken and she had invited half the town for Christmas dinner. With her five kids, well four since Steve lived out west, and Ken's five and their significant others. Plus, their children, neighbors and friends there was barely room to move. Ken and Mary Ellen shopped for days and stocked the spare fridge with beer. The morning would arrive, and they would work in unison like professional dancers in the kitchen. She would go right; he would go left. She would go to the stove, he to the fridge. The smells would fill the house. Turkey and dressing. Broccoli and Cauliflower. Mashed potatoes and homemade meat pies. The desserts were all prepared days in advance as well as an assortment of cookies. The guests would arrive, and Mary Ellen's stress level would rise with it. Everyone would hang out in the kitchen until she would finally be forced to ask them to go to another room. That's usually when Ken would step in and take charge. Clearing her kitchen so she could finish setting everything out. Once all the delectable choices had been set out Mary Ellen would take her glass of beer and her cigarettes and find a seat at the dining room table.

Never eating herself she would sit back and watch everyone enjoy the fruits of her labor. Those were the days, she thought. She and Ken would fall into bed a little tipsy after the last of the guests would leave, patting themselves on the back for another successful meal served to the masses.

Ken was such an easy-going guy. He spoke like a sailor, full of profanity. But always had a kind or gentle word for her. A lot of people were intimidated by Ken and that made Mary Ellen feel even safer. Ken didn't take and guff from anyone. He had a quick wit and a sharp tongue. He also had a great sense of humor, so long as the joke was on someone else. Ken had a different way of looking at life and Mary Ellen loved it. He didn't blame anyone for anything that happened in his life.

"It's just the way it is" he'd say. Oh, how she missed him. This would be an awful time for him though. As tough as he was, he probably wouldn't handle this very well. When he was diagnosed with cancer sixteen years earlier, he was all business. He made sure all their finances were in order, investments were on the way to make the most profits. He even made funeral arrangements for them both. Then he asked to be put on every drug trial available. He proved to be a real fighter. Well, he fought until he couldn't fight anymore.

Diane had stayed with them, giving everyone else a break. Diane and her husband had just moved back to the area, and she needed to be with them almost as much as they needed her to be there. She was the one who was with him when he took his last breath. Mary Ellen had gotten up at five am. that morning. Diane had been awake most of the night trying to keep Ken comfortable.

"Hi mom"

"Hi sweetheart, how is he?"

"Not good mom, he had a rough night." They had arranged to have a hospital bed brought in when Ken cold no longer walk. It was set up in the family room, so someone was always with him. On this night it was Diane. Ken struggled all night and Diane was ready at his side to meet any of his needs. Not that he really had any. He just wanted relief. Mary Ellen leaned over the hospital bed that held her husband and kissed his forehead.

"Good morning, Ken, I love you." She looked into his dark eyes, and he groaned. She kissed him again and went into the kitchen to put the kettle on. After filling the kettle, she turned the burner on and set the kettle over the flame. She reached into the cupboard and retrieved her favorite teacup. She took another one out for Diane. She reached for the tea bags and then the spoons. Next would be the place mats. Diane was standing in the kitchen with a look of anguish on her face. Mary Ellen knew he was gone before Diane said it.

"Mom I'm so sorry." Mary Ellen reached for her daughter's hand. They embraced as Mary Ellen felt her world shift.

She looked into Diane's eyes and said, "thank you." She then went to be with her husband. He looked so peaceful, finally. It had been three years. The doctors told him he would only live six months; they didn't know Ken. But they did now. They had all been amazed by his strength. None more than his doctor. She arrived ready to find Ken taking his last breath. Instead, she was greeted by a man who although looked frail was happy to see her.

"Well, hey there Doc, what's shaken?" Ken was leaning on the frame between the kitchen and dining room smoking a cigarette.

"Would you like a beer?" Mary Ellen simply looked at the doctor and smiled.

"Ah, sure Ken." The doctor thought, what the hell. Ken came and sat down and began a conversation that the doctor found quite engaging. Ken excused himself saying he was a little tired.

"Well, Mary Ellen, I really don't know what to tell you. He really is something else." Mary Ellen walked the doctor to the door and said thank you. No one could explain this man. He truly was one of a kind.

When dinner came Mary Ellen really didn't feel like eating. The food was really starting to annoy her. Was that possible? She looked at the tray that her daughter pushed toward her, and she wanted to scream. They had started her on a bland diet. White bread, mashed white potatoes, ground chicken breast. Are they trying to kill me? She thought. Her daughter explained that they were going to try this to help her stomach.

"Well shit, it's my stomach. Maybe someone should ask me what I want to eat!" She knew there was no point in arguing until she could get her speech back it was a futile argument. "God, do you hear me. Can you understand my thoughts? I know I only seem to come to you when I need something, but right now I seem to need everything. I think I remember being told once that every day is a gift. Well, I really didn't want this gift but I know it's rude to say that so I will start by saying thank you. Thank you for the doctors and nurses. Thank you for my children. Thank you for the life you've given me. My Meme told me that you knew my name. Dear Lord, maybe you could help me get through this one. Amen." Somehow speaking to God made her feel better. She still couldn't move, and her speech was still a mess, but she felt a peace that she hadn't felt in a long time. Maybe God really did know her name.

Her thoughts wandered back to the day she saw Ken in the grocery store. He hadn't changed a bit. She looked a fright. She was only in town to finish paying for the funeral expenses and pick up some groceries. It had been four months since Sean died. She had two weddings and finally gotten Sean's oldest daughter out of her house. It sure was good to see an old friend.

She was shocked when he said he was separated. She really didn't think Pearl would ever let him go. As time went on Pearl would come to regret her decision but it was too late. Ken would never give up Mary Ellen.

The morning Ken died was the hardest of her memories. One by one Diane had called each one of their children. His first, then hers. The family began to arrive, each spending a few minutes with the man who had always been there for each of them. Not always in the way they wanted, but in his way. Mary Ellen watched as they each kissed him and touched his hand or arm or just stared. How would she ever go on without him. So much had changed in the decades they had spent together. She wasn't strong or independent anymore. Ken took care of everything. And she had let him. She was so tired when he came into her life, she simply let him. The funeral came and went, and she was alone. She hated being alone.

Mary Ellen shook the memories from her mind and tried to focus on the here and now. But what did that mean. Her past was gone her future so uncertain, so she would live for now, right now.

Mary Ellen remembered being told when her oldest son died suddenly from a heart attack that when you lose your parents you lose your past, when you lose your spouse, you lose your present but when you lose your child you lose your future. How true she thought. Right now, Mary Ellen was living in a sort of limbo. Unable to move or speak. Trapped between her past, present and future. For now, she would just have to wait. Wait on the mercy of the Lord to reunite her with her parents, her husband, her child and her grandchild. So, she made up her mind to do just that, wait.

The End